The
Analyst

Fred Guilhaus

Wakefield Press
17 Rundle Street
Kent Town
South Australia 5067

First published 2002

Copyright © Fred Guilhaus, 2002

All rights reserved. This book is copyright. Apart from any fair dealing for the purposes of private study, research, criticism or review, as permitted under the Copyright Act, no part may be reproduced without written permission. Enquiries should be addressed to the publisher.

Cover design by Dean Lahn, Lahn Stafford Design
Designed and typeset by Clinton Ellicott, Wakefield Press
Printed and bound by Hyde Park Press

National Library of Australia
Cataloguing-in-publication entry

Guilhaus, Fred W.
The analyst.

ISBN 1 86254 582 0.

I. Title.

A823.3

Wakefield Press thanks Fox Creek Wines
and Arts South Australia for their support.

To Family

Prologue

Some years after the cataclysm of 11 September 2001, the world moved on from anxious to seriously neurotic. People scurried about in tight circles. The war against terrorism created a domino effect that saw attacks on oil installations and power plants push fragile economies over the edge into serious recession. Unstable governments in the Middle East were overthrown. The rest of the world looked on in disbelief as raging bands of armed tribespeople fought among each other.

The threat to the West dissipated in a false dawn. When oil stopped flowing from the Middle East, Russia was quick to fill the void. People rediscovered small cars. Then came the next wave of medical breakthroughs. Genes for every conceivable disease were discovered daily. Pharmaceutical companies were in a frenzy to fund research that saw the beginning of the end of cancer. The family goldfish became an expert in biotechnology. The recession was turned around by technology mania.

The veneer of normalcy was thin. Part of the world was in flames while the rest wrung their hands living the good life while it lasted. People looked at each other differently, contaminated by the global neurosis.

So begins the story of Henry Sinclair.

- 1 -

Henry Sinclair was an unlikely-looking character to be immersed in a stockmarket boom. On a Monday afternoon in November he was to be found rummaging for clothes at his favourite opportunity shop in the affluent Sydney seaside suburb of Coogee. The shop was a reflection of its contents, jaded on the outside, scuffed and worn on the inside. The times were such that wealth and poverty eyed each other warily.

The young woman who presided over this unremarkable enterprise knew Henry as an occasional customer. She was partially hidden behind a counter, fighting for space among the clutter of recycled clothes arranged in rows like refugees.

Henry was on a mission to ginger-up his appearance. Clutching his purchases, he approached the counter. 'Hello Melanie.'

'Henry. Guess what? I read your article in the paper. You're pretty clever,' she said, 'and cute.'

Henry shrugged. 'Cut it out, Melanie. Not r-really. How much for these?'

'Henry,' she sighed, 'you never take me seriously. By the way, I'm going to do a course on investing. I've been talking to my dad. All thanks to you.'

'Me?'

'You're the most famous person ever to set foot in this place.'

Henry acknowledged the dubious compliment with a smile. 'What will you be in-investing?'

'I have some savings. I was hoping you might advise me,' she said, then glanced down at his purchases for the first time. 'Henry, you can't be seen in public wearing these! Are you colour blind?'

Henry Sinclair lived as he looked. His one-bedroom apartment was in a state of denial. The sofa grimaced to be in the company of non-matching floral armchairs that threatened to march on the purple bookcase. The bookcase sagged against an orange wall. Colours did not so much clash, as plead forgiveness.

It was an exercise to find the telephone as it gurgled beneath an Everest of discarded clothes enjoying an open-air respite on their way to the closet from hell. Clothes, books and magazines were liberated in an eruption of discovery as Henry felt for the muffled ring.

Victorious at last, he stuttered into the receiver: 'Y-yeah?'

'It's Doug, from the *Herald*.'

'Yeah?'

'What's going on, Henry? Your articles are attracting more interest than Hollywood. I have a woman pestering me for your number. She's a publisher. Wants you to write a book. That relationship stuff, Henry. Maybe you're on to something.'

'A-amazing,' Henry said.

'Should I give her your number?'

'Umm . . .'

'Henry? Still there?'

'S-sorry. Just thinking . . .'

'Well?'

'Er, sure.'

Then, unusually, the telephone rang again.

'Sinkers?'

'You must have the w-wrong number.'

'How's your memory? It's Eric Schwartz, from school.'

Shocked, Henry led the cord around the sofa. 'W-what do *you* want?'

'Come on, Sinkers. Haven't you forgiven me yet? We were just kids.'

'Umm . . .'

'Look, Henry, we're all big boys now. I read your piece in the *Herald*. I want to meet for a chat, over coffee, catch up.'

*

For a somewhat shy man of thirty-three, living his life in material confusion, Henry was consistent when it came to his wardrobe. Socks, to offer just one example, were never married, but floated singly in his closet, and were chosen purely on the basis of convenient location. When a black and brown sock travelled on the body corporate with a bright orange shirt and green corduroy pants, the effect could be arresting. Henry now stood in front of his wardrobe annoyed with himself for agreeing to see Eric. He pulled on a pair of trousers, tightened his belt and glanced at the clock by his bed.

Henry sat nervously, clutching his cappuccino with both hands, and stared around the coffee shop through steamed-up glasses, wisps of hair dancing on his thinning pate. To Henry, Eric Schwartz was a thug, but had to admit the man had charisma, and that came at a price. Lateness, for example.

Eric arrived like a late train, gazed around the shop and nodded as he approached. 'Sinkers, it's been a while, how are you?' He grinned, thrusting out his hand in the manner of a man schooled in the rutting behaviour of the Canadian caribou. He gestured to the waitress, pointed at Henry's cappuccino, spun his finger in the air, then hunched over his hands and fixed Henry with the Eric look; an unblinking stare that sought to intimidate.

'Thanks for making the time, Sinkers. You haven't changed a bit. This won't take long. Are you aware I've made a few mill since school? Have you kept up with any of the guys? Some of them follow that technology mag you write for, and they reckon you know your stuff. Bit far-fetched, I always thought.'

Henry stroked his goatee with sweet patience. 'I-I've not really kept up.'

Eric rode roughly through his life, giving Henry a synopsis of his sometimes very public, and as far as Henry could remember, dubious achievements. The coffee arrived and Eric spooned sugar into the cup. Henry listened with glazed eyes.

'So, Sinkers, now you're getting syndicated? A regular run in the *Herald*. Well done.'

'Umm, thanks.'

'Coping with stardom? Why don't you use your name? We all know the Analyst is you.' Eric chewed the words with hidden sarcasm.

'S-stardom?' The same old dynamic from schooldays was affecting Henry. The man was a mudslide and Henry was in a tiny tent.

'How did you form your opinions, and what's inspired you to write about relationships, for God's sake? You're not married, are you?'

'No. I j–just listen and watch.'

'And you freelance, not actually employed by anyone?'

'That's r-right.'

'You're not well off then, I presume. Still dress like the Sinkers we knew and loved at school.'

Henry glanced down at his newly purchased shirt and the old cardigan that he wore as a soother.

'Why haven't you put your knowledge to use and made some money?'

'I'm o-often asked that question.' Henry stared into his coffee.

'I tell you what. I've spoken to my woman Rachael about it. She thinks your ideas are good fun, and wants to have you over to dinner. What made you write that stuff?'

'W-which stuff?'

'You know, the world's anxious. People are now so materialistic that partner choices are made exactly like share purchases?'

'Umm...'

'Anyway. I want you to attend one of my investment seminars. A friend has been trying to get your phone number from the paper. She had no idea that you and I were buddies.'

'B-buddies?'

'Just joking. There'll be a couple of others, keen to listen to you. Don't worry Sinkers, it's casual. Come as you are. There's nobody you want to bring is there?'

'Well . . .'

Eric gripped Henry by the shoulder in a gesture of true mateship, caught sight of his own reflection in a mirror, adjusted his tie and presented his card. 'Saturday night at eight.' He winked at Henry, flashed a ten-dollar note at the waitress and scurried away.

- 2 -

Henry had fought every instinct and accepted Eric's invitation. He arrived at the door in half a mind to turn back. The wind had blown his wispy hair about and he battened it down, pulled at his hound's-tooth coat and inhaled deeply. Clutching his bottle of Firly Creek Shiraz, he responded to some force that nudged him to ring the bell.

Eric lived in an apartment overlooking Sydney Harbour. Henry froze as he watched a huge container ship glide past windows that framed the entire wall of the living room. 'W-wow. W-what a view,' he mumbled as he reached out to shake hands.

Ensconced at the dinner table, the competition for air space resembled Sydney airport at rush hour. Henry was impressed that four people could have four conversations at the same time. He observed the two couples, acutely aware of the cleavage of Eric's partner, Rachael, who punctuated each of her conversational forays with a hand on Henry's thigh, making it obligatory for him to read the designer label on her bra-strap. She had decided that Henry was a man who would love her unconditionally, no matter how horse-like her laugh. On his other side was a woman introduced as Louise, with a mouth that puckered as she mined her words with care.

Caterers had been hired and the drinks and food arrived with understated efficiency, leaving the table to make short work of the exceptional wines that were poured with little regard for their label. Henry noticed that his own humble bottle had been put out of sight.

Eric took charge from the head of the table. 'To begin with, let's hear from Henry, our guest of honour. Henry, I'll introduce my guests. But just tell us a bit about yourself first.'

Henry cleared his throat, sat up straight and looked around the table. 'I-I have a slight stutter, and I'm sorry if it o-offends. I'm really not sure what I'm here for, but I'll be pleased to repeat what you r-read in the paper . . .' Finding himself under intense scrutiny, the words piled up in his mouth.

'Henry, you've always been hopeless at advertising yourself. Let me help.' Eric proceeded to tell it as he saw it. 'Henry and I went to the same high school. He was dux of the school, far too smart. His nickname was Sinkers, for Sinclair, and it stuck when he sank everybody in every exam. He topped the State in science and went on to get a PhD in biotechnology, then specialised in the human genome project. He's become a technology junkie, and now writes about the business side. He has a huge following, and probably doesn't even know . . .'

'How come you're now writing about relationships?' Louise said.

'Hang on Louise, before we go any further, I want Henry to meet you all.' Eric motioned for the waiter to top up his glass. 'Henry, we often get together to discuss our lives and loves and you are privileged to be in the company of some of this country's shakers and movers.' Eric raised his glass and everyone joined in to toast themselves. Henry raised his own glass gingerly.

'Okay, I'll introduce Andy,' offered Louise.

'Hang about. We introduce *women* before men at my table,' Eric thundered, winking at Henry. 'Come on Andy, tell us about Louise.'

Louise looked bookish. Henry guessed her pedigree from

the hurried application of her make-up, and the scant attention to detail in dress. This was a woman whose confidence transcended her looks. He began to think that perhaps Louise was a safe harbour in this stormy sea.

Andy raked his fingers through his hair and smiled at Louise in a very-naughty-boyish way. 'It's a challenge to present my darling in all her complexity,' he began, dripping charm. 'As we are presenting this sketch for Henry's benefit, it does focus the mind.' Andy edged in his seat, his chest puffed up as he sucked air through his teeth and surveyed his woman, allowing his chin to rotate just a little, his eyes narrowed. 'Louise is the foremost film and literary agent in Australia. She has a stable of the best film people and authors in the country. Many are household names because she has the insight, the skill and the flair to know what is going to sell. She is able to hold her own in any company, and has publishers knocking on her door, begging for the next discovery. More than that. My Louise, as you can see, is sexy, exceptionally bright, and a woman I love to call my own.'

There was an outbreak of applause.

'Okay Louise, you get your own back on Andy,' Eric said.

Henry noticed that Louise was rotating her wineglass nervously. 'How to draw an accurate picture of our Andy?'

There was a collective whoop, egging her on.

Henry could see Andy enjoying the attention. Andy had the physique of a sportsman, tall, muscular, with a shock of wavy brown hair and blue eyes.

'You see, I am in some doubt that such an attractive man could remain monogamous, and it fills me with reserve. Andy, like everybody here, including yourself, Henry, is successful. He has had multiple incarnations. Junior academic, solicitor, ministerial policy adviser and, at a similar age to all of us, he has an opportunity to make a real difference. Yes Henry, Andy is the Trojan horse for the people around this table. He is to be the future Prime Minister of this country, with the backing of this group, financially and emotionally. Andy is in a preselection contest for the Liberal party for the Federal seat of Bowers.'

'Hear, hear,' echoed around the table, followed by table thumping, leaving Henry agog. He was surprised that they considered him successful. He'd decided back in the last days of high school that his ideas of success differed markedly from those of his peers.

Eric, by now more than tipsy, stood up and called order. 'I have the very great pleasure of introducing Rachael.' He sat back down.

Henry wondered how Eric would present 'his darling', and who was behind Rachael's facade. Rachael flaunted her bosom as a weapon in the gender war. Beneath the gloss and make-up, Henry saw a face ravaged by excess, like a gleaming laminated bench top criss-crossed with knife marks.

Eric gathered himself like a weightlifter approaching a clean and jerk. He pushed down on the armrests of his chair as if he was about to rise, folded his arms in a minor body compression exercise, and stared at Rachael impassively. 'Rachael is a woman who knows what she wants. Few women do. It was Sigmund Freud, on his deathbed, who said there was one unanswered riddle in his life: "What do women want?"'

'Crap!' came in Louise.

'Don't start that again, please,' snapped Rachael.

'Don't get defensive, it's true,' said Eric, wide-eyed in mock surprise. 'Anyway. Rachael. She attended one of my seminars. She came looking for the river of gold, like all the marshmallows that have come to Daddy. And, unlike many of the no-hopers drinking at the well of fortune, Rachael has solid business experience and a mind to match. She is founder and principal of the largest niche recruitment business in the country, specialising in technology recruitment. She has built it up from nothing to an operation, ten years on, that is about to float on the sharemarket. Along the way she had two children by some motorcycle beast, who left her to look after his Harley Davidson rather than the kids he'd spawned. In sum, we have in Rachael a woman who has gone out there and done it rather than rely on some man to do it for her.' There was in Eric the capacity to incite warfare by dint of his mere presence in the room.

Henry wondered how this fabrication of towering egos would endure a night of alcoholic excess, and what, indeed, was the point of his invitation. All the while as the meal progressed, the caterers glided in and out invisibly.

Rachael picked at her food and then tapped her wineglass with a knife. 'I have yet to present Eric.'

'Oh yes, darling, I guesh Herry had better hear it from the horse's mouth,' Eric was beginning to slur.

'Henry, by the way, it's a highlight of my day to read your column,' Rachael said.

'It's n-not really a c-column,' Henry said.

'Anyway, my man Eric is that testosterone factory opposite. He is about to prove to this table, and the world outside this room, that he can make two-hundred million dollars in one year from a standing start. I feel privileged to be his woman, and I've not told him that before this moment. You would not know, Henry, but we are all newly coupled. Eric and I met nine months ago, at an investment seminar. Eric was the speaker. He strode into the room and announced that everyone there would be wealthy within twelve months. All they had to do was follow his instructions to the letter, fork out ten thousand dollars for his magic share selection program, and apply the Eric formula. You have never seen an audience more spellbound. It was like a cult.'

Henry saw Eric glow. The high-school football hero would pop the seams of his suit jacket if he flexed his massive hands around the wine bottle.

In the flurry of boozy conversation that followed, Henry gathered that these people were utterly convinced of Eric's money-making prowess. In an aside to Henry, Louise murmured that he was privileged to be at the same table as 'the group', saying this by placing imaginary quotation marks in the air. This was the core group, there were others who he would meet in time.

Henry listened as the plot was refined, clearly not for the first time. Eric had a fail-safe business plan that would not only generate wealth for each member of 'the group', but would create a pot of gold to finance the political ambitions of Andy. Eric had invited each of those present to commit to an investment in a listed mining company that he was transforming into a high-tech business. The prospectus for a new share raising was due in a couple of months. He had convinced 'the group' that within months a biotechnology boom would hit Australia. This was to be the real boom, unlike the bubble that had been the dot-com frenzy.

Henry had foreshadowed this in his newspaper articles, and he was beginning to see why he was invited. Well, sort of.

The food had come and gone, and offers of coffee had been rejected by all except Henry. As the others swilled cognac chasers Henry considered leaving the ship before it sank. He had been observing the amazing capacity of 'the group' to diminish the nation's grape harvest, counting a dozen empty bottles lined up on a nearby shelf. Except for an occasional word from Louise, he was more or less ignored. Each time someone swivelled in their chair and asked him a question, he was left swallowing a well-constructed riposte as their attention darted elsewhere.

Eric was nodding off. Louise, Rachael and Andy had been locked in a discussion that he'd half listened to. Then Rachael draped herself over Andy, imploring him to raise the status of small business in his cabinet when he became Prime Minister, and suddenly Louise seemed to remember that Henry was invited to talk about his ideas. 'Henry, God, it's nearly time to go home,' she said. 'Eric, wake up! You seem to have forgotten you have a guest of honour!'

Eric started and stared at Louise. 'W-what?'

'Henry!' hissed Rachael, shaking Eric by the arm.

'Oh yeah, Shinkers. Umm, what, are you sayin', Rach?'

Andy came in: 'Henry, sorry, we've been caught up. What about those ideas? The women love that stuff about people making partner choices like people buy and sell shares.'

'Yes, Henry. I *agree* with you that there's a balance sheet approach to marriage. We *are* all becoming consumerised,' Louise gushed. 'I'll phone you in a day or so. I have a proposal.'

'It's risk and return in marriage, just like the sharemarket,' Rachael offered.

'And you're now more a business commentator, rather than just technology?' Andy said, bleary-eyed.

'Umm.' Henry was startled by the sudden interest.

'Ya know, Sinkers, that stuff about companies and the seven deadly sins. You're bloody spot on. When ya said that BHP was a flamin' sloth ... you're right. Losin' billions.'

'And the downfall of Christopher Skase and Qintex *was* vanity.' Rachael almost shouted.

'And HIH was just bloody, umm, it was bloody avarice!' Eric said, pouring another drink.

'Jesus, Eric!' Rachael mopped the red wine he spilt with a serviette.

Henry took this as his cue to leave, scuttling off to catch the last bus home. Slurred protestations followed him out of the room: 'You're leaving? Great to meet you. Keep up the good work. Got your number ...'

- 3 -

The dinner party niggled at Henry like a burr in his shoe. He spent Sunday morning on his word processor, wrestling with the conclusion to an article, but found himself wandering into his kitchen to stare out of the window at the brick wall of the adjoining apartment block, where weathering had imparted imperfections to a fishbone pattern. Henry absorbed the detail as if in a trance.

Henry had never been a joiner. The boy scouts, football and surf clubs had been denied him because he was uncomfortable in circumstances where his thoughtfulness was interpreted as aloofness, and made others ill at ease. He was essentially a one-on-one person, and felt keenly the sense of aloneness that comes from watching a gaggle of Hare Krishna monks jingle their way through a shopping mall, blissed out in their own company. He wasn't at all sure whether he would join Eric's intimate group, if he was invited. And yet, there was something; a feeling that however vexatious to his spirit the four dinner guests were, there was some heady tinkering going on. What was all that about an exciting proposal from Louise? Why the interest in him?

Sunday was the day that Henry regularly paid a visit to his parents in Malabar. Henry could afford to live in Coogee only because he had an absentee landlord whose social conscience had been honed in a Buddhist conversion. The low rent that he paid would one day undergo a reality check. The apartment block had not enjoyed a coat of paint for the ten years that Henry had been a happy tenant.

Henry rode his bicycle to his parents' home. The ten-kilometre journey kept him fit, and besides, a car was out of the question. Horace and Mary had bought an old fibro cottage in seaside Malabar when the suburb was on the nose. Sydney's sewerage outlet had kept it off the tourist trail for decades and Henry, whenever possible, had timed his visits in those days according to the prevailing wind. But in the late 1980s the unsightly pungent brown slick had been transported by pipeline further out to sea. Horace Sinclair, like his son, reckoned that this was tantamount to a declaration of war on New Zealand. The result of this environmental sweeping under the carpet had been to ignite Malabar real estate prices.

Horace Sinclair reasoned that there were better things to do than gardening, painting, or generally renovating. On either side of the Sinclair cottage were grand houses recently built in a style that Horace described as Caesarean. Corinthian columns served notice that the inhabitants had been tutored in Renaissance Italian architecture. Armless statues and cherubs tinkling into goldfish ponds dramatically enhanced the contrast with the three-bedroom fibro cottage next door.

Agents and go-betweens were forever trying to convince Horace and Mary that they would enjoy their retirement in some warmer place, like Queensland. But Horace loved his home, and being able to wander down to the beach and dangle a line, and have a chat with some of the others in the community who were under siege. Mary created weavings, an activity not dependent on climate, so she screwed up her face at the mention of the Gold Coast.

Henry wheeled his bike into the backyard, pulled open the aluminium insect screen – its grating metal squawk making the need for a doorbell redundant – and responded to Horace's entreaty to 'just come on in'. He stepped over the cat, lost his balance and put out his hand to steady himself on a low cupboard. This act precipitated the collapse of an enormous pile of books that had found its way to that spot because most other spots were taken. As he bent to pick up the books he chanced upon his father's slippers.

'How are you Henry? Good to see you. Stay for tea?'

Henry had accumulated more literature than his thin arms could contain and as he got up, the books spilled all over the floor again.

'Just give 'em a shove and leave 'em, Henry. I'll fix it later,' Horace said.

Henry gave the pile a nudge with his foot. 'No, Dad, I'll fix it when I leave,' he said, and followed Horace into the living room.

This resembled an Indian carpet factory. A massive loom

occupied pride of place. Rolls of wool, thread, and boxes of material cluttered the available space. The light came from a hanging chandelier that had been a wedding present and belonged in the art-deco entrance of a vaudevillian theatre. Its numerous small globes were mostly burnt out, leaving the half-a-dozen residuals to shed a decaying glow below. Whichever architect had been responsible for the five-minute design imperative of the cottage would not have contemplated that the low ceilings could accommodate such a magnificent centrepiece, and anybody over five foot ten was forced to weave and duck.

Horace's spot in the room was an oasis in Mary's crush of enterprise. He mostly sat reading in his chair in one corner, while Mary banged away at her weavings.

Horace and Mary had named their twin boys Henry and Hugo. There was, for Horace, some magic in the letter H. He was fond of defending his choice of names with the observation that his two boys were the upright pillars in a letter bonded by a sturdy cross bar, namely himself; the capital letter was like a hurdle. Wasn't life a hurdle race?

'Where's Mum?' Henry asked.

The sound of a toilet flushing saw Mary stomping down the corridor, halt to glance at the mess newly fashioned by Henry, and smile at her son. 'Stay for tea, Henry? Where's Rosie?' Rosie was his girlfriend.

'Sure, Mum. Thanks. Rosie's back in a week. What's cooking?'

The question was a tad early for Mary, who screwed up her brow and pursed her lips. Henry always thought Mary Sinclair looked like a mum should look: grey hair tied back in a bun, and owl-like eyes that were magnified several times by horn-rimmed glasses. But a cordon bleu chef she was not. What she lacked in culinary skill was replaced by a fashionable approach to healthy dieting. Horace was responsible for implanting the latest fad in health-conscious eating in his wife, as he sat voraciously devouring his reading matter in the corner. So

Mary swung, unnervingly for Henry, between meals dominated by cabbage odours or soy beans, to lamb bits swimming in curry sauces, to thin wafers with Vegemite.

On this Sunday afternoon Henry was there hunting for clues. Henry wanted to know what had happened to his twin brother Hugo's business. But it was an Irish thing that the purpose of a visit had to be cloaked in the ritual of small talk. It was important for the visitor to offer casual observation about the state of the universe, waiting patiently for his host to ask whether there had been a recent death in the family, or whether the family pet had been run over, or whether there might be some point to the visit

'Finished that piece on investing in a mate?' Horace asked.

'It's on-going. Got a phone call from one of the people I went to school with. He invited me to a dinner party. All of his friends are high-fliers. I felt like a chicken in a fox den.'

'It's good you're getting feedback. You write well, son. Your mother thinks it's a bit callous to say that people choose each other like shares, don't you Mary? She said if that is the case then I'm a boring old coal company.'

'Nah, Dad would be a media company, like Fairfax,' Henry said over his shoulder to Mary.

'Yeah? Why's that?' Horace said.

'Because you devour information and churn out opinions. You pay the sort of dividend that appeals to women, keep things moving intellectually. You're a talker, Dad.'

The conversation ranged over a variety of topical and philosophical issues. Finally Henry felt the timing was right to ask his question. 'Dad, what's the latest on Hugo's business?'

Horace's face sagged. He lowered his bifocals to his lap and exchanged a look with Mary. A shadow passed over his face and his lips tightened in a grim line. 'It's bad. Hugo lost everything. I guess the bank will come knocking on our door.'

Horace reached for a letter inside his pocket. Slowly he opened it, and handed it to Henry, a tremor in his hand.

The letter was from Hugo, and addressed to 'Mr Sinclair'. The antagonism crept from the page and filled the room. Henry drew a breath and reached across to squeeze Horace on the arm, not looking up. The gist of Hugo's letter was a rejoicing that Horace now had to bear the pain of financial ruin. Perhaps it would be some compensation for the suffering that Hugo had had to endure. There was no point in trying to track him down. He was going to spend what little time he had left trying to enjoy himself. Any thoughts about his family only made him more ill. Good-bye.

There was silence. Mary sat at her weaving, looking intently at Henry.

The letter was a watershed, and Henry paused, gathering his emotions, wondering how to proceed. He looked at the crucifix prominent against the wall. 'Dad,' Henry began softly. 'It's time I was told the truth. Why did you assign a mortgage? You know what he's like.'

Horace fiddled with his glasses. 'I hate to talk about him Henry. We agreed not to.'

'But why would he write such a poisonous letter?'

'Son, he thinks I'm responsible for his disease.' Horace let out a long sigh.

Henry closed his eyes, then got up and walked out of the room. He went to the fridge and poured himself a glass of orange juice, then stood sipping and thinking. Horace had told him about the arrangement only a week ago.

Apparently Hugo had asked Horace to assign a mortgage over the Malabar cottage when he bought his computing business three years before. Hugo needed property security for a bank loan of four-hundred thousand dollars.

Hugo was as opposite in temperament to Henry as fraternal twins can be. Their father often joked that his sons were like two sides of a coin, Henry the head, Hugo the tail. As Henry stared out of the kitchen window he focused on his reflected image. The family's skeleton was etched in the shadowy double image of himself and Hugo. He deeply resented the Irish way of burying life's tragedies, of the fateful acceptance of some sort of destiny. He had once scoffed that if turning a blind eye were an Olympic sport, the Irish would have a gold medal in perpetuity. The Sinclair secret had become all-consuming. If the truth be known, every Sinclair action was motivated by something that nobody would discuss.

Henry's stomach tightened as he contemplated the awesome prospect of his parents becoming destitute, and thereby compounding the family tragedy. He inhaled deeply and strode back into the living room.

'Right. Enough of this,' he said, hands on hips, brow furrowed. He stared down at Horace. 'Your house is about to vaporise, disappear, poof, gone. I have a crazy brother running around, God knows where, with one of the worst diseases known to man, with bloody Huntington's disease ...' Henry took stock, in free fall. Nobody had ever mentioned the disease by name.

Horace and Mary looked at him, mouths agape. Henry had never raised his voice. Mary peered closely at the walls of her house, confirming that they were still intact, then examined her son with a perplexed expression. 'Yes?'

They looked at each other like statues. 'We sit around yacking like it's all happening to someone else. Well, it's bloody time I stopped sitting on my hands. I've got a fifty-fifty chance of getting the disease. Dad, you're going to become a basket case, needing constant care ... I'm going to do what I have to do.'

'Like what, son?' Horace asked.

'Well, like make some money. Try to find Hugo. Save your bloody house. The people I met on Saturday ...'

Horace leaned forward in his chair. 'Son, we've always agreed that money corrupts.'

- 4 -

Henry did not cope well with stress. This explained why he had rejected offers to become a full-time commentator for various investment magazines and newspapers. He had a genetic desire to please, and absorbed personally the disharmony of the workplace. He'd tried it, didn't like it. The trade-off was a life forever on the brink of financial collapse, which was ironic considering that he knew more about financial matters than most.

What surprised him considerably was the phone message from Eric Schwartz on Tuesday morning. A ringing telephone usually meant a solicitation to write an article, which happened infrequently because most of his regular correspondence occurred via e-mail. People who knew him found him to be a wee bit slow when it came to a telephone conversation. He rewound the answering machine to hear his messages.

'Henry. Come see me in action. Wednesday evening. Investment seminar. Come as one of the marshmallows. Just joking.' Eric then left an address.

A few hours later Louise, the esteemed literary agent, left a message insisting than he ring back and arrange a convenient time to see her.

Then Andy, the Prime Minister, rang and left greetings. The following morning it was the flamboyant groper, Rachael.

Henry reeled at his new popularity. Normally he would have declined an invitation from someone as aggressive as Eric. What was the point? He knew the score. Whatever it was that Eric wanted would be self-serving. But his parents' predicament had rattled Henry's cage, and he felt compelled to attend the marshmallows' briefing.

For once Henry spent some moments contemplating suitable attire. He considered the faded jeans a suitable match for his favourite hound's-tooth coat with the elbow patches that Rosie had said made him look academic. He thought to flatten his hair, but forgot about it, and thus exited for an evening as a marshmallow, whatever that was.

Henry sat at the back of a lecture theatre that accommodated one hundred, pleased that he could hide himself in the crowd. Free investment seminars were being widely touted. With the renewed popularity of the sharemarket, all sorts of organisations were enticing the uninitiated to buy into some black box system or other. Henry had written an article about technical analysis, and the dangers involved in the black box approach: the algorithm involved in assessing the momentum behind share price movements was not revealed, leaving the investor at the mercy of a system no more likely to succeed than the famous dart-throwing chimpanzee. Henry was made sceptical in the extreme by anybody who claimed to have a fail-safe system.

Out in front was an overhead projector beaming a welcome to the Internet Trader Share Selection System-acronym ITSSS Unbelievable. A couple of nervous-looking types in suits were wringing their hands and conferring in meaningful asides, jubilant that they had another full house of marshmallows.

Where was Eric? Henry was seated next to a woman in her early thirties who was poised, pen and notebook on her lap, ready to archive the gospel. On his other side was a middle-aged man who had failed to remove the grease from his stunted fingernails.

One of the suited men called the seminar to order and went through a welcoming patter, his voice climbing to a gushing introduction: 'The guru himself! Yes, this evening, ladies and gentlemen we are fortunate to have the founder of ITSSS, Eric Schwartz!' He hissed the esses like a snake, then turned sideways with a sweep of his hand.

There was no denying Eric's presence. The room hushed, and Eric shuffled some papers at the lectern. His close-cropped bleach-blonde hair glistened. He cleared his throat with a rumble, pulled his shoulders together, and stared out at the throng. 'You're all here to get rich. I'm here to make you rich. I've flown in from delivering a seminar in Melbourne and I'm tired. I am about to give you access to a learning curve that is steep, and requires discipline. You're all marshmallows. You know nothing. You're blank slates upon which we shall write success. You will be able to learn from each other and be tutored in the use of our program as you go. But listen here! I don't want you if you're not serious. If at the end of this session you are not convinced, then you're not for us. We don't want to waste our time or yours. You can go away and live your life as a marshmallow!'

Henry looked around at stunned faces. He saw the woman next to him scribble 'marshmallow?' and they exchanged a glance as she sniggered.

Eric gathered momentum. He ran through slides demonstrating the rationale of investing in shares as opposed to other types of assets, such as real estate. Then he expounded on the basis of all investment decisions. All investments were based on future projections of earnings, profit. All analysis came down to the future net profit divided by the number of shares that the company had on issue, throwing up the supreme importance of the first of a series of technical terms that HAD to be understood. He shouted this at the top of his voice, and the woman scribbled furiously, underlining 'earnings per share' multiple times. He raced through the difference between fundamental analysis, in which the entire gamut of a company's operations was dissected – management, competitors, product, market and technical analysis – essentially the ITSSS system.

And then he paused to whisper a question. 'The market is perfect. How do you win, when you have no insider information? The only way anybody can do better than anybody else is to know something that others do not. The only way this can happen is if you have an uncle on the board of directors.

There are laws that govern insider trading. The good news gets out, the share price rises. More people want to buy the share than sell it. Volume of trades goes up.'

Eric paused, stared around the room, then showed graphically how the ITSSS System highlighted the early momentum in share movements of a range of shares, signalling the best time to buy. He harangued and cajoled, and impressed Henry both with his oratory and his grasp of detail. Suddenly he packed up and left the room.

There was a hornet's nest of conversation. The woman next to him showered questions on Henry. 'Do you understand what he's talking about? I mean, I understand a lot of what he said, but this is my first time. Could you go over what he said about the "price earnings ratio" ... you're not taking notes ...'

Moments later one of the suited men appeared and dragged everybody away from their fantasies of early retirement. There was a noticeable sagging in the room as he exclaimed that all this was available for only six thousand dollars for the basic program and a series of on-going tutorials, or ten thousand dollars for the deluxe model. And by the way, he added conspiratorially, Eric had ignored the best news. Mr Schwartz was also principal shareholder in a company that was to float on the market in a couple of months. Members of ITSSS would be offered shares. Eric was not really at liberty to say, because of the law on insider trading, but — nudge nudge — it was predicted that the share price of Palamountain Ltd would rise from the initial subscription price of fifty cents to three dollars inside six months. The woman banged Henry's knee with her own.

People queued to sign up. Henry hovered, hoping to see Eric reappear, wondering what he would say to him. The woman singled him out and introduced herself. 'By the way, I'm Beth,' she smiled.

Henry shook the outstretched hand and radiated back that he was H-Henry.

'I think it's very interesting, don't you?' she said.

'Umm, yes,' Henry responded. Small talk was not Henry's strong suit.

She looked at him seriously. 'I can't afford the money. And then what do I have left to invest? I like the way you can do it with a partner, two for the price of one. You know, attend the courses, learn as you go. Do you know anything about the sharemarket?'

'Umm, yes.'

'*Do* you? Are you interested? I mean, we could go as partners, halve the cost.'

Henry looked around the room. Beth's open face was trusting as a child's. 'Wait here for a minute, p-please,' he said, and walked over to one of the suited men to ask him where Eric was, explaining that he'd had a personal invitation.

He was ushered to an adjoining room to find Eric waving one arm while stuck to a mobile phone. Eric pointed to a seat, growled at someone on the phone and held out his hand. 'What did you think, Sinkers?'

'V-very interesting,' Henry replied.

'You see what our group at the dinner party is on about now? I want you to participate in the course, for free. If you're impressed, you'll write about it. I know you have strong views about technical analysis, but I'm about to change them.'

'Th-thanks. I-it's generous of you. But, I may n-not change my mind.'

'I'll take the risk. Here, take this to the people at the counter, they'll sign you up,' Eric said, giving Henry a card. 'Nice to see you again, Sinkers. See you at the tuition courses.'

Henry found Beth and smiled. 'I think I can get you in for free,' he said.

- 5 -

His parents' predicament weighed on Henry. He paid them another visit the morning after the seminar, hoping for an honest confrontation.

He and Horace scrunched through the sand of Malabar beach. The south-easterly wind had kicked up a sea and the beach was strewn with the discarded remnants of a fast-food lifestyle. Henry maintained a vigil beside his father, who was exceptionally quiet.

At last Horace spoke. 'You know, Henry, it's as I've always said. If you take the struggle out of your life, you take the stuffing from it. Imagine having so much money that you didn't have to think about what things cost. I can't think what pleasure you'd get from merely buying *things*. The joy your mother and I have had over the years scrounging bargains, making do with the bare essentials. You remember how long we took to get that stove? I felt like Indiana Jones hunting the Stove from Doom, getting one that worked for twenty dollars.'

'Dad, you have to eat. Mum needs a hip replacement. The house, the disease. Your car is on its last legs.'

'I love that car. Wouldn't trade it in for anything. I suggested to your mum that we could sell it and pay for her hip, and she scoffed at me. She's as fond of it as I am. It's become a collector's item, did you know that son? Not many Morris Minors around any more. Some old geezer reckoned I'd get twenty thousand or more for it. Not in bad condition.'

'You never drive it, no wonder.'

'Have you spoken to Hugo, son?'

Henry's heart skipped a beat. This was the first time Horace had volunteered Hugo's name in years, and Henry felt his stutter come on. 'N-no. D-don't know what I'd say.'

Horace put his hand on Henry's arm and squeezed it gently.

'He's not like you Henry, never has been. Always wanted *things*, never happy. Then, when he married that Mignon – there's trouble, I said to your mum. Lots of ambition in that Fillet Mignon. Fancy calling someone Mignon. The wrong sort. Give me a woman with few needs, and I'll show you a treasure. Take your mum – you know, Henry, she made two hundred dollars on that last weaving, the one with the purple ducks flying over those funny-looking reeds. How do you talk about colours with someone like you or your mum? She says she'll make enough money to replace all of our hips.'

Henry's insides screamed for Horace to continue. Hugo had taken a trip to Ireland four years ago, and quite by accident discovered the family secret. Even before that Hugo had never wanted to be part of the family – he had moved away from home at twenty. But when Hugo returned from Ireland and confronted Horace with his discovery the doors slammed, the shutters were pulled down, and the lights went out in the Sinclair household when it came to any discussion concerning Hugo. And Henry never understood what happened that fateful night. There had been an argument. Horace had said that Hugo was like a wild man.

'Dad. I respect your right not to want to discuss Hugo, or the disease. But we're *both* sitting on a time-bomb. I've put it out of my mind as best I can. You *know* I've researched the disease?'

'Yeah. I figured you would have.'

'Dad, you have late onset. It will hit you, and probably soon.'

'I know, son. Your mother and I have our faith.'

'It's a lottery, Dad. Hugo is very unusual to get it so early. The fact that he's got it doesn't mean that I will get it. It's fifty-fifty. Now, on top of everything else you'll lose the house. What about Mum?'

'I know, Henry. I know. I've told you what I think. *Why* have a DNA test that gives you the kiss of death?' Horace blew air and stared out to sea.

'But Hugo had a right to decide for himself. *Why* did you argue about it?'

'I just don't want to talk about it. That's *my* right.'

They wandered back and paused to let a Mercedes drive into the driveway of the house next door. 'Oh, oh. That's Antonio and his wife, Francesca,' Horace said, stepping aside and tipping his old hat.

Antonio looked right through him. Francesca raised her eyebrows in a gesture of disdain.

'Funny people, our neighbours. I know our house takes the shine off their mansions, but that's no reason to be unneighbourly. You almost can't see our little place tucked in beside them. You know, he's offered to buy us out more times than I've had hot dinners,' Horace chuckled.

'Yeah? What's he offered?'

'Never comes to that. Just lays it on me whenever he has a chance. "Horace, itsa nice day. Whaddya think about land values in Malabar? My mudder, comin for a visit. Proud woman. Liddle village in Italia. Wants to see my place before she goes to heaven. You thinkin a'movin' yourself?" They're good sorts. I like Italians. You know he migrated out here when he was thirty? Very hard working. He's a builder. Done all right. But they're getting a bit pushy. Sign of the times. Henry.'

'It didn't take them long to build the house. Shot up overnight. The whole street is changing, Dad.'

'Yeah. Everybody except us, hey Henry?'

Henry sat at his desk and pondered whether or not to return the phone calls. The calm had disappeared from his life. There were so many bricks in his bed that he'd not slept well. He didn't have a clue what possible interest Louise, Rachael and Andy could have in him.

He phoned Louise first as the one least offensive to his

psyche. She talked on the phone like a woman used to talking on the phone. 'Henry. So pleased you called back. I'd love to speak to you. Strictly business. My office?'

The literary world was not entirely alien to Henry. He had a fair idea how an agent would operate, although he'd never met one. He inspected himself in the elevator mirror on the way to the fifth floor of the Sentinel Building in North Sydney. He had chosen to wear his favourite green jumper over a floral red shirt that argued loudly to be somewhere else. Henry had been told by Rosie that colour blindness was kind to the afflicted, but damaging to those who fashion their own self-concept on aesthetic considerations. She'd warned him that invitations to appear in public places could be curtailed. As Henry made his appearance in the open-plan office three people stopped talking on the telephone, and gaped as one.

Louise, whose desk was at the far end of the large room, stood up to greet him, grabbed her handbag, stopped in full flight to look him over, and put her bag down again. 'Henry, do come in. We can go into our conference room. Coffee?' She pulled him by the elbow firmly enough to let him know that the direction was implacably prescribed.

She shut the door, pressing herself against it as if she were shielding him from some horror on the other side. 'Sit down, won't you. Did you say you wanted coffee?'

Henry shook his head. Louise seemed agitated. She sat down adjacent to him at the end of a polished table that accommodated eight. Around the walls were photos of Louise and famous people, all autographed. One wall was taken up with movies and the covers of books that had been published through the intervention of her agency.

As Louise adjusted herself, Henry noticed the talons that were her fingernails. She looked harsher outside the soft light of the dinner party setting. Nature was bountiful in the many ways she could craft a personal history. Around Louise's eyes and down-turned mouth he saw wrinkles once destined to become laugh lines. They were reassigned to some more wretched preoccupation, like bitterness. Something was driving her, and hard.

'Henry, I'm interested in your writing. You have a wonderful turn of phrase, and we all love the way you make the business world understandable and human. I know some people think you're joking when you talk of the danger in us all becoming consumerised, and treat each other as share purchases, but I believe there's truth to it. Just excuse me a minute.'

Louise walked out and came back carrying a file. She opened it on the table and Henry could see that it contained clippings of his articles.

'Let's see if I can summarise some of this, and if I've got it right: if women want economic security, men want sex. If women make partner choices based on parenting potential, men make choices based on the waist–hip ratio. For women the analytical process of partner choice has become less clouded by strictly romantic notions and been replaced with hard-headed technical analysis.' She looked up. 'You know, as I applied your thinking to Andy the other day, I had to agree with you. I have chosen him because he has significant earnings potential, hence will provide a good dividend. He has a future with considerable blue sky, which you describe as "excitement value". You define this to be mystery, humour, and the attributes that imply a person has growth potential. This is like choosing a share based on an unknown but exciting future because of some research breakthrough, like a cure for AIDS for example. All in all you are prepared to pay more for potential, both in your partner and in the share. Those who take few risks should stick with predictability. Buying a share in a bank would be like marrying an accountant, engineer or other professional. But women who want a fast life should choose bio-tech companies, News Corp, or' – she smiled knowingly – 'Eric, or Andy?'

Henry realised that he was being taken seriously. He was about to point out to her that for him the idea was merely to provide a talking point, to satirise society's greed and mostly to enable people better to understand what share trading was all about. She rattled on about how wonderful it would be if people could get away from the glibness of astrology and size each other up as shares and investments. A whole new vocabulary could be spawned. 'Think of it. A prescription for love as easy as one, two, three when you know the formula. And you can tell us the formula, Henry. Could you refine your thinking and produce a slim volume?'

Louise tapped the table with a pen like a woodpecker. Was she excited, or did she just want to get this over with as quickly as possible? Henry couldn't tell.

'Well . . .' Henry had to think about it. She just didn't get him at all. But, the cottage, and Hugo . . .

Louise stopped tapping and started twirling the pen between her fingers. A deeper voice emerged. 'You know how we operate. Fifteen per cent of your cut, which is ten per cent of the retail price of the book. You look surprised?'

'Yes, I am. Actually . . .'

'I do all the negotiating. I've already interested a publisher. You'll get an advance. I don't know how much, possibly twenty thou.'

'Twenty thousand dollars?'

She scrutinised him, then pushed her chair back. 'What else? Agreed? What about three months to write and polish? You've already got most of it down.'

'Umm.'

'Okay, good. I'll call you to check on progress.'

- 6 -

Henry often thought of himself as a tiny rivulet gurgling along beside the Amazon. Aside from his close friend Alex and his girlfriend Rosie, who was this week visiting her brother in the country, he had acquaintances, but few close friends.

Alex and Henry were cut from the same cloth. Alex, at thirty-four, resided with his mother. He eked out a living by baking exotic breads in her oven and delivering them to shops in the area. His delivery van was a sixties Volkswagen Kombi, in which he could be seen early in the morning spluttering and fuming his way through the streets of Randwick and Coogee. Henry christened the van 'Acropolis', in deference to Alex's Greek origins and because it was an ancient relic.

Alex occasionally struck out on a new venture. Henry reckoned that Alex had about as much talent for business as Henry did for fashion modelling but was impressed when Alex rented a disused electrical shop on the main road in Clovelly and converted it to Alex's Seriously Slow Food Restaurant.

On the opening night Horace and Mary picked Henry up in the Morris, Henry bundling his legs into the back seat, a feat that could only be managed by sitting sideways. Horace wore his favourite old felt hat, which scraped on the roof of the car whenever he made a turn. Henry had tried many times to convince Horace that his driving days were over, and that it was dangerous to putter along at twenty-five kilometres per hour. 'What's the hurry, son?'

As they crammed inside the tiny car, Mary said that it was just as well Rosie had not made an appearance. Mary looked terrific in her floral number, and Henry complimented her, asking her what new fragrance it was that had drowned the car in a botanical garden of delight. 'Glad you noticed, Henry. You could take a cue from your son, Horrie.'

'What?' Horace was gripping the steering-wheel with feverish intensity. He had moved his seat forward to give Henry more room, and the wheel, uncommonly large by modern standards, was stuck under his chin, spread-eagling his arms and causing him to nudge Mary at every turn. 'Where to now, Henry?'

'I'm afraid you'll have to go up Arden Street now, Dad.'

'You mean that mountain?'

'Oh dear,' said Mary.

Horace reckoned that the gradient on some of the streets in Coogee made the Himalayas look like a desert. At the bottom of Arden Street he stopped, and they looked up the narrow incline. 'Oh well, we'll make it.' He gunned the little car to take-off speed, then rammed home the gearstick so that they took off with a kangaroo jump. Unfortunately this exhausted the one-litre engine, failing to provide the thrust that Horace intended, meaning that the rest of the climb was just achievable in first gear.

Henry noticed that an elderly woman carrying groceries beside them was making quicker passage than they were. She looked back at him in wonder.

So it was that the trip, all of two kilometres, took an uncommonly long time. Horace pulled to the side frequently to uncork the pressure of a long procession of cars fidgeting and dipping their lights behind. Mary thought it a bit over the top when somebody honked aggressively as he sped past, lowered his window, and yelled, 'The cemetery's next left, you old fart.' Henry looked at his watch and said that it was just as well that they had a reservation.

Eventually they parked the car and shuffled along the street looking for a sign, expecting to see some activity – like crowds, for instance. Alex had sited his restaurant among half-a-dozen delis and hairdressing salons, all of which lay dormant at night. They had moved past the only lit window in the strip before they realised they'd passed the restaurant. Tentatively, like a three-bodied animal, they craned over each other to peer through the window. 'There's Alex,' Henry said.

They opened the door and saw Alex's mother sitting at one of four otherwise empty tables. Mary and Effie Conomos exchanged pleasantries while Henry joined Alex, who was sidling from foot to foot eager for reactions to his new enterprise.

After everybody was seated on a motley assortment of chairs, Henry looked around to see that a skeleton occupied a chair at an adjoining table. 'Alex, what's that?' he asked in a hushed voice.

Alex grinned, 'It's to tell everybody not to expect fast service.'

Mary wondered aloud about the value of this promotion, but Horace beamed in full understanding.

Mrs Conomos had coped well with Alex's unusual flair over the years. She was a diminutive Greek lady who often complained to Mary that it was surely time for Alex to move out and get married. But Alex would have rated as a slow-moving share in Henry's mating game. He was terminally thin, tall, and bald except for a halo of long black hair that hung down from the extreme edges of his cranium. His distinguishing characteristic was a pair of the most colossal ears on the planet, which stood perpendicular to his head. Yet, as Mary often said to Henry, Alex had the loveliest brown cow-like eyes.

Henry took in the scaffolding that separated the kitchen from the eating area, and looked across at overflowing bags of potatoes. The choice of decor suggested that not too much renovating had occurred since the little shop's last incarnation as an electrical outlet. The offerings were advertised on a blackboard with considerable change of mind on the part of the proprietor, judging by the many crossings out. From a brave beginning of six main courses, the choice had narrowed to two.

Alex moved to the blackboard, pencil poised. 'Do you want to order? I'll go through the menu. I'm sorry that the choice is not as great as I would have liked, but Mum couldn't get round to more than two dishes tonight.'

'Are *you* the cook, Effie?' Mary asked.

'No, only occasionally, to help out. Alex is a wonderful cook, you know.'

'Yeah, well, I opened earlier than I should have. I still don't have a stove, and I had to bring the food from home. The council hasn't officially given me the all clear. I don't know what I'm going to do about toilets and a sink,' he muttered as if these were mere hiccups on the way to globalisation.

Henry reluctantly concluded that Alex had been a little too casual in his strategic thinking. 'Oh well, doesn't matter. We're here. It's early yet.' He glanced at his watch and had a sinking feeling that all the diners who were going to come were already ensconced. 'I'll start. I'll have' – he strained to read the scrawl – 'the bean soup as a starter.'

'Sorry. It's not ready, I mean it's still at home,' Alex said.

'Oh. Okay, what about the moussaka?'

'Yep,' Alex noted the request.

'I suppose we'll all have that, won't we dear?' Effie said.

'I guess you will,' Alex said, smiled, and turned into the kitchen.

- 7 -

True friendship is about loyalty, and Henry had immense respect for Alex as a pioneering, if often oblique, thinker. Alex had the most unusual ideas on just about everything, and could be relied upon to cut to the chase in any problem situation; well, almost. Henry had often said that many large corporations in Australia were moribund with management ideas that were about as creative as the menu at a fish-and-chip shop. They could usefully employ Alex to turn their ideas upside down, and inside out.

Henry had wanted to run his dilemmas past Alex, but had not wanted to bother his friend while he was preoccupied with his eatery. He sat in his office staring at the computer screen. On his left was a writing pad from which a number of phone numbers screamed at him.

He circled the name Andy, wondering if the future Prime Minister could cope without his intimate friendship. Then he swallowed at Rachael's name, remembering the horsey laugh and the wandering hands.

And what in the name of heaven was he going to do about Louise and her amazing offer? Twenty thousand dollars sounded like a lot of money. She was right that it would only take a bit of spit and polish, and he'd be a published author.

He'd committed to Eric's investment tutorials, principally because Beth was now counting on him but also because he could have an intimate view of a share-trading system. The various offers were attractive because of the compulsion for him to change. He could not face the prospect of his parents' financial ruin when he had the skills to rescue them. Besides, there was the looming shadow of Hugo. Henry wished that he had Rosie around to chat and offer her opinion, but it would be another week before her return.

Finally, deciding he had nothing to lose, Henry steeled himself to return the phone calls.

He eventually got through to Rachael, who absolutely insisted that he visit her on Thursday evening at her Potts Point apartment. Andy was as urbane as you would expect of the Prime Minister, and arranged for Henry to see him in a week.

He sighed, put down the phone and stared at his piece on the computer screen. Minutes later the phone rang. He was about to allow the answer machine to kick in when he ran into the living room and picked up the receiver, thinking it might be Rosie. 'Hello?'

There was silence. 'Hello, who is it?'

'Henry, it's Hugo.'

Henry switched the receiver to his other hand and felt his heart racing. 'H-Hugo?'

'Still stuttering? Haven't you outgrown it?'

Henry could hear a bang, as if Hugo had dropped the receiver. 'Hugo? W-where are you?'

'I'm clumsy, Henry. Are *you* starting to get a bit clumsy? Should I say more clumsy than usual? How long since we've spoken, Henry? Five years is it? How did Horace like my letter? Before you say anything, just hear this. He's a bastard, and you'd better go and have a test. After all, you've got a girlfriend now. Have you told her yet, you weak shit? I'll bet you haven't. What if she wants a baby, Henry?' Hugo's voice changed to a gurgle.

'Hugo?'

'Just having a little turn. It's starting to catch up with me, Henry. You wouldn't recognise me. Have you thought about that? Mignon's left me. Good riddance. Just a good-time girl. Have a test, Henry. I'm watching you . . .'

The line went dead. Henry slumped onto the sofa, the phone dangling from his hand. Watching me? Why? Wouldn't recognise him? Horace is a bastard? He sat, confused, then got up, opened a cupboard drawer and pulled out a photograph. There they all were, in happier times, when he and Hugo were about fifteen. Hugo stood beside Henry. He looked at his brother. Hugo was the sports star, womaniser, man-about-town. It was as if Henry had deliberately fashioned his own character to be as opposite as possible to his twin brother's.

Hugo had kept his distance ever since moving out of the family home. Now and then they heard from the police that he was in trouble. The ultimate shame came when Horace had to get Hugo out of jail. He was just drunk and disorderly, but it affected Horace none the less.

Hugo's diagnosis of Huntington's disease hung over Henry's life like a guillotine. What was it about the wild argument between Horace and Hugo?

Henry remembered how he had tried to help his brother.

But after Hugo had defied Horace and had himself tested, he had been in total denial. He had refused to speak to his family, later rushed into his business venture, and otherwise lived life frenetically. Henry knew that Mary had occasional contact with Hugo's wife, Mignon. Mignon spoke of Hugo's womanising, and his gambling. Mary bottled up her sorrow.

Henry tucked the photo under some clothes. He had a sinking feeling that it was all about to come crashing down around him. When would Horace succumb to the disease? Would he himself begin to show signs of memory loss, clumsiness? Henry still carried a torch for his brother, although it had faded to a flicker. What about Rosie and Alex? They knew nothing. They'd never met Hugo.

It was only possible to enter Rachael's Potts Point apartment through an elaborate security system. Henry pressed the bell and waited, not realising that intimate details of his nostrils were being beamed in to Rachael's living room. He whacked at his hair, blew his nose, and jumped when Rachael's unsubtle squawk to 'come on up' echoed around the entranceway.

As she opened the door Henry recoiled with the realisation that he'd prefer to be anywhere else in the world. She wore an orange Lycra bodysuit that clung to her like Glad Wrap. Her chest was suppressed within the suit like an innerspring. Her shiny blonde hair billowed in a cloud that would intimidate a tribal headdress. 'Henry, so nice you could make it.'

Martini in one hand she led Henry into a living room that featured the latest in modern living. Henry gaped at the shiny-yellow, plastic-looking circular lounge that swept around a thickly carpeted floor, and felt dwarfed by enormous paintings that bombarded the room with leering Bosch-like images of people being strangled, or eaten. Rachael thrust a drink in his hand and pressed a button on the stereo. Rushing water and carping seagulls descended.

Rachael sat close to him on the modular lounge, allowing

Henry to be in no doubt about her perfume. He contorted his backside in a sideways shuffle, just to create a little more space. 'Marvellous dinner party the other night?'

'Umm.' Henry nodded, sipped on his martini and coughed.

'Oh dear, too strong for you?'

Henry cleared his throat, thinking that at last he knew what it was like to drink methylated spirits. 'No, i–it's fine, thanks.'

'What did you think of the other guests? We all had a little too much to drink. Poor dear, you must have been overwhelmed.'

'N-no. Although . . .'

'Where do you live Henry? I don't know anything about you.'

'Umm, Coogee. A flat.'

'By yourself?'

'Yes.'

'Andy's a darling. He and Louise are so good together. You should hear him give a speech. Eric is going to pull it off, you realise.' She paused. 'You know, I must confess, and I hope you don't take offence, but I've not read as many of your articles as the others. I hear them talk, and it's good enough for me. After all, we have Louise in "the group", who must know, and Eric and Andy who are experts. I'm really too busy. I'll be floating my company soon.'

'Y-yes. I m-mean no.'

'You know Henry, you're really an attractive man, in an academic sense. Those John Lennon glasses really suit you. You have wonderful hands, it's one of the first things I notice about a man.' Henry turned his left hand over, seeing it for the first time.

'And you have the cutest smile, and wonderfully expressive eyes. I'd shave off the goatee though – makes you look a bit alternative.'

Henry, who was caressing his goatee, quickly stopped.

She then concentrated her gaze on Henry's attire. She paused at the quagmire, which was an honest appraisal of Henry's dress sense. Henry looked down at his clothes, wondering what it was that held her attention. Rachael forced a smile, which was designed as a clear signal that she was not yet prepared for a comment that would change Henry's life.

'I suppose you must be wondering why I asked you to call in briefly tonight? I have a confession to make, and I hope you don't consider me crass. I'm an extremely open sort of person, and I want you to feel free to say anything.'

She got up and began to pace up and down in front of Henry. 'I find this difficult, because we hardly know each other. I trust Eric's judgment, and he's said that you have a huge following from your column, and that people trust your opinion. He says you're incapable of lying, which makes you a pretty special sort of man these days.'

Henry followed her progress as if he were watching a tennis game.

'But Eric is such a tough act. I love him dearly. He's everything I could hope for in a man, but he's so *competitive*. I'm afraid that if I don't succeed, I'll lose him. He hates losers.' She paused, stared out at the impressive view of the harbour, then looked down at Henry meaningfully. 'Do you have any idea how hard it is to make a success of life as a woman? I have two children—they're with my mother tonight, otherwise I would have loved for you to meet them. I juggle work with motherhood. You write about personal issues; perhaps you would understand better than most men. The fact is the float of my company is incredibly important to me, and the children. I know we're well off by normal standards, but you can imagine how hard it is to keep up?'

Henry was concentrating hard, trying to figure out how he could possibly be of assistance in this tragedy. Rachael swooped down next to him, made to reach for his hand, and changed her mind. 'Would you have a look at my prospectus, and only if you like it, of course, would you support the float in your column?'

★

Disgorged from Rachael's apartment, Henry found himself waiting for a taxi. It was routine that at a certain point in any proceedings there would be a sudden urgency for his host to attend some emergency or other, and a speedy exit was deemed necessary. Still, it meant that he occasionally sat in the back seat of taxis wondering what the evening had been all about.

He noticed that the taxi driver was sitting behind a plastic shield, and smiled when he remembered Alex's reaction the first time he saw one of these shields. Alex, who hadn't been inside a taxi since his mother made an emergency dash to the maternity hospital, reckoned that since the role of a taxi was principally to ferry drunks, the shields were there to prevent passengers from vomiting over the driver.

Henry conjured up the memory because Alex had made this comment during Henry's first real date with Rosie, and he missed her. Rosie and Henry had met via e-mail. Henry's email address was appended to each of his articles and his readers' replies were a source of constant inspiration and frustration. Rosie had written in response to Henry's first foray into his thesis about partner choice. She was struggling to educate herself financially, and found Henry's opinions a beacon in a flat sea. They had begun a dialogue which lasted for about three months, until eventually Rosie rang Henry to organise a 'date'. Rosie, an experienced cyber-surfer persuaded Henry to meet her in an electronic chat room. She assigned Henry the chat-room name 'Lancelot', while Rosie was 'Drawbridge'. She explained that she felt like a castle surrounded by a crocodile-infested moat, and that she would only lower the drawbridge for her Lancelot.

He arrived home and listened to his answering machine. Rosie apologised, but she wouldn't be able to get back until Monday.

- 8 -

On Saturday morning Henry woke to glorious sunshine streaming through his window. He decided that he would unravel his thoughts by going for his favourite stroll along Coogee Beach and the pathway to Clovelly.

He hurried through breakfast and pulled on his walking shoes, then checked his e-mail. There were the usual messages from readers and analyses of stock movements on foreign bourses. Financial analysts were in disarray. Events in the Middle East were a constant reminder of the volatility of the times. No one would commit to a forecast beyond the next weekend.

And Alex wanted him to call in during the day. He'd left a lengthy message. It appeared that the council had refused his restaurant licence. There was some bureaucratic objection to letting his clients use the public toilet down the way. Alex was upset. 'We need to share resources, Henry. What's wrong with the council? There are enough toilets for an army with diarrhoea.' And the fact that he was going to use bottled gas also met with disapproval. He couldn't understand why it was against local regulation something-or-other for him to cook outside the back door. There would be natural venting, no need for an expensive exhaust. And he could wash up in a big plastic container. He was looking for a refrigerator. So what if he only had four tables? He was appealing to an exclusive clientele.

The end of November had brought early sun-seekers to the beach. Henry gloried in his good fortune at having such a beautiful environment on his doorstep. He strolled along the esplanade and absorbed the spectacle of a young woman removing her bikini top. He was as programmed as any male to gawk. Men couldn't help themselves. It was all so Darwinian.

As he gazed back up the hills that formed the Coogee Beach basin, he saw that the streets glinted from the reflected sun on endless car windows. Cars clogged the streets. Coming toward him was a pair of beach-goers shepherding a tribe of small children. The father was buried under a shop of beach accoutrements, boogie-board tucked under his arm. He was dripping with towels, inflated toys and assorted bags. His staggering gait was pitiful. His crimson-faced wife was screeching at the children and using the beach umbrella as a crowd-control weapon. Henry figured that they had been forced to park their car about five kilometres away, such was the pressure on available spaces – the council's efforts to beautify the beach had made it accessible only to families that ventured out before dawn. He wondered why this family did not squat on the beach in protest rather than contemplate the return journey. Alex had said that the beach of the future would only be experienced from the window of an airliner.

But then, the walk was magnificent as usual. The waves crashed against the northern headland of the beach, and he looked out at Wedding Cake Island, a kilometre from shore. His eye was drawn to the island as it would be to a lone ship at anchor. It was the first point of resistance for the ocean's swell and huge flukes of water gushed into the air. He stood on the precipitous cliff and sucked in the salty air, glad to be alive. Then the shadow of Huntington's disease descended, and the bitter saga of his parents' home, and he reflected on life's fragility.

Henry walked along Brook Street and looked up at the Conomos residence. It was set back on the high side of the street, a former stately home that had been somewhat neglected for fifty years. The house was contained behind a formidable sandstone wall. A magnificent verandah stretched out underneath a shingle roof that had become a patchwork quilt of tarpaulins. Alex had worked out the cost benefit of repairs to the shingle roof and calculated that he could purchase second-hand tarpaulins for a fraction of the investment. He had convinced his mother that he could replace the tarpaulins every five years and be miles ahead.

Henry followed Alex into the kitchen, said hello to Effie, and fought his way around the flotsam of the true engine room of Alex's restaurant.

'It's frustrating to live in a world of bureaucrats,' Alex complained as he waved his arms at bags of onions, carrots, flour and enough provisions to make a significant contribution to world famine relief. Henry nodded sympathetically. 'Anyway, come outside and sit in the sun. Want a tea?'

They sat outside the kitchen window at a rickety table. The up-sloping backyard was a jungle of waist-high weeds and grasses. 'What are you going to do now?' Henry asked.

Alex stared into the distance. 'I'll have to convert the restaurant into . . .'

'You'll come up with something,' Henry said.

'But look, I've been absorbed. What about you, Henry? How's it going with that matchmaking idea? You seem a bit flat.'

Henry described his extraordinary fortnight, omitting any reference to his brother's phone call but telling Alex about the failure of Hugo's business.

'Amazing, Henry. Incredible.' Alex was more interested in the plight of Henry's parents than the machinations of 'the group' at the dinner party. Horace and Mary were family to Alex. Henry saw Alex's cow eyes turn down at the corners, and felt warmed by his friend's concern.

'I have an idea.' Alex scratched his chin. 'You say that Horace's neighbours want him out of there. They're all loaded to the gills. What say we make it even more urgent for them to offer a really good price for your folks' cottage?'

'Hey?'

'You say the bank will call up the mortgage and it's worth four-hundred thousand dollars? What would the neighbours offer if Horace went to them and said the cottage was for sale at six-hundred thousand dollars?' Alex was winding up.

'I don't have any idea.'

'Imagine we made the cottage even more of an eyesore. Made the neighbours *really* think about shifting Horace. We'll have to act fast, before the bank moves. It's just land value, the cottage is worthless.'

Henry's heart lifted at the sight of Alex's eager expression. 'You know, Alex, I love you like a brother I've never had. We're two halves of a whole person, have you ever thought about that?'

'You're definitely the top half, Henry. I make a very promising sphincter.'

'You're the extrovert to my introvert.'

'The excrement to your increment, more like.'

'Okay shithead, let's get cracking.'

When Henry told his father about Alex's idea there was silence over the telephone. Henry could almost hear Horace's brain shifting gear. It was a long shot. Henry knew what would happen if the bank took possession and forced a fire sale. There was never any incentive for a bank to get more than the principal debt.

'I don't know, Henry. It may not work, what then?'

'We've lost nothing, a few dollars. It will also delay the bank. They have to give you fair notice. These things take time. You always said that you have to take action when you're forced to the edge, as long as it doesn't hurt anyone.'

'Your mum is going to get a shock,' Horace said. 'But, you know Henry, it's a bit of fun, isn't it? I guess we could argue that I've become a sculptor, or a collector of antiques. Will the council allow it? Car bodies have interesting histories, Henry. I could spend hours speculating about the life of each of them.'

Sitting inside Alex's Kombi, Henry began to have doubts. When Alex got a bee in his bonnet there was no stopping him. He began to talk of the Kombi as an ambulance speeding to an accident, deflecting Henry's concern that it didn't have the power.

'Course it does, Henry. It's just a bit slow.'

They pulled into the wrecker's yard and began to hunt for car bodies, seeking out the most derelict, cheapest, rustiest, nastiest auto corpses they could find. Would the wrecker loan them the flat trailer? Four bodies.

The wrecker, a shrewd operator, had seen his share of unusual customers over the years. He looked like a wrecker, as wreckers do. Henry could see that Alex mystified him. He couldn't believe that anyone would relieve him of wrecks that had been stripped of any useful parts, and he became suspicious. 'What do you want them for? Scrap?'

Alex explained the true purpose and the wrecker's face lit up. 'Great idea!' he chuckled, identifying with Horace's tragedy. 'We'll help. No charge.' He wrung his hands and raced off to make a phone call. Moments later he came back and said that his sons wanted to be in on the game.

The wrecker and his sons, two clones who arrived in trucks with much fanfare, immediately took over and began to load car bodies onto the backs of two tip-trailers.

Late in the afternoon an odd procession of vehicles took off for Malabar. Alex's Kombi led the way, belching out an impressive smoke screen that camouflaged the two trucks following. The wreckers were accustomed to cars on their last legs, but were forced to drive with their heads straining out of the window.

The convoy's arrival outside Horace's cottage was a noisy and smoky affair, resembling an invasion. Even the totally deaf would have felt the vibrations.

Mary watched anxiously as the wreckers tipped the car bodies onto her front lawn. Horace wondered what make of car each one was. It was impossible to tell. He nudged Mary and pointed to the shell of one old bomb, then bet the wrecker that the body was a Standard Vanguard. He and the wrecker walked around the rusty hulk debating the point.

Alex, watching the impact of his brainchild on the houses next door, elbowed Henry when he saw curtains move. Nobody appeared in the street to celebrate the arrival of a tangle of rusted wrecks other than a clutch of local children, whose eyes danced at the prospect of the strange new playground being nurtured in the front yard of old man Sinclair's hovel.

Sunday was a working day for Henry. He was putting the finishing touches to an article due to be published the following week in which he wanted to advance his hypothesis about partner choice, and he was applying himself to research that he had uncovered on the internet.

There was emotion involved in an investment decision just as in the choice of a partner. Henry scratched his head and sucked his teeth as he wrestled with some far-fetched notions. He was treading on dangerous ground. He wrote:

'Neural research on the brain is throwing up some interesting ideas. There is a gulf in the brain between the neural connections of emotion and intellect. The reptilian brain, responsible for heartbeat and blood pressure, is capable of survival even when one is judged to be brain dead. Quite a few politicians appear to operate on this level.

'The neocortex is that portion of the brain which allows a person to be considered clever; it's responsible for smart chat at the dinner table.' He remembered his own awkwardness at the group's dinner party. 'Modern research tells us that the limbic brain determines emotion and instinct. Love and partner choice are guided by the limbic brain, and a person has about as much control over them as an economist has over the outcome of his models.

'It is all about the early imprinting of strong love images. The reason a woman is drawn to a man against all rational argument is because somehow it feels right, because, to take a ridiculous example, somewhere in that woman's limbic brain a man with crossed-eyes' – or maybe a stutter, he thought – 'has made an indelible love connection. Unless crossed-eyes feature in a prospective mate, there is no long-term chance for him. Some people refer to this as "chemistry". And because men are generally more primitive, it explains their fascination with female body parts.'

Henry adjusted his glasses and read what he had written. Satisfied, he continued: 'So what does all this mean? While it is useful to be aware that rational choices are in vogue, there is no way the head can ever make the correct lifetime choice. In choosing a dividend-paying cash cow, the woman is doomed to fail unless the cow has crossed-eyes. And this is precisely why men are accused, correctly, of thinking through their penises.

'In the same vein, men are swayed by the opinion of admired peers who exhibit a machismo or intelligence that they think themselves to lack. This is the tribal dimension. Men are inclined to follow someone they admire over the nearest cliff.' Henry thought of Eric. 'A crowd of men whipped up by a charismatic leader is the single most dangerous force on the planet – witness the events of 11 September. Thus it was possible for the sharemarket to reach ridiculous heights as the crowd became "irrationally exuberant".

'Fortunately for humankind, learning and new imprinting is possible. It is possible to resist the crowd. But unless there is strong imprinting to erase what has been laid down before, then it will not work.' Henry concluded by saying: 'This fact highlights the continuing importance of romantic love. In time a woman can shift from a man with crossed-eyes, to a man with only one gammy eye, however difficult it may be for him to focus by candlelight.'

He closed down his computer and ran his eye over his calendar of events for the following week. In light of what he had written he wondered what it was about Rosie that had attracted him. Certainly not the waist–hip ratio. Men were supposed to marry their mothers. He loved his mum, but could see little of her in Rosie. Maybe there was something of Horace about Rosie?

- 9 -

Henry milled in the throng waiting to participate in the first ITSSS Unbelievable tutorial.

Beth tugged him on the elbow. 'Hello Henry. Isn't it exciting? I've been reading the financial pages of the newspaper. I don't understand half of it. It makes me mad when I have no idea what they're talking about. You said you understand the sharemarket?'

Henry had been looking about for her. Her down-to-earth nature made him feel instantly at ease. 'I think I do. But, maybe no one does,' he said with a smile.

'I'm so glad that I have a partner to do this with.' She beamed back at him.

They sat down and soon Eric Schwartz strode centre stage. 'Welcome to the river of gold, to the Babylon of dreams. You are about to embark on an empowering journey that will allow you to take control of your lives. No longer are you marshmallows without options in life. If your boss is giving you the shits, if you hate going to work, I'll show you how to make a living sitting on a yacht. I have a yacht. I made a cool hundred thou last Friday between sips of champagne while I watched dolphins frolic. I am on a mission to make two-hundred million dollars in twelve months. I'm going to take you with me.'

Eric explained the format of the tutorials. He used a projector connected to a personal computer to show the basic method of the program and to highlight movements in share prices that had occurred during the past week. He was able to call up any number of shares and illustrate graphically how they had traded. Each time he clicked on aspects of the program he created new graphs and began to analyse buying momentum. When Eric finished his demonstration everybody moved to another room arranged with aisles of desktop computers.

Henry explained the basics to Beth at the screen.

'Henry, I want to ask you something. This is gambling by another name, isn't it?'

'Well, you can stick your head in the sand, but I believe people should get involved.'

'Why?'

'Because most people own shares. That's where your superannuation money goes. If people only realised how much their future depended on the sharemarket.'

'Do you own shares?'

Henry was cornered. They were staring at the screen, talking sideways to each other, and Beth looked at him. 'Beth, I, er, write about this stuff for a newspaper.'

'*Do* you?'

'I'm trained as a scientist, but accidentally went down the business path. I analyse technology and often write about companies.'

'Is that right?' she said, then paused. 'What are you doing this course for then?'

'It's a long story. To make an informed judgment.'

'But why don't you own any shares yourself?'

'Because the moment I do, I have a conflict of interest in what I say.'

'Conflict of interest?'

'Well, if I own shares in company X I really can't talk about that company. If I declare that I own shares then I can't really talk about competitors of the company. It would be unethical. Anyhow, I haven't got any money to invest.'

'Oh, yes, I see. You're obviously not rich. Oh God, no offence. I mean, you don't dress like you're rich.'

Henry took no offence. 'What about you?'

'Don't ask. I've saved a bit. I'm divorced and have a young daughter. I need to do something to look after her and get our own house instead of renting. I'm a relief nurse.'

The day his article appeared there was a message from Louise. 'Henry. Just brilliant. Makes me see Andy a little differently. Maybe I'm only attracted with my head, not my heart. You've unsettled us all. I phoned Rachael and read the article to her, and she's *desperately* worried that maybe there's no limbic brain connection with Eric.' She laughed and ended by asking if he was on track with his manuscript. She needed a chunk of it soon to show publishers.

This was the day he was due to meet Andy, the Prime Minister. He chuckled when he imagined inviting the 'group' to Alex's restaurant. Rachael turning up in her body suit, Louise looking for an angle, Eric striding in to see what was on offer. And how would they feel when he introduced Alex as his best friend?

So here he was, standing outside yet another fine example of top Sydney real estate. Andy was working from home, he'd said, preparing for the contest of his life – the battle for pre-selection as a candidate for the seat of Bowers. Henry pressed the intercom button on the gate of the Killara mansion and watched the huge gates slowly open.

Andy met him at the door and ushered him inside. Again Henry felt like a trespasser. Andy was ingratiating, and Henry felt his stutter coming on.

'Henry, sit down please. I won't take too much of your valuable time. In fact, I noticed you came by bus.'

'Um, yes.'

'Would you like me to Cabcharge you home? Taxis often take their time getting here.'

'S-sure. Thanks.'

Andy pressed some digits into his mobile and commandeered Henry's attention.

'Can I get you coffee, tea?'

'I-I'm f-fine thanks,' Henry said.

'Okay, let me get to the point.' Andy brought his hands together under his chin as if in prayer, then knocked his fingernails against his teeth. He looked deeply into the carpet as he cogitated. 'I'm about to run my most important race. Do you know much about politics?'

'Um, n-no.'

'To be preselected for a blue-ribbon seat in the Liberal Party is the biggest game in town. I have connections. Born here, went to Kings, rowed, played rugby for the first fifteen. Captain of the cricket team. Short burst playing inside centre for Gordon, not first grade, of course. Law degree Sydney Uni. And I go up in four weeks. It will be a huge night. The vote will be close – I'm contesting a seat held for twenty years by an old war-horse. Whoever is selected will have a seat for life. My main opponent is getting on. Dead wood. I have the support, I know it. But it'll be bloody, he won't go down without a fight. Do you understand?'

Henry didn't, but nodded as if he did.

'If I get up, I tell you, it'll be smooth sailing – all the way to a junior ministry, then treasurer, or foreign minister, then the job itself. You saw the power of 'the group'?' He paused. 'Anyway, I suppose you're wondering why I have brought you here?'

'Um.'

'By the way, great article about the limbic brain, and that bit about men thinking through their dicks. Can't fault you there. Old Eric was having a good laugh about how Rachael would react. He loves that girl but, you know, he can't help his hormones, can he?'

Henry really didn't want to know about all this.

'So, Henry. You've got everybody guessing, but I may be

a bit smarter than the others. You can rely on a politician to smell the real angles. Tell me honestly, do you believe that stuff you write? You're too clever by half, I think.'

'Um, which s-stuff?'

'The bit about partner choice, us all sizing each other up like shares.'

'W-well . . .'

'I didn't think so. Anyhow, I'm getting off the track. One thing's for sure, you've got influence, and you probably don't even know it. So I'd like you to write for me and, if our association is fruitful, to have you along for the ride of your life, all the way to the Lodge. I'm going to give you a dossier of my policy proposals. I'm policy driven, you have to be these days. You can't do it on personality alone. I'd really appreciate it if you absorbed where I'm coming from. Anybody who writes about business has to be a Liberal Party man. And economics is where it's at. I need editing, a succinct summary. A good beginning is to tell people what I think about globalisation.' He pushed a thick folder of notes at Henry.

'Th-thanks.'

'You'll be well rewarded. Could you let me have a summary of my thoughts as you see them? How about a week? Don't have much time. I'll need some speech material.' He paused and fixed Henry with a Prime Ministerial glare. 'Henry, you're perfect for me. You have no political baggage. A truly innocent man.' He beamed like a father.

- 10 -

Yearning for days past, when the biggest calamity was to find the telephone, Henry sat at his desk, stared at the dossier and shrank in his seat. He'd been caught in a maelstrom and saw no way out. Rosie was due back, and he figured he may as well convene a meeting of his kitchen cabinet. Henry often had been buoyed by sharing his dilemmas with Alex and Rosie.

But these issues had been trifles when compared to the conundrums now facing him. He began to doodle, writing down his problems in no particular order: He had to make four-hundred thousand dollars to save his parents' cottage; Louise had asked for a manuscript in which he was supposed to offer a formula to resolve the world's most intractable problem – partner choice. Andy wanted a policy statement, which would mean applying cement to a straw house. Eric and Beth expected to see him at the seminar, and Eric was an insufferable bag of self-serving hot air. Rachael wanted him to promote her company in his column, which was contrary to his ethical stance. He had to find Hugo to be of help as Hugo degenerated. The disease might strike himself and Horace at any time. And, the most difficult of all, he had to find a way to tell Rosie about the disease.

As he circled his list with a pen, he glanced at the headline of the newspaper on his desk. 'Iranian militia invade Iraq'. What's the point of worrying? The world's gone mad, he thought.

Rosie was due for dinner on Monday night. Alex said he would love to join them. He offered to bring some bean soup, saying that he had about twenty litres surplus to requirements.

Henry went shopping for fresh ingredients for Thai chicken curry. He was an accomplished cook when he put his mind to it, and could serve a meal that dumbfounded Rosie. He found that whenever he was pressed, a good solution was to expend energy and thought on something totally unrelated, like cooking.

Henry was ambivalent about women. Not in the sense that his sexuality was in doubt. But because he had an easy-going temperament, he found it unsettling when women were thrown off-course by the merest trifle – his untidy apartment, for example. Upon his return from shopping he cast his eyes around the bedlam and had a think. While things were cluttered, nobody could accuse him of being unclean. He wondered how long it would take for Rosie to begin rearranging his furniture and buying him clothes that were scratchy. What was it about women that made them want to mother him?

He spent Monday afternoon rearranging his apartment. This was an exercise in precision logistics. Even Henry had to admit that a good cleanup had been needed for some time, and he reluctantly gathered the old newspapers that he'd kept for reference and made numerous trips to the garbage bin downstairs.

Surveying his efforts, he marvelled at the spaciousness of his living room. He dragged in the kitchen table, covered it with a white sheet that was a tad wrinkled but imparted a suitable facelift when stretched and tacked underneath the table, and dotted the room with candles. He put his only vase on the table and arranged the chrysanthemums.

When Rosie and Henry had first met the air was electric. Henry had brought Alex along for support, just in case he found himself stuck for words, such had been the build-up in the chat room.

For months, as Henry chatted with Rosie over the internet and he told Alex what was happening, he had got the same response: a rolling of Alex's eyes. 'You haven't even met the woman!'

It transpired that Rosie had been a wee bit understated in her self-description, while Henry had been as clear as he knew how. Rosie had pestered him with questions. If famous actress such and such was a 'ten', then she was a 'two'. What was Henry, if Brad Pitt was a 'ten'? Henry, who was vague about Brad Pitt, had to guess the relativities. If Rosie could be so self-deprecating, then surely Henry could hardly argue for a higher position on the food chain. They had resolved, through intense negotiation that Henry was a 'minus three'. But, as it became manifestly clear to Rosie that Henry must be joking, and that he was bereft of the normal male propensities for inflation, she became ever more cautious about his reaction to seeing her for the first time. She began to probe him about his inclinations toward women who were a smidgen overweight. Henry had never really been pressed on the issue, and stated quite honestly that personality was more important. What about women who were *quite* a bit overweight?

Alex had taken the challenge of the couple's first meeting personally, as a good friend would. Throughout the journey in the taxi Alex had been optimistic and had overridden each of Henry's reservations. Shyness was an attractive quality. They'd established rapport electronically, what was to lose? But then, Alex had to shove Henry into the coffee shop in Randwick.

The two of them bursting into the coffee shop with the energy of Alex's shove had made it appear momentarily that a hold-up was underway – except that they tripped on the step in the process, and Henry fell to the floor. Coffee drinkers looked up in alarm.

As Rosie later explained, she'd been waiting nervously for about fifteen minutes. Her first impression had been that the tall balding man with the ring of long black hair was attempting to mug an equally strange-looking man, and that they had crashed into the coffee shop in the struggle. Then she had become aware that perhaps she was looking at her chatroom Lancelot. Neither of these odd men remotely fitted her preconceived notions. But a goatee, puce cardigan . . . yep, it added up.

For his part, Henry had a momentary respite as he groped over the floor for his glasses. Alex came to his rescue and placed the glasses on Henry's face in a show of concern that totally diminished any lingering mugging hypothesis. Henry looked around for Rosie and spied a woman in the corner who was dark-haired and appeared to be gesturing with her hand, the fingers of which were waving independently in a meek sign of recognition.

There were faltering introductions. Henry and Alex had sat down and a massive silence had engulfed them as they tried to think up an appropriate way to proceed. Fortunately a waitress came to the rescue, and coffee was ordered with gusto. Then Henry had looked at Rosie for the first time. She had returned his gaze and the moment had frozen. Alex had become aware of an unusual transaction taking place before his eyes.

For Henry, Rosie had the face of an angel. Her large, expressive eyes dominated a totally round face framed by a confusion of dark hair. A Botticelli angel in full bloom.

Alex could only think that she was rotund – well, overweight. Fat, to be precise.

Rosie did not cope well with inclines, hills or, for that matter, any gradient above horizontal. She viewed each visit to Henry's apartment as equivalent to an hour in an aerobics class, which of course she could only imagine. She would gather herself at the bottom of the three flights of stairs and inhale deeply before beginning her climb. This usually meant that she arrived at his door breathing heavily, which Henry initially interpreted as excitement until he was better informed. This time there was a mixture of genuine excitement and exhaustion, because they had not seen each other for more than a week.

Alex, who was busying himself in the kitchen, had decided to bequeath Henry the full twenty litres of bean soup, for leftovers. This thoughtfulness was a bit untimely because Henry's two available pots were occupied with curry and rice, so Alex was forced to heat up a Sydney Harbour of bean soup in a pot suitable for cannibals. Fortunately he was able to use every one of the stove's four burners, so there would be no delay.

The reunion was an emotional affair, doubly so because Henry's spring-clean and candle-lit table made a huge impression. Rosie was mightily pleased.

They sat down, three convivial diners, slurping bean soup.

After Rosie had given a synopsis of her journey, Henry outlined events. Rosie was spellbound. Occasionally she sought clarification. She found Alex's inspired stratagem to dump car bodies unusually oblique, even for Alex, and could only nod her head.

Finally Rosie offered an opinion. 'I do see it's up to you to save the cottage, but Henry, this group sounds like a peculiar bunch. How could you be comfortable mixing with that lot?'

'Henry's just going for a ride, aren't you?' Alex asked.

'Well ... It's the only quick way to raise money. The publishing offer, the seminar, the future Prime Minister wants me to write his speeches.'

'You're on a roll, Henry,' Alex grinned. 'Besides, who knows whether the car bodies will do the trick?'

'It's not you though, is it Henry?' Rosie asked, reaching across the table to put her hand on his.

Henry gripped his upper lip with his lower lip, a mannerism that showed he was seriously reflective. 'You're right. I went to school with this Eric guy. Still calls me Sinkers. My nickname.'

'Hey?' Alex and Rosie exchanged a look.

'You mean Stinkers, don't you?' Alex wrinkled his nose.

'He was a thug then, and hasn't changed from what I can make out,' Henry said.

'So you're consorting with thugs?' Rosie said.

'Well, I don't know.' Henry bit his lip. 'I've read odd bits and pieces in the paper over the years. He's attracted a bit of attention, not all of it good. I find him arrogant and aggressive. But I can make up my mind as I go along. There's no harm in it. Anyhow, what does the kitchen cabinet advise?'

- 11 -

The biotech revolution had created a frenzy of investment in start-up companies seeking to exploit new discoveries. Commentators likened it to the internet revolution. Henry had a more balanced view. He wrote a piece exhorting his readers to be cautious. It was a revolution but, like the dot-com mania, it was likely to have many false starts. For biotechnology to work as a business model that actually generated profit, there was a need for people to broaden their time horizons. And patience was in short supply – instant gratification was the order of the day.

Henry, still awash with bean soup, turned from his monitor and opened the window. In his mail was a prospectus and a covering note from Rachael, telling him to read with care and consider the imminent float of Techpersons Recruitment Ltd. He read the usual background information and flipped the pages looking for the proposed board and management structure. It was as he had suspected: Eric Schwartz was chairman, Rachael was principal shareholder and executive director, and each person at Eric's dinner party was a foundation shareholder, with Eric owning twenty-five per cent of the total shares.

Henry calculated that if the float came on at the issue price of fifty cents, then Rachael would be worth six million dollars, Eric would be five million better off, and each of the dinner party guests would be hundreds of thousands of dollars in the black. If the opening price on the day of the float was driven up beyond fifty cents, as appeared likely, then the wealth of each person was going to be enormous. As in the not-too-distant past, float fever was gripping the country, and he hadn't seen a float that opened lower than the issue price.

He felt, on close reading, that Techpersons was indeed a sound business, and that Rachael, as the founder, had done extremely well. It was a credit to her, and he tried to marry the image of the Lycra bodysuit with that of a successful businesswoman.

He thought back to the previous night, and how helpful Rosie and Alex had been, hotly debating whether Henry should go along with 'the group'. Alex said that Henry had a great opportunity to be a voyeur on the lifestyles of the rich and famous. Rosie, more sensitive, encouraged Henry's protestations that he felt horribly ill at ease with the idea. But then she suddenly went quiet and stared into her empty soup bowl, spoon poised. Henry was about to refill her bowl for the fourth time, thinking she must be unusually peckish. Then she burst forth.

'Henry, Alex, I've got it!' Rosie said, looking at each of them with zealous conviction. 'This Andy, the Prime Minister. Imagine 'the group' is successful, and they do help Andy get into parliament. He wants you to help write his material, Henry. How often have the three of us talked about the idiocy of government policies? Couldn't we hop inside a Trojan horse? Imagine we're able to slip in some really important policy initiatives, you know, the sort that the politicians are too gutless to do anything about?'

'*Trees.* Trees, trees, trees,' Alex almost shouted.

'Free childcare. Free childcare.' Rosie banged the table with her spoon.

Henry gazed at Rosie with the look that comes into a man's eyes when he feels vindicated in his choice of car. 'Maybe,' he said slowly.

The following week was one of the busiest Henry had experienced. Rosie had reminded him to gather his thoughts and respond to Louise's timetable for a book.

He digested Andy's thoughts, as set down in the notes that he was given, and pondered. Naturally he could be forgiven for his lack of intimate knowledge of the policy aspirations of a future Liberal Party Prime Minister. What surprised him, in a reading of Andy's world view, was the boring predictability of the man – he had seemed sharp enough to try on some new shoes. Andy rolled out the platitudes as if he had no strong personal convictions. Rosie's outrageous idea gathered steam.

Andy had salvaged aspects of Coalition policy from brochures and mixed in some home-spun philosophy. For example, he advocated an immigration policy that could only be described as racist. He was strongly opposed to welfare for single mothers. Capital gains taxes should be abolished. Lowering welfare and medical expenditures would fund the tax cuts.

Andy was the sort of man who had sailed through life on good looks and charm. If Henry could manage to convince Andy of legitimate causes, he might just change tack. But how to talk to a man who couldn't hear a train whistle?

A smile came over his face. Andy had written down his ideas in no particular order. It would be interesting to see what happened if Henry arranged Andy's policies in a more humane hierarchy. He would leave out a few unmentionable policies, and see what happened. Deftly he reconstructed Andy's thoughts.

There were other goings-on that week. His father phoned and said that Henry would never believe what had happened. Horace had the sort of laugh that was highly contagious, and Henry hadn't heard him in such a good mood for ages. Antonio, the neighbour on the left side, had snatched a moment of Horace's time while Horace was out inspecting the car bodies. He had walked over, hands in pockets, and stood next to Horace in the front yard. Mentioning yet again that his mother was due for a visit in a week for Christmas, he had looked at the car bodies as if for the first time, and asked how anyone could have made such a terrible mistake as to think Horace's house was a garbage dump. Could he help clean up the mess?

'Well, you should have seen his face when I said I had become a collector of antiques! "You makin' a big joke, Horace?" There were a few kids mucking around in one of the shells. I said, "Isn't it wonderful that the kids have a playground now?" He stared at me like I had flipped my lid. He put his hand on my arm and said that it would be all right, not to worry.'

'Well, guess what?' Horace went on. 'The car bodies have disappeared!' Horace couldn't understand it. Mary slept with balls of wax in her ears to deflect Horace's snoring, and had heard nothing during the night. Horace usually died at night and had a legendary incapacity to be woken up, but he thought that even he would have heard something. 'Pretty difficult to cart that lot away without a squeak, Henry.'

Henry chuckled. 'Antonio has taken matters into his own hands.'

'What? That'd be *stealing*, Henry.'

'Who else, Dad?'

Horace thought about it. 'Do you think they were worth something?'

'Of course not.'

Horace signed off, still chuckling. 'Mary wasn't too upset to see the end of them, Henry. I'd identified all the bodies. They were interesting, son. One *was* a Vanguard Spacemaster Deluxe. And there was an old Hillman.'

Henry phoned Alex.

'Very interesting, Henry. I'll bet that they've been dumped at the same wrecker's.'

'Of course! I'll phone you right back,' Henry said.

Moments later: 'You were right Alex. There's only one wrecker in the area. He said he was having a good time as a wrecker for the first time in his life. He'd charged a mint to take back the bodies. Did we want to deposit them all over again? He said he could see himself getting rich. No charge.'

Alex pondered on this. 'Brilliant, Henry. We'll have to start charging the wrecker a commission. You told him to go for it?'

'Of course.'

The children in the street had been making good use of the corpses as cubby-houses. Horace had seen to it that there was no possibility of injury, and had encouraged them, pleased that they were playing outside rather than sitting glued to the television. Accordingly, the return of the bodies was greeted with much enthusiasm, this time by a horde of children who immediately set about reconstituting their cubby houses. Horace took it all in his stride, and thanked the wreckers by inviting them in for a cup of tea.

That afternoon Henry received a surprise invitation from Louise. 'Henry, I'm having a lunch for some of my authors, my place on Saturday afternoon. I'd like you to call in briefly. Rachael and Andy will be here. A few wines, some nibbles, nothing flash. Can you bring whatever you've written? I want to introduce you to a publisher. Oh, and Henry. Please dress for the occasion. We want to make a good impression.'

He telephoned Rosie in a panic.

She lived in spartan circumstances in a one-bedroom flat in Matraville, a suburb adjacent to Malabar that hosted a sprawling chemical factory, an activity that required enormous infrastructure, like an oil refinery. Unfortunately, unlike Malabar's sewage, the factory waste could not be piped out to sea. As a consequence, newborn babies were checked very closely for signs of deformity. Rosie joked that she was ready for a bit of rearranging, so any noxious influence was welcome.

She revelled in the challenge of making Henry over, and Henry despaired that she was showing her latent female desire to buy him scratchy clothes. Then he wondered how Rosie could possibly be of help. As he thought about it – not that the matter had ever surfaced before – Rosie was not the person to inspire confidence when it came to fashion. He could only recall seeing her in massive tent-like dresses.

The shopping trip was uncertain from the start. 'How much do you want to spend, Henry?' Rosie asked as they trundled through Target, he holding her hand as always.

'Not much,' Henry responded, appalled by the variety of clothes on offer. He hated shopping, and generally got it over with by buying the first cheap item he laid his hands on.

Rosie scanned the store for a sales assistant, and Henry was impressed when he noticed one flitting around doing her level best to ignore them. It was the first sign of sanity in a time-wasting exercise. Rosie held scratchy shirts up and put them against Henry's body, clucking and cooing. Henry sighed. She asked him to go try them on, and his face dropped. Henry was about to ask whether she'd ever bought clothes for a man – she was getting giddy with the adventure.

'Can't I just buy this shirt and go?'
'What's your size, Henry?'
'I'm about six foot.'
'No, your shirt size, silly.'
'I really have no idea.'

So, armed with a new shirt, a pair of trousers and even a gleaming pair of shoes, Henry was depressed. They sat in the bus clutching Henry's transformation, and he calculated that he'd spent nearly two hundred dollars, more than he'd ever spent on clothes. He said in an aside to Rosie that he thought his entire wardrobe wasn't worth that much.

When it came to getting ready for Louise's lunch he discovered that the shirt *was* scratchy. He gritted his teeth and decided that he wouldn't be comfortable. The trousers seemed all right as he held them up, but there'd been a slight miscalculation in the size, and he bit his lip, realising now that he should have tried them on when Rosie asked. The trousers were incredibly tight, and he sucked in his stomach – not that he had any stomach to suck in. He looked down and saw that they were a bit short in the leg. He couldn't cast them aside as well. Rosie had cautioned him to wear matching socks and he pulled out two that appeared to belong together, but were in fact distantly related, incorporating the same wool fibre but possessing two different colour genes. This wasn't noticeable to Henry, as always, but to normally sighted people they were definitely different shades of brown. He hunted around for a favourite shirt, and put his hand on one that would have felt at home in Hawaii, but perhaps not at a trendy lunch in Paddington. He gathered the first thirty pages of his book, and set off.

- 12 -

If there was a graph for 'Establishment', Paddington would be off the page. Or so Alex had remarked one day when he and Henry went to the Paddo market. The herding instinct was so powerful, he said, that the chic people simply *had* to live in terrace houses even if the frontages were only as broad as Rosie's outstretched arms. As for the backyards ...

Henry pushed open the front door, which bore a sign that instructed guests to go through to the back. He heard the cackle of conversation and emerged into a tiny yard filled with people holding wineglasses.

He was fighting an urge to leave when stiletto-heeled Rachael swayed by; dressed in shiny black leather pants and a jacket that was unzipped at the front. She elbowed Louise, who stared at Henry like she'd just seen evidence of extra-terrestrial life but sailed across with a stuck-on smile. Making sure that she was not being overheard, she pretended to give Henry a kiss on the cheek and whispered, 'Didn't you get my message?'

'W-what message?'

'This morning, the publisher couldn't make it.' She smiled through brittle eyes. 'Doesn't matter.' She stared at his shirt like a headmistress. 'You're here now.'

She tugged him by the elbow and led him to Rachael, who was winding up for a hello. 'Henry, I'm *so* glad you could make it. Did you get my prospectus?'

'Um, y-yes.'

'What do you think?'

'I–it's very good.' Louise handed him a glass of wine and he nodded his thanks.

'Will you be writing about it this week?' Rachael asked, coals glowing in her eyes.

Andy appeared through the crowd. 'Henry! It's good to see you. I told you that you'd made an impression at the dinner table – and you also saw Eric, I hear?' He looked Henry up and down, then stared at a woman passing by.

'Um, y–yes.'

'Henry is going to give the float a plug in his column, Andy,' Rachael gushed.

'And I want him published,' Louise said.

Just then a dishevelled man appeared at Louise's side. He had a wild hairdo and was dressed in a corduroy jacket that made Henry feel at home.

It turned out that the man was one of Louise's finds, a new author who Louise later extolled as 'prize-winning talent'. He took her away for an earnest conversation just behind Henry.

Henry was engaged by two conversations at once, though no one was talking to him. He couldn't help but overhear snippets of Louise and her author, and listened to Andy discuss the float with Rachael.

'What does Eric think, Rachael?' Andy asked.

'He's delighted. Now he expects the price to open at two dollars.'

'Really?'

'I think we may do better than Palamountain,' she sniggered, referring to the forthcoming float of Eric's own company.

Louise was assuring her find that she would definitely ring him next week, and apologised for not being in touch. But, the man insisted, she'd promised to ring a fortnight ago. So busy. Things take time. Doesn't matter, the man said. Just do what you say you will do, no more no less, and we'll get along fine.

As the conversation became emotional, Henry noticed Louise escorting the man out of earshot.

Rachael turned her attention on Henry. 'Dear Henry, I do feel we're getting to know each other. You know, I'm going to have the best party when we float. Nothing spared. You must come along, be sure you dress just like you are. I think you're setting a trend – did you notice those women gawk at you? I told you that you were attractive. By the way, do you have a woman in your life?'

'Y-yes.'

'You *do*? Pity, I was thinking of lining you up. In fact, there's a girl you'll meet at my party who will sweep you off your feet. She's so sexy. By the way, I loved that bit about the limbic brain. I really thought about it, and feel that there's something about Eric that has imprinted on me. You know, my father was like Eric,' she said proudly.

'Um.'

'I think you may have cemented our relationship, because I no longer have any doubt that we're together for keeps. I really can't understand why men hate the "commitment" word. I couldn't possibly discuss any of your ideas with Eric. He can't stand to talk about wussy stuff. He's a self-made man.'

'And relieved G-G-God of all responsibility,' Henry said.

Rachael looked at him closely, furrowed her brow, then threw her head back. 'You *so* funny, Henry,' she laughed.

Henry was a piece of driftwood at parties. Pushy people elbowed to be at the centre of things, and Henry was gradually shoved aside. He found himself with his back to the fence, watching as usual. He hated parties almost as much as shopping, but they fed his material on the human condition. He noticed Andy, distinguished in a fine jacket that he wore draped over his shoulders, holding a couple of attractive women spellbound. Louise had finished with her author, and Henry watched as he beat a lonely exit. He wondered about that.

Soon Henry sidestepped his way slowly out of the door breathing relief as he sped away, his manuscript still tucked under his arm. He felt guilty about not saying good-bye, but figured Louise had been too busy. It must be extremely difficult to be an agent, he decided. So many authors, so little time.

- 13 -

Former marshmallows, now acolytes of the Babylon of dreams, were asked to attend a huge gathering of new members. ITSSS Unbelievable had hired a giant theatre to accommodate the throng.

Henry sat with Beth in row thirty-nine looking down at the stage. Spotlights stabbed the darkened space and the crowd talked in hushed tones, as if waiting for the curtain to rise. Out in front, centre stage, was a lone podium. Behind it was a giant screen that beamed the usual welcoming logo: Excalibur stuck in a rock.

Suddenly the theme from *Chariots of Fire* rang out, and Eric appeared in a dinner suit. He strode to the podium and faced his audience. Beth nudged Henry. 'Looks like an Oscar for best actor,' she whispered.

A ripple of applause gained momentum, fanned by Eric's prompters, until people rose from their seats in ovation. Henry looked on in amazement.

Eric raised his arms and hushed the crowd. He began with a low rumble. 'This is the first true milestone. Today we gather on the road to Eldorado. We welcome those who are new, who in due course will look back on their dark days of poverty. While the Middle East is in chaos, we shall make sunshine. We will not be deterred. The world will thank us for showing the way to prosperity!'

Eric dug his hands in his pockets and walked away from the podium closer to his fans. His microphone travelled with him on his lapel, and he used it like a pop star, crooning his promises of the dawn of financial independence.

Then he paused: 'My inspiration. I want you to meet the wind beneath my wings, my one true love and friend.' He gave a snapshot of Rachael's past, dwelling on her struggle as an ordinary single mother who had achieved a stunning success, and was about to swim the river of gold. 'Each one of you members of ITSSS Unbelievable will be able to share in her fortune, and *this* is an example of what is to come. Now, the woman of the moment, the ravishing *Rachael*!'

Eric turned side-on and clapped Rachael to the stage. She emerged in a black evening gown that shimmered with sequins, and scampered for Eric's outstretched hand. Together they turned to the audience with Eric's arm around her waist. It was product endorsement at its best. The audience erupted.

Henry saw Eric and Rachael as exotic specimens of worldly success. They stood entwined in black, hairdos shimmering in the spotlight, testifying to the power of modern gym equipment and the skill of surgeons' knives. At any moment he expected to be singing 'Onward Christian Soldiers'.

The strategy became clear. Each member was invited to participate in the forthcoming float of Rachael's company. Anyone who signed up would gain priority access to shares that would become dollars from heaven. Eric couldn't discuss the likely opening price on the sharemarket because he was chairman and a founding investor. But, if it was good enough for him ...

During the interval Beth turned to Henry. 'Wow, that was slick. What do you think? Should I buy some shares?'

'Beth' – Henry paused to look into her hopeful eyes – 'I think I understand what's going on. All these people have dozens of friends and relatives, who have dozens of friends and relatives. This is going to create a whole market of buyers all thinking they have the inside running. They'll follow Eric all the way to Eldorado, just as he says.'

'Well, what's wrong with that? If it works ...?'

Henry, in a dilemma, went quiet. They were standing in a roaring crowd of excited investors. Henry could hear people proposing to mortgage their houses to get as much of the action as possible. 'Beth.' He moved closer to put his mouth near her ear. 'This is dangerous stuff. Somebody has to end up holding the parcel.'

'What?' Beth strained to hear.

'This is a game of pass-the-parcel.'

'What?'

Henry raised his voice, which he seldom did. Unpractised, his larynx switched to treble and his comment came out as a piercing shriek. *'This is a game of pass-the-parcel.'*

The crowd around them hushed and Henry found himself drilled by suspicious eyes. A very large woman placed her implacable face squarely in Henry's. 'What do you mean?'

He tried to back-peddle. He couldn't focus, for one thing. But he was hemmed in on all sides. 'Umm.'

Beth was shunted aside as others wanted an explanation for the outrageous comment. They hadn't understood it, but it sounded critical of the gospel according to Eric.

'N-nothing,' Henry gasped.

There was a spontaneous getting of wisdom as closer inspection of the source of the dissonant outburst revealed an obviously harmless and clearly stupid marshmallow. Henry grimaced apologetically and, as one, the crowd turned in on itself again.

'Phew,' Henry gasped.

'Poor Henry,' Beth said. 'Come outside, will you?'

They fought their way into the foyer, which had been taken over by the smokers who were too excited to observe the welter of no smoking signs. While the inner crowd could only be described as zealously committed, the smokers made them look like lukewarm car buyers. There was such energetic puffing that cigarettes shrank with amazing speed. The atmosphere was dense, and Henry suggested to Beth that they should go into the street before they became addicted themselves.

'What was that all about?' she asked as they arranged themselves on the pavement.

'God, I thought I'd be lynched,' Henry said. 'What I meant was that everybody buys and sells until somebody ends up holding the shares at a ridiculously high level. It's called ramping, or momentum buying, or just plain greed.'

Beth was perplexed. 'But, isn't that the name of the game?'

'I suppose it is, but for each winner, there's generally a loser.'

'Well,' she looked at him uncertainly, 'should I buy some shares? My mum told me she would lend me some of her savings if I thought I was on a sure thing.'

Jesus, Henry thought. Then, remembering Rachael's comment at the party that Eric had said the shares would open at two dollars, he paused, and looked at Beth's eager face. 'Beth, I do think there's little risk. I've read the prospectus, and the float is cheaply priced, so there will be a profit on listing.'

'Really?' She did a jig on the pavement. 'I'll invest as much as my mum can spare then?'

'It could all turn very nasty, very quickly. If the New York market turns sour, it will take Australia with it, and even though Rachael's company is no pie-in-the-sky, it may be savaged.'

'Oh, so what then?'

'If I were you, I would sell on the day of listing, pay back your mum, share the profit, and keep your share of the profit to reinvest in something else.'

'Great! But Henry, aren't you going to invest? Don't you need any money?'

- 14 -

Louise left a message on Henry's answering machine. 'Henry, you didn't say good-bye. I was so busy. I need your manuscript. Please send me what you've written.'

Andy had phoned. 'How's my running mate? The pre-selection meeting is on Thursday night, two weeks. Getting close to Christmas. Have you got my thoughts together, old son? Ring as soon as you've finished.'

There was a twist in the saga of the car bodies. Horace phoned Henry and asked if he wanted to come over on Saturday afternoon. The neighbours had asked for an urgent meeting. The request had come in the mail, which was rather formal, Horace thought, given that they lived next door. The letter was signed by four couples and written by Antonio, who must have worked on it for days. It had taken Horace ages to figure out what was being said.

'Henry, do you want me to read you his letter?'

'Sure Dad.'

'Here goes: "We's all living together happy in the street. We all like you, and the Mrs Horass. You make no trouble. We make no trouble. It's a time we meet you, like we do in Italia. We sorry that we no taking the trouble before. It's important for people to be friends. We have lotsa friends. Do you have lotsa friends? Maybe we bring some cake. Do you like cake? Francesca, she's a good woman. She makes very good cakes. Does Mrs Horass make cakes? You know, it's our good friend Luigi, on the other side, who is worried. He thinks that maybe Horass's house is the target for terrorist. He making a joke. I tell him that's rubbish, but he's worried about you. We all a bit worried. Maybe we just have cake and talk?"'

Horace asked Henry if he wanted to come. With all the cake, it could be a party. Horace was concerned that the house would be a bit cluttered – maybe Alex could bring some of his folding chairs?

Alex was enthusiastic. The car-body scheme had been his work of art. He wanted to see it reach its inevitable conclusion.

It did mean that the front yard had to suffer another wreck, because Alex needed to park his Kombi close to the house to unload all the chairs. As Henry was helping with the chairs, he walked past the back of Alex's Kombi. Alex had plastered some new slogans over his van: 'Want a friend? Get a tree'; 'Population control? Keep smoking'.

Mary was in a panic trying to rearrange her weaving enterprise to make room for all the guests. Henry and Alex were directed to move things here and there and it seemed to Henry, after some considerable energy was expended with no visible improvement, that people should just sit on boxes and piles of material. Alex praised the rich atmosphere of productivity. Horace agreed, saying that the neighbours were builders and no one appreciated productivity more than them.

Mary still looked anxious when the delegation arrived. There were only four couples, not an army as Alex had hoped, and Horace met them at the door. Antonio, the spokesman, set about introducing everybody to everybody on the way into the living room. He did this with Italian exuberance, and became confused when Alex stuck out his hand.

Horace reckoned that the neighbours must have spent days getting ready. The men were dressed in suits, and the women in floral dresses that made them difficult to tell apart, particularly as they all appeared to be exactly the same height, which was not very tall. Mary squeezed past the long line of people in the hallway in a mercy dash to her bedroom and a change of outfit.

One by one people entered the living room as Henry pointed to various accommodations. It was obvious that the delegation had never seen a weaving enterprise before, and they were either considerably taken aback or hugely impressed – it was difficult to tell. Perhaps it was the chandelier, which was often a talking point.

Finding everybody a seat was a challenge, but Alex carried it off with authority. One of the women, attempting to rest on a cardboard box, lowered herself gingerly like a chicken over her eggs. Unhappily, the box was nearly empty, causing her to collapse in an unfortunate display of thighs and stockings that stopped just above the knee. To make matters worse, she flattened the cake she was holding to her chest. Remarkably good-natured about her unseemly contortion, she smiled apologetically then retreated to the bathroom to powder her nose, leaving everybody to stare at the flattened cake.

Alex's chairs were redundant because there really was no room for them. Antonio started to pass the folding chairs around and all the men took part in a circular game until Antonio once more took charge and issued clearer instructions. He had passed the same chair twice and was obviously tiring. Just then Mary made a timely appearance in her best dress and everybody looked at her. 'Tea?'

Eventually the throng settled, and silence dropped on the room. Horace was sitting happily in his rocking chair looking out over his bifocals. Two of the women had gone to help Mary in the kitchen, and Henry noticed that the remaining women were doing their level best to avoid looking at Alex, who looked unusual, even for Alex. He was sitting in the lotus position on the carpet and the back view was absorbing – a bald head and very large ears, with long bits of black hair hanging down like a back-of-the-head beard.

Antonio took charge, again, and began to talk energetically, throwing his arms around the room and informing all those present that he was confident Australia would make it to the next soccer World Cup. No way, said one of the other men adamantly. Again there was silence. Then Luigi said that the war in Iraq was terrible, and everybody agreed.

The conversation was stop-start until Horace piped up and

welcomed everybody, saying that he was delighted to have them visit, and that they had only ever said hello in the street, and how typical this was of modern life. This got the party going, and Antonio stood up, crowned by the chandelier, to pass around the tea and cake that Mary was offering. It was impossible to eat cake and drink tea at the same time because there was no place to put things, so Mary concentrated on cake while Antonio held the floor.

A consummate public speaker, he regaled everybody with his worldview. He skipped over some large issues making it clear that he was a thinking, concerned citizen. In a brief outburst he established several new agendas for the government. It was terrible that kids were watching so much television, and there was far too much sex on SBS, and it was really asking too much for people to cope with all the new taxes. He kept returning to sex and violence on television, leaving all those present in no doubt that he watched a lot of it. Eventually he petered out and focused on matters immediate to the visit. 'Now, Horass, and Mrs ...'

'Please call me Mary.'

'Oh yes, Maria. I forget. We all come to help. Somebody making your life difficult, always dropping old cars in your house. We no understand who? You know who?'

Horace was concentrating hard. 'Who?'

'Yes, who?'

'*Who* is dropping the cars, Horace?' Alex explained.

'Oh, them.'

'Yes, them.' Antonio became steely-eyed with purpose.

'Well, we have a friendly wrecker ...'

'Not so friendly,' Antonio was cross-examining.

'Oh, yes. He's a fine fellow,' Horace said.

'Forget about that.' Antonio was becoming impatient.

'About what?' Horace asked.

Antonio sucked air. He tried a different tack. 'Horass, we all neighbours, friends. You want us to be unhappy?'

'Of course not.'

'We unhappy.'

'What's the matter?' Horace showed some real concern.

'Horace, we unhappy with the cars.'

'Yes. I'm sorry – it was meant to be ...'

'We wanna help you getting rid of them.'

Henry wondered what Horace might say now, but Alex came in. 'You're right Mr, er, Antonio. It's my fault. I wanted to make Horace happy.'

Antonio had been confused since first seeing Alex, wondering if he was a Sinclair relative, disbelieving in any possible genetic connection with Horace. Now he stared at him, doubly unsure what to make of this strange man. Alex's alien appearance took the wind from Antonio, and he sat down on a box.

Alex looked up from where he sat on the floor. 'Yes, you see, Horace has always been a collector of fine motor cars, like his vintage Morris Minor. The trouble is, he can't afford collecting cars that actually work.'

The neighbours chewed the bone, obviously taken aback by the distant plausibility of this motive.

'Oh, well, that's nice,' Antonio said, deflated.

'Yes, and we want to encourage him. It gives Horace a purpose in life. He hasn't got too many more years to enjoy his favourite pastime,' Alex said morosely.

Henry saw a concerned look come over Horace's face, as if he'd just been told he was seventy-four when he'd thought all along he was only forty.

'But' – Alex brightened up – 'we're hoping to buy him a bigger place with more room for cars. The trouble is, nobody is prepared to offer what we think is a fair price for this house.'

'You thinkin' a selling?' Antonio whispered.

'Well ...' Horace tucked his head into his neck and shrugged his shoulders.

'How much?' Luigi obviously couldn't contain himself.

You could hear a feather drop. Horace had never enjoyed such singular attention. 'Well . . .'

'For it to be worth their while, Horace and Mary would need six-hundred thousand dollars,' Alex said, passing the sum off as a trifle.

There was an enormous venting of air.

The neighbours all suddenly needed to be somewhere else, and the delegation shunted out of the house. After farewells, Horace convened a meeting. 'Jeez Alex, that was a bit over-the-top, wasn't it?'

'It's an enormous amount of money,' Mary said, wringing her hands.

'If it's worth it to them, they'll pay it, Mum,' Henry said.

'I hate to ask that much, though. It sounds like we're ripping them off,' she said. 'What did we pay for the house, Horrie?'

Horace scratched his balding pate. 'I don't remember. Wait, wasn't it about ten thousand dollars?'

Henry asked Alex for a lift home and he stowed his bike in the back of the Kombi. Alex was confident that the wrecks would have the desired effect on the neighbours. 'When Horace gets six-hundred thousand dollars, he'll have to pay the bank four-hundred thousand dollars and he keeps the rest. Your folks could live comfortably on two-hundred thousand, couldn't they? They only buy beans and wool.' Alex clutched the wheel.

'We'll see. It's a bit of distraction for Horace,' Henry sighed glumly.

'What's wrong Henry? Not yourself lately.'

'Alex, I haven't told you that I got a phone call from Hugo.'

'No shit?'

Henry told Alex the gist of the conversation, omitting any reference to the disease, but mentioning how Hugo had gloated over the letter to Horace. As far as Alex was concerned, Hugo was a bad egg who didn't want to know his family. But Alex had been curious for a long time, wanting to make his own assessment of Henry's twin brother.

Henry mentioned that Mary carried the pain of Hugo's estrangement around with her and was still in touch with Mignon, Hugo's wife, who had left him. Alex's brain whirred with possibilities.

- 15 -

Mary didn't know what to say when Alex phoned. 'You say you want to find Hugo and surprise Henry?'

'Mary, you know I've been curious. I've never met Henry's twin and I'm Henry's best friend! Henry mentioned that you were still in touch with Mignon.'

'Yes I am. Alex, I don't think you'll find him approachable. You know he wants nothing to do with any of us? *I* don't even know where he lives any more.'

'I know. I promise I'll not bug him. What could happen?'

Late that afternoon Alex pushed the Kombi through the narrow terrace-lined streets of Newtown. He checked the address written on a piece of paper and stopped a couple of houses away from Hugo's tiny one-storey terrace. Alex could see from where he sat that the postage-stamp size front yard was overgrown, while the grimy windows looked like they had never been opened. Loose pages of a newspaper moved in eddies on the verandah. The place seemed deserted.

Alex parked the Kombi and, to the consternation of a woman leaning on her elbows looking out of the window of her house, stepped onto the pavement. Smoke from the exhausted engine billowed around him.

'Hey. Can't ya read?'

'What?' Alex looked around for a street sign.

'Residents only. Ya can't park that heap in front of my place. My son'll be home soon.'

'Sorry. Won't be long.' Alex started to walk towards Hugo's house, then turned back and spoke to the woman. 'I wonder if you could tell me if anyone lives in number twenty-two? The one with the rusted gate.'

'You on drugs? Havtabe, drivin' a crate like that.'

'Hey?'

'Yeah. Some poor fella lives there. Has a nurse come visit him. Should be here now. Comes every day, same time. Waddya want to know for?'

'I need to give him something personal from his wife.'

'He married?'

'Thanks. I'll be just a sec.' Alex wandered down to number twenty-two and pushed open the gate. He rang the doorbell and heard the sound reverberate inside. The upper half of the door was split into two tiny windows, and he strained to see through the grime. A car came hurtling down the street abruptly pulling up in front. He read the insignia of a district nursing organisation on the car, and saw a woman fossicking for something. Deciding she hadn't seen him, he stepped quickly onto the street and pretended to be tying his shoelaces.

The nurse slammed the door of her car and swept past him to ring the doorbell, giving Alex a quick look. She waited for a moment then opened the door with a key. Alex peered over her shoulder inside the house. Someone stood in the gloomy corridor and there was an exchange as the nurse turned around and looked at Alex. He saw a man, his face contorted in a spasm, pointing at him. Alex moved on nonchalantly bending down and half-hopping, as if he hadn't quite finished tying his laces.

The door closed. Alex looked to see whether the woman was still leaning out of her window. He could see her looking down the street in the other direction. Quickly he re-entered the front yard and carefully stepped over some discarded guttering in the tiny passage that led between the terrace and its neighbour. He could hear voices through a window halfway down the passage. He stopped, nervous, as a man shouted inside.

'I won't. Get away from me! *Piss off!* You're just like the others.'

He heard the sound of smashing glass. Half turning in the metre wide space, Alex wondered whether to sneak a look through the window. He edged forward and braced himself, facing the wall, heart pounding. Bit by bit he shifted his face to see inside the window.

His timing was unfortunate.

A man's voice roared: 'Who's that? Get him!' An object smashed through the window as Alex pulled his face back. He sounded like a platoon of soldiers as he clambered back over the guttering and tore out the gate.

Speedily he opened the door to his van and inserted the key. The nurse had appeared outside the house and was looking in his direction. He caught the eye of the woman leaning out of her window and pulled a face. The engine coughed and belched smoke as he engaged gear and crawled forward. The man was coming toward him, fist clenched, then appeared to trip on something and fell over as Alex passed by. The nurse rushed to help.

- 16 -

Rosie had been at Henry to visit her brother Bruce, who lived in the country. Henry sighed at the prospect of this unwanted digression from the storm of his commitments, but he relented.

When first the idea was raised, Alex had suggested that they make the trip in his Kombi. He wanted to test it on a longer journey, and was confident that it could travel to Goulburn.

Alex hadn't mentioned that he had found where Hugo lived. The next time he would arrive before the nurse. In his mind he held the vision of someone who didn't resemble Henry in the least. In fact, Alex was unsure just what he had seen. The man's face was strangely misshapen. Alex could only focus on the rage. The man was out of control. Definitely no twin of Henry's.

Because Rosie accounted for more space than both Alex and Henry together, and because the Kombi had only a front seat, the trio had never travelled in Alex's van before, always preferring public transport. Very early on Saturday morning, outside Rosie's Matraville apartment, actually sunrise, a flurry of getting in and out could be observed.

First they tried Rosie in the middle, but Alex found it impossible to shift gear without becoming very familiar with her inner thigh. With Henry in the middle, shifting gear was only possible if the gear-shift was between his legs and Rosie's door was left open a bit. Alex managed this by tying an elastic strap to the door.

Alex didn't have seat belts; his Kombi came from a less complicated era. To give an aura of safety, he buckled together several wide leather belts, and draped them around Rosie and Henry. 'For cosmetic reasons,' Alex insisted. 'The police have tyrannical agendas these days.'

They finally set off, enjoying the natural air conditioning. Because the Kombi could only manage the speed of an average cyclist, and that only down hill, they had wisely chosen to leave before the Saturday morning traffic began in earnest – this, they reasoned, would allow sufficient time to arrive before nightfall. Alex definitely wanted to avoid driving by night: the Kombi's headlights had lost their former sheen, and were barely able to emit enough glow to see more than a couple of meters. Besides, he'd not replaced the battery in one of the flashlights that doubled as a tail-light. He was always on about the van's electrics, and how unpredictable they were.

To start with the trip was a joy, even though the door kept bumping against Rosie's thigh. She had prepared a snack, and Alex complimented her on the 'moveable feast' as chickens, sandwiches and salads materialised from an esky just behind the seat.

The smoke grew thick at traffic lights. The arthritic Kombi protested at being constantly asked to stop and start. Gathering speed was a complicated affair in precise gear shifting. Many times the Kombi was not ready for second gear – it was quite content to relax in first gear for another kilometre or so. Ever hopeful, Alex said that a downward slope might be around the corner. Rosie congratulated Alex on the relationship he had with his Kombi, suggesting that it was more dignified and sensitive than the treatment she'd received from men – except Henry, of course, she added.

Road rage grew around them as they puttered. Henry could see that some men were almost apoplectic with frustration – shaking their fists, honking their horns, yelling obscenities. 'Oh good, that's an interesting insult,' Alex chirped as he saluted a passing driver and gave a saintly smile. 'I'll add it to my road-rage journal. Where's everybody going in such a hurry on a Saturday, anyway?' he asked.

'You're used to the eastern suburbs, Alex. You've never seen cars travel faster than twenty kilometres an hour,' Henry said.

The freeway was sheer luxury. It had been a while since Alex had been on a freeway – perhaps he'd never been on one – and he was hugely impressed. He was just exclaiming how peaceful it was not to be bothered by cars queuing up behind, although the speed at which some cars passed them was unnerving, when a flashing light came up behind them.

A policeman got out and walked up to Alex's window. He took off his sunglasses, peered inside, then walked around the van with his note-book, scribbling as he went.

The policeman, having asked for Alex's licence, seemed mesmerised by his photo, and kept comparing it to the real thing. He didn't say anything, just handed Alex a sheet of paper, and said that the Kombi should be scrapped. And were they aware that going too slow was an offence? Alex was genuinely confused, and was about to engage in a debate about this contradictory revelation, when Henry nudged him. The policeman, who seemed world-weary, signed off by saying Alex had a bit of work to do, then sped away.

Alex was aghast when he read that virtually every part of his beloved van contravened some bureaucratic opinion or other. He was given notice immediately to effect changes to lights, tyres, exhaust, seat belts, on and on – and the note concluded by fining him six hundred dollars. He was so offended that he scrunched up the paper and threw it into the back of the van.

Henry, alarmed, told him that he had to comply. Rosie said that he'd be thrown in jail. Alex grinned. What would they do, hang him? He wasn't going to let this spoil their adventure. Once more they set off.

Rosie's brother Bruce was a man with whom Henry had found instant rapport. Years ago Bruce had decided that he wanted to live in the country with his horses. He actually lived in a small flat in Sydney during the week. He had been a teacher, then a psychologist of sorts, and now had an impressive job with the government. Bruce had purchased his forty-acre property near Marulan, north of Goulburn, for a good price because huge power lines traversed the area and there had been a scare about cancer from microwaves. Dotted with eucalypts, the property rose to a rocky outcropping from which vantage point the power lines were an impressive sight. It was here that he had decided to build his dream home, a log cabin fashioned from gum trees.

Bruce, it had turned out, was not as practical as his dream might suggest. But he had a way with people and had organised working bees to help him cut trees and saw logs. Rosie had told Henry the story, and it probably became shonky with the telling, but Henry had believed it all when he first laid eyes on the cabin two years before.

Rosie had speculated that 'working bee' must be an oxymoron. Either the bees weren't living up to their name, or somebody had to invent a new term. Like, let's see how many people have fixed ideas and are expert at directing other people with fixed ideas about something they know bugger-all about.

Rosie felt that the problem lay with the individuality of Australian trees. Unlike North American trees, which are uniformly, superbly, boringly symmetrical, no two Australian trees could claim any relationship, she'd said. This was a nightmare for a working bee attempting to construct a log cabin. There was no question that the trees, when cut, were approximately the same length, but there was no way that they were straight. When piled on top of one another to make a wall, this posed a problem of detailing.

Fortunately Bruce was not obsessed with detail. He had scrounged a number of window frames, with and without glass, from surrounding demolition sites. They were square, or rectangular, as befits windows, but belonged to a veritable suburb of different houses, so no two window frames were alike. This was but a hiccup for the ingenuity of a working bee. The result, when frames were inserted to fit orifices cut into logs that seemed to be struggling to be as distant as possible from their partners, was like a jigsaw put together by a strenuous one-year-old. The resulting gaps were quite breathtaking, speaking of an entirely new direction in man's pursuit of shelter. Aesthetic considerations were no contest in a struggle with functionality. From afar, the windows were at random heights, random intervals, and generally random.

Bruce was unperturbed by the challenge to keep the weather out. He made all those who volunteered for the next working bee bring an unwanted pillow. These had been prodded and stuffed into the gaps between the logs and windows, until Bruce had time to think of a more permanent solution.

It was just as well that the trio set off at sunrise because they arrived in the late afternoon, jubilant that the old Kombi had prevailed. They bumped their way over the rough track leading up to the cabin and paused at the bottom of an incline that led to the rocky outcrop. Here the Kombi decided, at last, that enough was enough. Alex climbed out, untied the elastic strap that held Rosie's door and helped her out. They were bum sore, the seat hardly suited for a journey of ten hours. Rosie mused that it was just as well Marulan was 180 kilometres away from Sydney and no further.

Henry walked up the hill to meet a beaming Bruce at the top of the rise. Rosie's brother was a bachelor by default, Henry reasoned, due to the failure of women to apply proper perspective. At thirty-six Bruce was in his prime and quite trim, especially considering the scope for other outcomes offered by his genetic makeup. He was considered a god by his sister who now gazed up the hill and gulped, gathered her strength and plodded up defiantly.

For Henry, a visit to Bruce's cabin rekindled childhood memories of running amok in fields, and adventures in creek beds.

Bruce had prepared dinner, which was always a stew bubbling away in an iron pot over the massive open fire. The four of them sat around the fireplace in comfortable tatty armchairs, while Bruce told stories.

He had a spiritual connection with his cabin that was difficult for the women in his life fully to comprehend. His entire life, so Rosie said, was an example of the potency of dreams. He had thought about creating a polo field on the flat and breeding polo horses, but stony ground had waylaid that plan. Then there was the dam that he built to create a lake for canoeing regattas – unfortunately the water used to drain away after rain (but this yielded an occasional crop of yabbies). Then there was the plan to create a trail-riding business, with campers flocking in from Sydney. The lack of shower facilities, and the amazingly off-putting drop toilet, cancelled that ambition.

Rosie complimented Bruce on the new repairs to his walls — he'd filled in the gaps with mud. He was sitting stroking Cattle Dog — his cat — and nodded in appreciation. 'Had to get rid of those pillows, Rosie. They'd had their day.'

Changing the subject he boasted that one of his six horses had foaled. He was a proud grandfather.

'Where are they at the moment?' Alex asked.

'Let's see.' Bruce said, and stood up to sniff.

'What're you doing?' Rosie asked.

'I can tell where they are by my horse sense,' Bruce replied, probing with his nose.

The horses wandered around the far-flung reaches of the property in a desperate search for blades of grass, and their precise location was always unknowable. But Bruce looked after them well. He stored hay in his bedroom, which was a tack-on to the original cabin, as a temporary measure until he built an appropriate shed. In the early days he had slept in the loft, a platform suspended above the kitchen area, until his girlfriends complained about the possum family that dropped each night through the gap left for Cattle Dog. During a recent drought the horses had smashed the bedroom door to get at the hay.

Bruce claimed to be the original 'horse whisperer' before that term became known via the popular novel, and Henry reckoned that Bruce's whispering had less to do with horse ailments, than with a surfeit of wine.

So Henry challenged Bruce to prove his claim. 'I'll bet you get it wrong. Tell us where you think the horses are, and then whistle.'

Bruce's whistling was far more potent than his whispering, and they'd seen him summoning his horses before. They all trooped out to the verandah, where Bruce once again concentrated his olfactory armoury, sniffing the wind. He pointed confidently to one side of the hill and let out a piercing whistle at which Cattle Dog scurried away in fright.

Bruce stood smugly with his arms folded, while the others waited in suspense. Then they felt the thunder of hooves — coming from the opposite direction.

Following this minor dent in Bruce's credibility, they sat around waiting for the stew.

'Henry, I've wanted to ask you about your book. Imagine we're all meeting each other for the first time, judging each other as shares,' Bruce said, stirring the pot while hunched in front of the fire.

Everybody looked at Henry. 'What do you want to know?'

'What sort of share is Rosie? My sister doesn't seem to me to be a good investment,' he grinned, looking sideways at her.

Rosie shoved at Bruce with her foot and toppled him from his haunches. 'Henry sees me as a sugar company. He noticed my surplus capacity. I'm the big Australian.'

'What about Alex, then? What's he, a windmill manufacturer?' Bruce guffawed.

'Hey? What about you Bruce? The Holiday Inn?' Alex waved his arms, like a windmill. 'Come to think of it, what's Henry?'

'I'm a company in receivership,' Henry sparkled.

'A bad debt.' Alex nodded sombrely.

Lighting in the cabin was always in short supply until Bruce made his concession to modern living and turned on the generator. He'd muffled the chugging sound as best he could by placing the generator down a ravine behind the cabin. Nobody liked the invasive sound but they conceded to it in order to appreciate the stew. It was difficult to divine aspects of the stew by candlelight.

After the meal Henry explained his parents' predicament.

'Jesus, Henry. How could Horace be so reckless?' Bruce asked.

'You don't know about my twin brother Hugo, Bruce. Horace felt he owed him something,' Henry said, cradling a glass of red wine.

'Your folks are like parents to Rosie and me. We'll have to do something,' Bruce said.

'Yeah. Maybe find Hugo and tie him up over an ant's nest,' Alex proposed.

'Henry, Hugo is a constant mystery to us. Why are you so secretive about him?' Rosie asked.

'I've told you. He wants no part of the family. We can't force him to like us.'

'Umm …' Alex was about to say something about Hugo, but he didn't know what, when he was interrupted by Bruce.

'Anyway' – Bruce got up – 'on a brighter note, now is the time to tell you about my surprise. Henry, I owe it to you. Remember when I asked you about that biotech discovery? I invested in the company. Yep, first time I've ever taken a punt on the market. I've made a killing!'

'That's fantastic Bruce. How much?' Rosie asked.

'You're going to squirm.'

'Come on, stop teasing,' Rosie said.

'Two hundred thousand dollars profit.'

'Bloody hell!' Alex yelled.

'I want you all to come here for Christmas, including your folks, Henry.'

The Kombi expired. It died the sort of death that you would expect from a soldier of fortune. The next day on the freeway the Kombi ground to a halt in a billow of smoke that might have come from a crashed airliner. They shunted it to the side of the road, and performed an inspection. Alex was overcome with grief. Head inside the engine compartment, he grunted that perhaps the engine had seized, or worse. Henry asked what could be worse than that. Alex had no answer.

As they stood by the freeway attempting to hitch a ride, they must have presented as an odd troupe of performers. Certainly they generated considerable interest from passers-by: Alex thumb out, Henry immediately behind, Rosie perched forlornly on the esky, they enticed many a child to remonstrate with his stony-faced parents.

Then along came another Kombi. It took a Kombi to respond to a Kombi in need, and the driver stopped. He could easily have been part of the troupe, so instantly was he absorbed. As the young man raved and nodded looking at Alex's dead Kombi, Rosie whispered to Henry that she thought he was stoned out of his brain.

The man's Kombi was a sprightlier version of Alex's. It was six years younger and, would you believe, it was for sale. The transaction was negotiated over the next seventy kilometres. Alex's final offer of five hundred dollars – 'let's forget about the GST' – convinced the man that he had a fair deal. This Kombi had a back seat, was once an attractive orange colour, and could manage a top speed of eighty kilometres. It blew hardly any smoke, by comparison. Henry chastised Alex for being so fickle. 'You've not even buried the last one.'

The old Kombi found its final resting place in the yard of the very same wrecker who had become embroiled in the car-body scheme. He agreed to tow it to his yard, saying that he would be able to salvage some parts. Old Kombis were making a come-back. Alex said that at least he had a cemetery he could visit to relive some great memories.

- 17 -

The whirl of commitments started afresh. Louise gushed a message congratulating Henry. A publisher was interested and had offered an advance of ten thousand dollars. This was less than she had hoped for, but very good in the difficult publishing environment.

Rachael repeated the invitation to her celebration party, saying it was unusual to float a company just before Christmas, but Eric wanted all his investors to have a Christmas present. 'Would you watch the opening on the market, and maybe say something in support? You know, I can still get you some shares. We wouldn't want the price to collapse shortly after opening. Remember there's somebody very keen to meet you at the party. Dress just like you did at Louise's. I've decided to make it fancy dress anyhow. The theme is Hollywood. Imagine! I've invited just good friends.'

Ten thousand dollars represented a tangible beginning to his money-making quest, yet Henry was a trifle unsettled. The pursuit of wealth meant an uncertain new direction that, among other things, had the potential to estrange him from Alex and Rosie.

Just before the next ITSS Unbelievable seminar, held a week before the close of applications for Rachael's float, Henry met Beth in the small coffee shop around the corner. She swept in with a spring in her already jaunty step. 'Guess how much Mum gave me to invest?'

'I have no idea.'

'She said it was just sitting in the bank and only collected bank charges.'

'Beth, she should put it in a money market account,' Henry said, concerned.

'Oh well, too late.'

'Well, how much?'

'Twenty-five thousand dollars!'

'God!' Henry's eyes widened. 'Wait a minute. There's still a risk. Can she afford to lose it?'

'Of course not. It's her nest egg, or most of it. She said she had some more in a super fund that was paying her a regular pittance. What's the matter? You said it was a good bet.'

Henry exhaled and began to fidget with the sugar bowl. 'I think it will be all right Beth. But I hate to feel responsible . . .'

'Oh, is *that* all? Don't worry. I wouldn't blame *you*. I've got such plans. If the price does open at two dollars, the shares will be worth four times what I paid! One hundred thousand! Aren't you going to buy some shares, Henry? You know, I may have the deposit for a house!'

'You promise me you'll sell on the opening day? You know you have to pay tax.'

'Oh, God, I'd forgotten about that. Can you help me with the tax? By the way, I'd love you to come to dinner one night.'

The following morning Henry sat daydreaming at his computer. He reflected on Beth's dinner invitation. It was time that he told Rosie about Beth. He had thought about it before – Rosie had a right to know that he was partnering a woman at the seminars. But now his sense of duty became more urgent, and Henry didn't quite know why. Women were extremely unpredictable about other women, and Beth was attractive. If ever Rosie found out that he'd been helping Beth, and that the relationship extended to having coffee, well, he had no idea what Rosie might think.

Rosie had also been pressuring him to stay overnight more often, whether at her place or Henry's. Henry knew that she really meant her place, because she couldn't sleep in his rickety double bed. Henry recalled their first attempts to sleep together, remembering well how he had ended up on the floor. His bedroom was too cramped for a full-size bed, and the inflatable mattress that he blew up at a juncture in the night was a hopeless solution. But how was he to tell her, gently, that her weight meant he rolled toward her all night, and she was like a furnace?

And another thing. His work commitments meant that staying at her place was just too difficult at the moment. He recalled how cuddling Rosie had been awkward at first. She was a lusty, open woman, but nevertheless had inhibitions, brought on by a world that presented mainly anorexic images of women who looked close to death. The obsession with thinness was one of the most perplexing things about women. Henry had discussed it with Alex, plumbing the depths of his friend's feelings on the matter. Alex's female adventures were something else again.

It was obvious to Henry, and Alex agreed, that beauty was definitely in the eye of the beholder, and men were beholden to their eyes, no question. But the limbic brain was inexplicable. Skinny, hollow-eyed women were definitely off the horizon for most men. Men wanted meat on the bones of their women, and some men were more carnivorous than others. Throw in a good-hearted attitude, a sense of humour and adventure, certainly a brain, and your typical man was able to imagine his woman as the most desirable thing in a negligee. Throw in a man healthily unconditioned by even normal media images, and you find Henry and Rosie.

But Rosie had her hang-ups, and it was obvious to Henry that he had a lot of convincing and gentle loving to do to reassure her that he found her attractive. Not that Henry was a bedroom athlete. Far from it. It was difficult at first, but it was also hilarious, as they examined how many ways it was possible for a relatively fat woman to accommodate a relatively thin man. Sometimes, of course, hilarity and sex make poor bed partners, at least when it comes to the serious end of the business, and Rosie did insist that the lights were out. However, what made it all work was that Rosie found all sorts of ways to please Henry and, he being ill-experienced in matters of the flesh, was transported to unimagined places. As was the case with all women, Henry realised, the surrounding issues were far more important than the mere recreational aspects anyhow. Rosie was in heaven.

But Rosie was a woman. And there was Beth. And Beth was attractive. And therein lay a festering vat of trouble. And one more thing. The biological clock was ticking. Rosie had become clucky. She kissed enough babies to be running for the Presidency of the USA. Any hint of children on the horizon pressed the murky Sinclair button, and had the potential to shove Henry over a cliff of high anxiety. It all added up to an unavoidable conclusion. It was high time that he replaced his rickety bed, his apartment, his wardrobe and a few other foibles.

Henry, worried by Beth's exuberance, double-checked his calculations. The forecasts in Rachael's prospectus were realistic, capitalising on the expected growth in technology recruitment. The profit expected in the following year resulted in a prospective price-earnings multiple of seven times, based on the subscription price of fifty cents. Comparisons with other recruitment companies, whose price-earnings multiples were twenty times, suggested that indeed shares in Rachael's company were cheap at fifty cents, and purchasers would be guaranteed an immediate increase in value.

Henry found this curious. Rachael was giving up a lot of money. She could sell her company for much more than fifty cents a share. He was satisfied that Beth's money was safe but market conditions on the day of the float as well as the peculiar timing of the float, so close to Christmas, were risk factors. He returned to the cheapness of the offer price. Then it occurred to him. Eric. He had a hunch.

Horace phoned. He'd witnessed an extraordinary exchange in front of the house. Antonio had been visiting Luigi and was making his way back across Horace's front yard with a full head of steam, eyes to the ground. He had almost run into one of the car bodies, and hadn't noticed Horace standing there. Horace was about to say hello when Luigi appeared and yelled at Antonio in Italian. It didn't sound good, and Antonio had turned around shaking his fist. Then Luigi gave Antonio a very convincing finger, and Antonio had responded in kind. A few of the kids playing in the car bodies had stared at them. 'What do you suppose is happening, Henry?'

'Don't know, Dad. What would they fight over? Wait a minute. Maybe they're arguing about who will buy your property.'

'Oh, and Henry, I wasn't going to tell you, but you would want to know. I got a letter from the bank, demanding $430,000. It seems Hugo's business was a total flop.'

'Jesus.'

'What does it mean, son?'

'It's the first notice, Dad. Now they jack on interest on the unpaid amount. You're supposed to fork over the money. If you don't, they'll sell your house.'

'Well, it's what we thought, isn't it?'

'Yes, Dad. Not a good Christmas present.'

'We'll make do. I can always sell the car bodies,' Horace chuckled.

Andy the Prime Minister thanked him in an unctuous message. 'Henry, I was right about you. Thanks for the summary. I didn't realise I made that much sense. The meeting is in a week. I'm confident. You may be smarter than I thought. That's a compliment, because I already thought you were pretty smart, Dr Sinclair. I'll let you know what happens. If I win we're on the way. I hear you're invited to Rachael's party. Maybe we can celebrate there. Hollywood, hey? Who are you going as? Woody Allen?'

Woody Allen? Henry thought this over. He'd always liked Woody Allen. Smarter than he thought? How smart was Andy? Rachael's party. Ugh. No way on earth would he set foot in her place again.

- 18 -

Rosie came to visit with a hang-dog expression. Henry wondered whether this had to do with his apartment, which somehow had reverted to its former chaos. She wanted to talk about something, she said, and Henry squirmed on the sofa, preparing himself for a conversation that he knew was overdue. He was sliding into defensive mode, and hated himself for it. He wondered whether she wanted to talk about staying overnight more often.

First off Rosie talked about work and problems she was having with her boss. Then she started. 'Henry, we only ever have fun. We never talk, I mean *really* talk.'

'Umm.'

'I think about us a lot. I think you're wonderful, Henry. I can't imagine what I was like before we met. You know we've been together for nearly two years?'

She was sitting in an armchair across the room from him and wrung her hands as she spoke.

'Two years?' Henry was taken aback.

'I'm going on thirty-five Henry. I know you're wonderful putting up with me, and my, um, weight problem. And I know it's on your mind, constantly. Don't tell me it isn't, because it is. I know what men think.'

'Rosie, we've been over this. You know we have a true limbic brain connection. Why don't you believe me?'

Her eyes brimmed with tears, and Henry went over to put his arms around her. He surveyed the landscape for a handkerchief and settled on a T-shirt. He dabbed at her eyes.

'Oh, Henry, it's all right. I'm a bit emotional, I'm sure I'll get over it,' she sobbed, pushing him away.

He retreated to the sofa and saw other clouds in the sky.

'I have to get a few things off my chest. I'm an ordinary

person, Henry. I work in an office. Nowadays you're rubbing shoulders with the rich and famous, and you're about to become an author.' Beginning to sob, she grabbed the T-shirt and wiped her eyes. She inhaled deeply, and looked at him forlornly. 'One day I want a baby, Henry,' she said in a wavering voice. 'Not straight away. Please don't take this personally. I love you Henry.'

She didn't want him to comfort her. Henry, all at sea, raced out to the kitchen to put the kettle on.

'Where are you going?' she mumbled, blowing her nose in the T-shirt.

'Cup of tea?' he called over his shoulder.

'*Henry*,' she screamed.

He was shocked, and stood wringing his hands. 'What?'

'You're *always* so, so, calm. Don't you *ever* get upset?'

'Umm. Yes. Do you want me to get upset? I am upset.'

'Oh, get me the tea,' she said.

This was a crisis and Henry was definitely not one for a crisis. He stood over the kettle and thought furiously, hating the idea that he was causing her all this worry. Of course he'd be more passionate. He was working on it. But he'd spent most of his life trying to be calm. Why go around being upset all the time? He loved her, and had told her often. But a baby? He could barely support *himself*. And, of course, there was more to it than that. The Sinclair tragedy. Until he had a test for Huntington's disease a baby was out of the question. Why not tell Rosie? He was ravaged by guilt. He'd have the test! That would put an end to it. He did have ten thousand dollars – how much did a baby cost? The kettle was spewing steam.

'I'm sorry, Henry. I feel better now. I don't expect any response from you right now, but I have to speak my mind.'

As usual Alex threw the bomb. Henry had to discuss Rosie's visit, and the following night they sat in Henry's apartment.

The idea of having a child was appealing to Alex, provided

that Henry was the father. 'Henry, you worry about supporting a child. You worry about your mum and dad. You worry about this Beth woman. Why don't you make a mint yourself? You just made Bruce rich. Why don't you use the ten thousand dollars and save the world?'

Henry gaped at Alex.

'Henry, you're pretty dumb sometimes.'

'Alex, I'm a bloody idiot. But, I'm trying to steer through a minefield.'

'You're no saint, are you?'

'I guess not. God, no.'

'I'm the saint around here. Tell Rosie I'll be the father. As long as I see the kid after its fortieth birthday,' Alex chuckled.

'Don't you ever want a child?'

'Henry, Adonis I'm not. I'd have as much chance of a woman falling for me as going to the Olympics as a wrestler.'

'Not true. What about Olivia?'

'Yeah, what about her?'

'She loved you. You got scared. And Alex . . .' Henry paused and looked away. 'There's something about our family I haven't told you . . .'

'Yes?'

'If one day I tell you the real story about Hugo, you have to promise me you'll try to understand why we keep it quiet. It has a lot to do with whether I will have a baby, but it's too painful to talk about now.'

'Really, Henry? You having a baby? Come on, cut the drama. You can tell me, you know that.'

'I'm trying to protect Horace as well. I just can't talk about it right now.'

'You're a worry, Henry. Am I ever going to meet him?'

'Not likely.'

'Do *you* want to see him?'

'Of course I do. But it has to be on his terms. He's family.'

- 19 -

Phoning Rachael to ask if he could subscribe for shares was going to be difficult. The problem was that he had never asked anybody for anything in his life. It would change the balance. But now his parents' plight was becoming desperate. He had little confidence in the car body scheme.

He was leaning out over a huge drop suspended by a thread, and the thread was unravelling. He had a nightmare, which was a first. He was sitting on a toilet that suddenly opened up, and he was falling in.

He was no better in the morning. He stared at the phone and racked his brain for another way out. He hated the idea of asking Rachael for anything. What about Eric?

He found Eric's card and dialled. Eric acted as if it was only natural that Henry would want some shares. It was just as well Henry had rung when he did. Final allotments were occurring at that moment. 'How many? Ten thousand dollars worth? Is that *all*? No cheque?'

He could hear Eric's heavy breathing. 'Look Sinkers, you'll have to stump up with a cheque. I can't process the application without it. Well, wait a minute. You're going to change your mind about what we do, aren't you? You love technical analysis these days, don't you? You're going to support the float of my company Palamountain, I'd say? Be a bit more effusive than you were about Rachael's float? That's worth ten grand to me. I know you're as good as your word. I'll fill out the application for you. What's your address? By the way, I expect to see you at Rachael's party. And Andy says you're doing a great job. What's your address?'

Henry was floored. He was about to tell Eric that Louise had said his advance cheque would arrive in a couple of weeks, he could pay then. He put the receiver down. What had he agreed to? Jesus. He was another ten thousand dollars richer, and he'd done nothing. Or had he?

Henry wandered around his apartment. He turned on his stereo and placed a recording of Beethoven's *Eroica* on the turntable. There was already a cacophony of noises drumming away in his head. He couldn't accept ten thousand dollars from Eric for supporting something he may not believe in. What sort of company was Palamountain?

To cap it all off when he opened his mail he discovered a glossy invitation to Rachael's party. It contained a photo of the Hollywood letters strung out on the Los Angeles Hills and invited everybody to come as their favourite actor. If people were stuck, there was an excellent costume hire place that hired masks.

And another burden weighed on Henry's mind. Alex had to shell out money for his new Kombi, as well as pay a hefty fine. Henry felt responsible for the fine; it was a combined excursion, after all. Alex would never ask for money – Henry wondered how he'd financed his restaurant, and how he would extricate himself from the lease. And what, if anything, would Alex do next with his slow food idea? Alex was not one to air a new direction until he had thought enough about it himself.

But Alex had not been idle, although he'd postponed going back to look for Hugo because he had a brainwave in another direction. He only ran things past Henry if he thought Henry was not going to worry too much – which is why he had simply announced his restaurant idea after the fact. Henry was hugely clever when it came to global issues, but Henry was not the man to choose when looking for inspired leadership. Alex took on the council.

Somehow he must have caught the local councillors napping. At a meeting he argued eloquently and with passion that it was the responsibility of a council to foster local enterprise. He had embarked on an ambitious, novel idea, which would have emblazoned Coogee on the restaurant map of Sydney. It would have been franchised around Australia, maybe the world, and employed thousands. But no, he had been turfed out of his restaurant because he didn't have enough toilets! (He glossed over the fact that he didn't have any at all.) There were public toilets inches away, but oh no, they weren't good enough. Didn't the councillors have confidence in their own toilets? What a disastrous waste of ratepayer funds.

Alex could tell when his arguments were making an impression, and he gathered himself for the negotiation of his life, as he later explained to Henry. He knew, from experience, that councillors were very short on detail, and long on comforting ideas. He sallied forth: Coogee Beach had few snack outlets right next to the beach. People had to walk across a busy road to buy a pie. It would not be long before a major accident occurred as someone ate a pie while crossing the road. There was a need for a pie cart. In fact, it was outrageous that Coogee didn't have a pie cart!

An elderly, influential councillor sat listening to Alex present his impassioned plea. He was an Anzac who loved things Australian. He also had very poor eyesight, a handicap that was sheeted home to a war injury, part of the folklore that surrounded his considerable stature in the community. He saw Alex as a bit of a blur, but recognised a Jesus-like figure with a good argument. Pies were as Australian as kookaburras. He hadn't been for a walk along the beach for a while, but the memory of his aching joints told him that Alex made sense. People had a God-given right to buy a pie and not walk miles to do it.

How Alex overcame the next bureaucratic obstacle was a miracle. He got approval from council, in principle, provided his pie cart was positioned in the reserve and conformed to planning regulations. It should be moved each day, and not become a permanent structure. Alex asked if he could use a van. How about a converted Kombi, for example?

The wrecker was thrilled to take a profit share. He thought the idea was brilliant, and loved pies. It would be no problem to fix a tow-bar to Alex's new Kombi, nor to weld his old Kombi into shape. As he babbled, it became apparent that the idea appealed to some dormant creative sense. He was sick of merely destroying cars, and would love to resurrect the Kombi and turn it into a work of art. Gut the inside, install a pop-up roof, cut open one side for the serving window, make some shelves. It only needed room for a pie heater. What colour?

When Alex revealed his astonishing coup, Henry was enraptured. 'Alex, you'll be in Kombi heaven.'

- 20 -

On the day of the float of Rachael's company Henry sat with Beth at the computer screen. The computer room was overflowing with eager acolytes all talking in a frenzy. Henry overheard people speculate that they'd heard the shares would come on at three dollars. Beth couldn't believe it. 'Henry, is that possible?' she asked with fire in her eyes.

'I don't think so, but you never know. These day traders are likely to push the price along.'

Henry explained that there would be an initial rush, then a stall as appetites were satisfied, then a slump, and another rise. Around the end of the day the price would settle down to some reasonable level. He'd argued that they should sell into the first strong wave, sell half, and wait. If he was right the price would dip, and they would have to hold their nerve. If it seemed that the stock was in serious retreat, then they would have to bail out.

'Why not sell all on the first rise?' Beth asked.

'Umm, we could Beth. It is the less greedy thing to do.

I just wouldn't want you to become disappointed if the price goes higher later. I think you should always take the profit that you might have expected. Never be greedy.' He looked at her and saw the significance of the moment for her. Each time they'd met he'd found new things about Beth that he admired. He looked at her exceptional blue eyes and the full mouth, and wondered if she could find Alex attractive. He'd decided that they would be good for each other.

The float was due to come on at eleven o'clock. They punched in the stock's code and waited for the first transactions.

The opening bid and ask flashed like lightning and soon there was a whirr of numbers. The crowd roared as the shares opened at two dollars twenty. Then the price fluttered up, and up, and up.

Henry couldn't believe it. 'Jesus, Beth. This is madness.'

'Henry!' she cried, putting her arms around his neck and hugging him.

The price faltered at two fifty. Henry was poised to sell Beth's fifty thousand shares. 'Now, I think, Beth.'

'Are you sure Henry? Just wait.'

Henry was getting worried. The price dipped to two thirty-five, but still Beth said to wait. He decided to sell his 20,000 shares at two twenty-nine. The price was coming down and sellers all around them dumped their shares.

'Beth, what do you want to do?'

'Hang on.'

The price fell to two dollars twelve. Time marched on, and the trades slowed down. The total volume of shares traded was eight million, and Henry told Beth that unless the mutual and superannuation funds came back into the market, the price would continue to crumble. There was a flutter back up to two dollars nineteen.

By two-thirty in the afternoon most of the room was empty. People had sold and bought and were happy to leave it. Not Beth. She came back with a sandwich for Henry, afraid to let him leave the screen. If it was going to happen, Henry told her, it would happen about three thirty. She was quite happy. After all, she'd decided that two dollars was her dream price – anything over that was a bonus.

And then the volumes started to flash like a roulette wheel. Back up went the price, as the mutual funds became serious buyers.

Wrung out, Beth and Henry looked at each other at the close of trading. She'd decided to sell her fifty thousand shares at two fifty-five, almost the high for the day. She was sitting on $127,000. Henry calculated that his shares had netted him $45,800. They were rich – well, kind of – and Beth was overcome. 'Henry. I can buy a house!'

Two days later Henry, who had not told a soul about his stockmarket success, stared at the invitation to Rachael's Hollywood party, which had been confidently arranged with a dual celebration in mind. Henry had no doubt that Rachael would be boiling over with her success, while Andy was supposed to have won preselection and be on the way to the Lodge. It augured well for quite a shindig – that he'd been determined to avoid.

But that night, as he tossed and turned in bed, he realised that he couldn't avoid going to the party. He now had a business relationship, of sorts, with Andy. He had made money from the float of Rachael's company. Louise, after all, was his agent. And, maybe the party would be the place to return the ten thousand dollars to Eric. Eric would interpret it as a back-down from an agreement, but would probably be too drunk to remember.

Saturday night beckoned, and Henry had resolved to get it over with. Rosie expected him to be working on his book. He wondered whether he should tell her that he was going. He recalled her outburst about mixing it with the rich and famous and how unsettled she was. No, he'd tell her later. He couldn't face the thought that she might be upset all over again.

He needed to get a costume. Might as well use the hire shop Rachael's invitation recommended.

The man who hired out costumes was perfect for the job. He had apparently worn most of the costumes himself at one time or another – Henry began to think that he was walking around in the man's wardrobe. Each costume was associated with some failed or imminent conquest, so that he spruiked the rental of a costume by way of its association with his love life. As he pulled the Dracula outfit from its hanger he became reflective and sighed, 'Johnnie, dear, darling Johnnie,' then hurriedly stuffed it back, almost teary, before Henry had a chance to comment. There was no way Henry would go as Dracula when Johnnie had proven to be unfaithful. This went on for a while, and Henry became worried that the man had such an effusive way about him that he would never ask Henry what he wanted.

'Umm, I really only want a mask. I want to go as Woody Allen.'

'Wooodieee? Darling boy, why didn't you say so? Everybody's going to the same party. I've rented out all my masks, but not Woooddiie!' he shrieked and scampered away.

He came back and Henry tried on the mask.

'Oh my God! You *are* Woody!'

Henry looked at himself in the mirror and couldn't believe it. The man was right. The combination of Henry's thinning pate, head shape, and even his choice of clothes was perfect.

'Darling, I have to tell you in all honesty that not everyone makes a good Woody. Some big beefy characters come in here wanting to be Woodies when they're only cut out to be Schwartzeneggers. But you can't tell a customer.' He put his fingers to his chin and examined Henry more carefully. 'Darling, you're perfect. You're not available are you?'

- 21 -

The party was due to begin at ten o'clock, which struck Henry, a morning person, as almost bedtime. It was ten-thirty before he actually arrived outside Rachael's door feeling absolutely lousy. He'd come with a bottle of his favourite shiraz, a bunch of flowers and a congratulations card. He pulled the mask out of a bag, and put it on his face.

Rachael's apartment was actually the penthouse suite, a fact that had escaped his attention previously. It made an excellent venue for what he was about to endure. A huge 'Congratulations Rachael and Andy' banner was fastened above the door. So Andy did make it, Henry mused.

Noise hurled itself at him as he pushed the door open and peered inside. It was horrible. The room was filled with misshapen replicas of stars any movie buff would instantly recognise. Henry stared, his head around the door, afraid to make an entrance. Just then Tom Cruise and Dolly Parton appeared from behind him, and he was shoved inside with their arrival, as if they all belonged together. He stood looking around at people shouting and shrieking at each other, the music a din of late-sixties Led Zeppelin, clutching a bunch of flowers that looked a little under-cast for the occasion.

Because nobody paid him any attention whatsoever, he started to relax. Slowly he edged his way to a sheltered spot near the balcony. It became obvious that nobody cared who anybody was, and Henry placed his offerings on a sideboard and decided to have a drink. Waitresses dressed as cigarette girls were carrying drinks on trays slung around their necks. A woman passed him in a Shirley Temple mask; she looked out of place alongside four Marilyn Monroes, each of whom was vying for the 'nearest thing to' award by wearing a dress so tight that laughing was a threatening gesture. As Henry reached for a glass of champagne, Shirley Temple congratulated him on his appearance.

A miraculous transformation occurred. Henry was not in the least bit afraid of stuttering. He was Woody Allen in hyper-confident mode. He looked through the eyeholes at Shirley Temple and found someone gazing back at him through her own eyeholes. The view was blurry – he couldn't wear his own glasses behind the mask. He downed his drink, and before she moved off, had reached for another. 'I used to love Shirley Temple movies,' he said.

'I've never seen one,' she replied.

He wondered where the members of the 'group' were, and scrutinised the crowd. If only he had been to more movies. Horace and Mary loved the old-time cinema, but had given up when each movie became a car-chase and only ever watched anything made before 1960. This meant that Henry knew the Lauren Bacalls and Humphrey Bogarts, but would have trouble picking Mel Gibson in a crowd. Who was Rachael? Or, more precisely, Rachael was who? And Andy, and, Jesus Christ almighty, what about Eric, and Louise?

He had another glass of champagne. Henry had a recently acquired taste for booze that had been sharpened by trips to Bruce's cabin. Rosie and Bruce enjoyed a tipple, and the quality was occasionally suspect. Beverages emerged from brown paper bags, and Henry had been forced to educate himself about the subtle differences in bag labelling. One night in the cabin he had boasted that he was adept at picking bouquets of plum and hint of oak on his back palate from paper bags. But by then he'd been well on the way to becoming a giggling wreck.

Henry actually began to enjoy himself. He flitted around the room offering unsolicited witticisms – as might be expected from Woody Allen – and ignoring jibes. And then he heard Rachael before he saw her. That laugh! She was Morticia from *The Addams Family*, and a damn good one in her magnificent black wig and long black gown. Eric, of course, was Gomez, the self-professed womaniser who was nevertheless devoted to his Morticia. Henry was pretty sure that George W. Bush, standing to one side of Gomez, was Andy. And Nicole Kidman over there, wasn't she Louise? Well, maybe in twenty years.

Slightly more tipsy than he would ever acknowledge, Henry made his way through the press of people and tapped Rachael on the shoulder.

'You did come as Woody Allen. It's Henry isn't it?' Andy/George W. Bush said.

'Wooooddiee!' Rachael/Morticia crushed him to her bosom, then raised his mask and smothered him with a kiss. She was drunk out of her mind. Eric/Gomez, was half paying attention.

Henry almost gagged, quickly stepped back, lowered his mask and collected himself. He congratulated Rachael, and Andy.

'We've done it!' Rachael brayed, and everybody in the room roared with wealth.

'We've done it!' Andy yelled, and everybody screamed like a voter. He grabbed Henry by the shoulders and shook him. Everybody whooped it up again.

It seemed to be some sort of primitive signal because until that moment the party, which had been the wildest of Henry's life, was a wake by comparison. The noise edged up ten decibels, people started to jig, rock and roll, and crash into each other. There was no scope for conversation, which was just as well. The lighting dimmed from subdued to almost non-existent. Rachael swayed toward him and he backpeddled for fear he would be resuscitated all over again. 'Herry, I mean Woollie,' she slurred. 'I want you to meet Angie.'

She dragged him by the hand and he was pummelled through the crowd and through a door to another room. There were people everywhere. This room, he thought, must be reserved for serious actors, or accident victims: everyone within was more subdued. There were no hi-jinx, crazy dancers or semi-naked Marilyns.

Rachael, Henry in tow, came to rest alongside Sophia Loren. Henry, quite giddy by this stage, was thunderstruck. His male fantasies had been given a good leg-up in boyhood by the pouting lips of Sophia Loren, and her huge vulnerable Italian eyes, in *Two Women*. Horace had watched this movie over and over until Mary became suspicious.

Sophia stood voluptuously in the very outfit she had worn in that movie. The mask returned an inscrutable, constant visage. There was something erotic about masks, as if Henry could do the most outrageous thing and it would go unnoticed. Morticia said something about Woolie being Herrie, and disappeared again, leaving Herrie to indulge his fantasy.

Sophia placed her mouth six inches from Henry's ear, and asked why he had chosen to be a child molester. Henry's Sophia Loren fantasy had never anticipated this question, and he searched for a suitably Woody riposte. He weighed various responses – 'I was bored with being an axe-murderer'. 'I'm a Noo Yorker and it's a requirement'. By the time he'd swung a number of cats around in his mind his answer was a tad overdue.

'My shrink said it was therapeutic,' he said proudly.

'What is?' She was looking in the direction of an ensuite bathroom. Henry followed her gaze and could see a queue forming there. Perhaps he needed to relieve himself as well? This was the time to establish his indifference, as an actor would, and he excused himself and stood behind Madonna – though she might have been a basset hound – who examined him dispassionately from behind a long cigarette holder.

Just then the door to the ensuite opened and Henry could see someone inside, mask up, holding what looked like a straw to some talcum powder on the sink. Madonna asked him if this was his first line of the night, and he had to say yes, although he was taken aback by her familiarity. Then, through the fog of the champagne, Henry saw what was going on. These were serious drugs. Not that he hadn't had the odd hash cookie, or been enticed by Alex to smoke a joint, coughing and wheezing in the process. He had decided that he didn't enjoy it. Alex had once been a regular pot smoker, until he decided that it had reduced his motivation to bake bread.

Henry certainly didn't want to use this bathroom, and retreated to Sophia who was by now wrapped around Gomez. Gomez? Eric. This was not just an ordinary how-dee-doo – Gomez, mask-up, was doing his level best to ravage Sophia. Henry was fixated on the spectacle, which seemed not at all disconcerting to anybody else. Gomez was manhandling parts of Sophia that definitely could not have been displayed in her movies.

Gomez looked up over Sophia's back and saw Henry staring. He extricated himself momentarily, still holding Sophia's shoulder, and snarled into Henry's ear. 'Sinkers. You're one of us now. Enjoy yourself. She's a real goer.'

Eric went back to his plunder, and Henry about-turned and stood against the wall, his mind working furiously. One of them? If he now insisted on giving back the ten thousand dollars, Eric would think Henry was judging him for ravaging Angie. Oh shit, Henry thought.

The rest of the evening was a nightmare. Louise, as Nicole Kidman, was seemingly very close friends with every second man. She was flying, and at one point was within inches of Henry, but oblivious. He witnessed a disturbing exchange between her and Andy, with Louise storming away.

The masks started coming off as guests tired of having to lift them up to drink or go deep-sea fishing with their tongues. Henry, repelled yet intrigued by the goings-on, certainly was not going to remove his mask. He saw Rachael unmasked, staggering around, her dress hanging off her shoulder, her face bloated with excess. Somehow she spied Henry, and to his horror made a circuitous beeline for him. She was upset.

'Herry, Herry, gimme a hug.'

As she leaned against him, he put one reluctant arm around her shoulder.

'Eric shot frew with Angie, the bish.' Ready to cry, she grabbed him by the hand, led him down to a bedroom and collapsed on the bed. Henry looked at her lying face down, sobbing, then sat on the edge of the bed and wondered what to do.

Slowly he began to see Rachael as a victim. He stroked her back, trying to console her. There was a mirror on the wall, and he caught sight of himself, Woody Allen stroking the shoulder of a heaving, sobbing woman. His mind had cleared. What the hell was he doing here?

The sobbing stopped and Rachael fell asleep. He found a pen and scrawled a note on a piece of paper: 'Hope you're all right. Thank you for the party. Henry.'

- 22 -

Henry took stock. In six days it would be Christmas, and preparations were underway for the trip to Bruce's cabin. The money had started to arrive. First a cheque from Louise for eight-and-a-half thousand dollars, being the ten thousand dollars advance less her commission, with a note asking him to work to the deadline for completion of the manuscript. Then came the cheque for the sale of shares in Rachael's company. He stared at his wealth.

Horace received an offer from Antonio. He was subdued about it, saying it was nowhere near what Alex had asked, but still Horace struggled with the number of zeros. 'Henry, four hundred and fifty thousand is an awfully large sum. Mary couldn't believe it. What do you think?'

'Dad, it's not enough to get you out of trouble. You have to give most of it to the bank. Where will you live? How will you pay for mum's hip? If Antonio is keen, he'll come up with a larger offer.'

'And Henry, we had a "please explain" letter from the council. Someone has lodged a complaint about the car bodies. By the way, we have a month to respond to the bank before they take action, isn't that right?'

'Yes, Dad.'

'That makes it about the middle of January. What will happen then, son?'

'They'll begin to sell you up. It'll take another month, but an agent will auction the house.'

'Oh, right.'

'Are you looking forward to going down to Bruce's for Christmas, Dad?'

Henry felt he *had* to see Alex. He knew that Alex was due to pay his fine, and that the former owner of the new Kombi also wanted his money.

Alex picked him up on the way to the wreckers, where he was going to oversee the construction of the pie cart. He was ecstatic about his new venture.

Henry waited for Alex to finish raving. While the old Kombi sounded like a threshing machine with a live sheep stuck in the blades, this Kombi sounded like it at least might make it comfortably to the corner and back. Eventually Henry raised the matter of Alex's finances.

'Yeah things are a bit tight, Henry. I don't want to ask Mum, you know how it is.'

'What are you going to do?'

'I owe five hundred on the lease for the restaurant. I owe the guy for the Kombi, and that's really urgent. I know I have to pay the fine some time. But I'll be selling my pies.'

'Can you afford the stock and the fit-out?' Henry asked.

'The wrecker's charging me nothing. He just wants a share of the profit.'

'How much?'

'I offered him fifty per cent.'

Henry thought this was a huge cut, but said nothing. 'Will he pay for the stock?'

'Don't know, haven't asked him.'

'Alex,' Henry began slowly. 'I don't want you to argue. I have the money. I'll gladly give it to you. And by the way, I want to pay the fine.'

They turned the corner into the wrecker's yard. Alex stopped the Kombi just inside: 'You know we don't mix money with friendship, Henry.'

'Please, Alex. It's burning a hole in my pocket.'

'Where'd you get money from, did you get the advance on the book?'

'Yes, and . . .'

'Wow, that's brilliant!'

Alex was genuinely happy for his friend. He agreed on a short-term loan, definitely not a gift, to tide him over until he made money on the pies. Henry hinted that he needed to have a more involved chat, but realised why this was difficult when he saw the wrecker apply his blowtorch to the old Kombi, and how distracted Alex was.

What had started as cosmetic surgery was assuming a grander design. The wrecker, who saw no need for a pop-up roof had cut the whole lot away, then welded supports for a permanent roof that now protruded high over each side of the Kombi, giving it the appearance of a new-age gipsy caravan. As Henry stood watching, the wrecker and one of his sons were hoisting an old car seat onto the flat roof. 'What's he doing now, Alex?'

'He's a genius Henry, just watch.'

The men added another car seat, facing the first. They welded a steel ladder to the side – and Henry could see divine inspiration, the sort that he'd come to expect from Alex. This would be a double-decker pie cart – one that offered, as Alex exclaimed, 'an outdoor pie-eating area with a view'! His happy customers could gorge themselves above the hustle of ordinary street-level pie-eaters. Weren't outdoor cafés all the rage? People would be fighting to eat up there. He might charge extra for each pie.

Alex climbed inside and, being thin, was able to move around with his head clearly visible. Because of the overhanging roof there would be no need for windows. It was an impressive structure, even without a new paint job, although Henry noticed that the cart was starting to look a bit toppy.

Alex, however, would brook no criticism. He said that the end product would be stunning. It would be a new concept in pie carts, and he was seriously thinking that Volkswagen would be better off building pie carts than Kombis. He would send the company a photo of the first model. At the very least they'd want to display an identical model in a hall of fame. Perhaps he would joint venture pie carts with the wrecker, who was having the time of his life.

'And guess what I've decided to call it?' Alex climbed out and grinned. 'Come on, have a guess. I'm going to paint it in big letters. What's the name?'

'Pie Floater?'

'Pie in the Sky!' Alex swooned.

- 23 -

Henry had almost shoved the party from his mind when a note came from Rachael: 'Thanks for being so sweet Henry. I do apologise. Eric was just drunk. I'm certain that Angie was on something and didn't know what she was doing, but I can't forgive her. I've forgiven Eric. He was just being a boy. Have a very merry Christmas, and I'll be in touch. You're really one of the few truly nice people.'

He was pleased. As for Eric – the man was a rat. He'd have to find another opportunity to return the ten thousand dollars.

Rosie came to dinner two evenings before the trip to Bruce's, and Alex dropped in on them to help plan the trip.

Henry was delighted to find that Rosie was in better spirits, and felt the time was ripe to tell all; about the money, Beth, the Hollywood party. They were talking about the Christmas arrangements when the phone rang. Alex mentioned that the phone was ringing, which was obvious. Rosie asked Henry if he was going to answer it. Just as he replied that the answering machine was on, the message toned around the apartment:

'Henry, it's Beth. I wanted to wish you a merry Christmas. This will be the best Christmas of my life. I'm looking at houses, and will get your opinion if I find one I like. I promise to have you over soon. It'll be really nice to repay you for your help. I think about you a lot, Henry. Bye for now.'

Henry was gob-smacked and looked it. Rosie stared at him, incredulous. Alex could see black clouds forming above her head.

'Who was that?' Rosie asked, steel in her voice.

'Umm.' Henry was not good at this.

Alex stepped in. 'Rosie, I know who it is, and you have to listen. Please don't get upset. It's all very innocent, isn't that right, Henry?'

'Yes, totally.'

'No, Alex. Henry's a big boy, he can speak for himself.' She was a taut ball of string, sitting with her arms folded, lips pressed in a tight line, her eyebrows lifted in anticipation of a very suitable explanation.

'Umm, Beth is a woman I met at the investment seminar. I told Alex about her.' Henry felt the million-watt glare of Rosie's eyes, and the words came out clumsily. Out of the corner of his eye he spied Alex's nodding head. Rosie noticed the exchange and her frown deepened, as if Alex was a co-conspirator.

'She's a very nice, umm, woman. A s-single mother . . .'

Alex shook his head imperceptibly.

'Umm, she needed a partner...'

Alex widened his eyes.

'Umm, she chose m-me because we were sitting together... I thought she needed help. I got her in for nothing. She couldn't afford it, and we m-met for coffee, and she got a loan from her mother, which she couldn't afford, and she's a n-nurse, and, umm, she's attractive...'

'What?' Rosie was really starting to wind up.

'I m-mean, for Alex...'

'For me?' Now Alex was perplexed, leaving Henry on a very thin limb.

'Umm, yes. I-I haven't told you, because I thought I would have dinner first...'

'*Dinner?* Henry, you pig!' Rosie was on the verge of tears.

'Oh shit, I'm not very good at this...' Henry mumbled, wanting to put the kettle on and the situation to just go away.

'No, you're not good at this at all, Henry. In fact you're the worst, most pathetic liar I've ever heard...' Rosie was raising her voice, and would have stood up but for the effort.

'Wait just a minute!' Alex banged both his hands on his knees. 'Henry doesn't lie, Rosie.'

'All right, yes. Will you explain, Henry?'

'I was going to tell you the other night, Rosie, but you were too upset...'

'Well, I'm *really* upset now.'

'Shut up, Rosie, let him finish.' Alex was stern.

Henry finally got it out, in his way. When he finished by saying that he really thought Beth may be good for Alex, Alex became interested. Henry proposed they all go for a coffee sometime, and Rosie relaxed.

Henry was exhausted. He had to tell them about the money, and the party. But, oh hell, it was all so unlikely. 'I made some money. Beth's talking about her win, with her mother's savings. I made fifty thousand...'

'*What?*' Alex and Rosie stared at one another.

'Umm.' Henry let out a huge sigh, as if he'd scored the money by robbing a bank.

'Henry, you're a wee bit secretive sometimes,' Alex said, and Rosie nodded.

'I'm really sorry, there is something else ...'

'*What next?*' Rosie was starting to doubt her hearing.

He sailed into the murky waters of the party and explained his reason for going.

'What a night. Wish I'd been there. Would've gone as Prince Charles. He's got my ears,' Alex said.

'I wanted to tell you, but the pie cart ...' Henry mumbled.

'And when were you going to tell me?' Rosie said, softly. 'What *am* I to you, Henry?'

'Oh Jesus Rosie, you're everything to me. I just didn't want to upset you ...'

'You're not good with conflict are you Henry?' she said. 'You lied when you said that you would be working Saturday night.'

'Yes. Not very, no, in fact, I'm ...'

'Doesn't matter. Henry is Henry,' Alex said, 'and whatever he did, he did it for good reason.'

'I suppose so,' Rosie said uncertainly.

- 24 -

Arranging everybody in the new Kombi was an exercise in logistics made possible by the availability of a back seat. Alex was able to drive in relative isolation, with Rosie in the front beside him, and Horace and Mary behind. Henry volunteered to sit in the space at the rear of the back seat, perched on some pillows, surrounded by food baskets and Christmas presents. The load presented a problem for the van, but thanks to Alex's experience in nurturing Kombis they plugged along at sixty kilometres an hour – singing Irish folk songs.

In Ireland, as Horace often explained, a night at the pub, which was most nights, would finish with a sing-song at someone's house. Each person would be called upon to contribute a song, or poem, or yarn, depending on his talent. No matter how woeful the singing, it was never criticised, but applauded, because the taking part was the important thing. So it was that Henry had grown up surrounded by wailing chants and morose ballads which, unfortunately, were sung off-key by both Horace and Mary. This was understandable because the feedback loop had been circumvented throughout their lives, and they both considered themselves near professional standard.

It was warm in the Kombi, so the windows were wide open. The singing had an interesting effect at traffic lights. Dogs, some trigger in their limbic brains clicked by the wailing, took off in pursuit. Then the singing had to stop for a while, as Mary couldn't bear the thought of leading the dogs all the way to Goulburn. But the freeway was the hilltop in *The Sound of Music*, and the Sinclairs were the von Trapps. Alex, who knew some Irish songs, like 'Whiskey in the Jar', which was his favourite, could easily have partnered his old Kombi in a duet. Henry loved to sing, but his voice was no match for the basso profundo of Horace. Rosie, keen to diversify the agenda, after two hours of uninterrupted Irish numbers, launched into 'The Little Drummer Boy', and made quite an impression. She sang in key and caused some moments of introspection.

Bruce, who had never hosted a fully-fledged Christmas party at the cabin, had decorated the lone gum tree standing at the front door. He had purchased shiny baubles and miles of silver frizzy tinsel. A lone angel perched on top of the tree was lost among the foliage, which, belonging to a gnarled and twisted gum tree of four metres, was not totally conducive to the transformation.

Bruce had surveyed his handiwork and decided that it would not make a huge impression. The tinsel looked like a rare fungus. Accordingly, and because he had the view that it was silly to try to imitate a snow-covered landscape in heat-wave conditions, he applied an Australian perspective. He festooned the tree with shoes tied by their laces, pots, tins and assorted clothing. He'd not quite finished when the Kombi arrived.

The tree was the first thing that the troubadours noticed when, armed with baskets and presents, they staggered up the incline to greet Bruce, who stood to one side of his creation. Everybody complimented Bruce on his remarkable effort, although Rosie said that it would have been better to lay his stuff on the ground if Bruce was going to have a garage sale.

Bruce, an average electric guitarist and singer, had isolated one corner of his living room as the sound stage. The generator powered enormous speakers, several microphones and sound equipment, and was capable of belting out an ocean of noise. The singing in the Kombi had been mere practice for a night of Carols by Candlelight, Horace inspired by the idea that his voice would carry all the way to Dublin.

Mary and Horace loved Bruce's cabin instantly, although Mary had been primed by Rosie to expect truly rustic accommodation. Rosie had been quite elaborate in her description. Bruce, an adopted Sinclair family member, had insisted that everybody should treat the cabin as their holiday home. For her part, Rosie had long ago put her foot down when it came to the laying out of food and tidying things up around the place. As they stood in the doorway she remarked to Mary that to properly apply a woman's touch would take some centuries, and not to bother. Mary, being a latent feminist, wholeheartedly agreed. The men had never seen the need for Rosie's defiant stand on the matter, it being assumed that the cabin was a male sanctuary, but the women had to suffer the consequences.

Horace and Mary were offered the luxury of Bruce's own bedroom – the tacked-on lean-to – while Henry and Rosie were assigned the loft above the kitchen area. Bruce would sleep on the sofa, in front of the fireplace. Alex would sleep in the Kombi.

As Rosie showed Mary around the cabin, Mary whispered that she hadn't seen a bathroom, and Rosie nodded and led her by the elbow. 'Mary, you remember I warned you about the toilet? It's a typical bush dunny, you know, a hole over which they've put the thunder box. That's what it's called in the bush.'

'Rosie, I'm an old sheila. Sat on a few myself,' Mary tut-tutted.

They wandered outside and Rosie pointed to a forlorn structure made of logs with a rusty tin roof. 'You shouldn't go anywhere near it.'

'Goodness, why not?' Mary asked.

'Look at it. It could feature in a glossy brochure designed to keep foreign tourists at home. There's nothing wrong with the hole; a hole being a hole. The dunny is an afterthought put together by one of Bruce's working bees. It's far too narrow. A person of normal size has to enter backwards, because there's no room to turn around. I've never used it. The logs have huge gaps and the door doesn't fit.'

'My, my. It looks like it's going to fall over,' Mary said with a smirk. 'You did warn me.'

'Yeah. Bruce thinks there must have been an earthquake. Enough said, but I guarantee you that it's a challenge for anyone spoilt by toilet arrangements on a flat surface. Henry reckons he has to lean to the left while sitting on the thunderbox.'

During their stay, the women were often to be seen walking over the rise.

Bruce had gathered half-a-dozen casuarinas and placed them around the cabin, propped up against the walls, and had run the tinsel, in which he had cornered the world market, liberally through everything. It made the cabin look like a wrapped present.

Eventually they settled, and sat in anticipation of the evening's carol singing and the opening of presents with a welcoming drink. Mary suggested it would be more appropriate to open presents in the evening, because she was doubtful she'd get a good night's sleep. 'Who knows how I'll be in the morning, Horrie.'

Alex topped up the wine glasses.

'We're here celebrating while much of the world is at war,' Horace said, reclining in an armchair, holding his glass at arm's length.

'The world's changed, Horrie. Thank God we have each other. There's nothing as important as family,' Mary said, as Alex refilled her glass.

'It's too bad that Hugo isn't here then,' Alex responded, catching Mary's eye.

Henry started and watched Horace's face darken.

'When am I going to meet him?' Rosie said.

'I have to make a confession,' Alex began, and sat down in an armchair. 'I found out where he lives. I was about to ring the doorbell when a nurse arrived . . .'

'*What?* When?' Henry stared at Alex.

'A couple of weeks ago. I got his address from Mignon. She sounded pretty upset.'

'Why didn't you *tell* me?' Henry asked.

'Calm down Henry. Look, Rosie, Bruce and I have often wondered about your twin brother, and why we haven't met him. I wanted to mend fences for you. To surprise you for Christmas. Tie Hugo up in the back of the van and wrap him like a present.' Alex smiled.

'So, what happened?' Horace asked, exchanging a look with Mary.

'As the door opened I saw someone in the corridor who seemed to be jerking, or twitching as he looked at me. Then I snuck a peek through a side window. Whoever it was saw me and threw something. Nearly hit me. Smashed the window. I got the hell out of there. Couldn't be Hugo, he was wild. He ran out of the house and tripped, flat on his face. I thought I'd go back another day. If Hugo lives there he, he lives in a dump in Newtown,' Alex said.

'Oh dear,' Mary said.

'Mary, why didn't you tell me that you'd given Mignon's number to Alex?' Horace asked.

'Horrie ... this is really difficult. When Alex asked, he put me on the spot ... Don't you think we should tell everyone what's going on? This has gone far enough.' Mary's eyes, magnified by her glasses, showed her sorrow.

Henry stood up slowly. The moment played itself out in his mind. His mouth went dry as he gathered himself to deliver the revelation that had plagued him. He glanced at Rosie and wondered if this would end up being the worst Christmas of his life. Like a damp fog seeping under a doorway, the tension flooded the room. Henry took Mary's hand in a gesture of support and looked meaningfully at Horace. 'You're absolutely right, Mum. If it has to be on Christmas Eve, so be it. We Sinclairs have kept a secret from you all that has eaten away at us like a cancer ... Horace is the carrier of a disease called Huntington's Chorea. It's been passed on to Hugo, and I have a fifty-fifty chance of coming down with it ...'

'*What?*' Rosie sat up.

Henry went to the sofa and sat down next to her. 'It will soon hit Horace. When Hugo visited Ireland about four years ago, he found out by accident that there was an illness in Horace's family. When he confronted Horace there was a wild argument. This is the part that I don't understand ...'

'Henry, what are you saying? You might get it? What are you talking about?' Rosie hushed.

Horace put his hand to his forehead and sighed heavily. 'I wanted to avoid this. But you're right Henry, we have to get it out in the open. Rosie, it does affect you. Not only may Henry come down with it, but so may your child, if ever you and Henry decide to have one.'

'That's what you were on about the other day, Henry?' Alex asked gravely.

Horace continued: 'Hugo was livid. He ranted at me for not telling him about the disease. It's hit my family every so often, but they've always thought it was some crazy variation of Alzheimer's disease. It's very rare. When my brother told me, twelve years ago, I was shattered, and thought it best to ignore it. Mary agreed with me. If you know you have it, there's nothing that you can do but wait for the symptoms. So I tried desperately to stop Hugo from having a test. If he found out that he had it, it would have meant that I was the carrier. Then there was the chance that Henry had inherited it too.'

'So, *what* is it? Henry, you've kept it from me? You know how much I want a baby.' Rosie was ashen-faced. She took her hand from his. 'And you've already got it, Horace? You don't look sick.'

Henry exchanged a look with Horace, raising his eyebrows, waiting for Horace to respond. Horace hesitated and leaned over to reach for the bottle of wine.

Henry saw that Horace was agonising over his answer. He turned in his seat looking into Rosie's eyes. 'The disease is called Huntington's Chorea. Chorea, meaning dance. You degenerate slowly. You get wild mood swings, depression, coordination problems, dementia, uncontrollable jerky movements, grimaces. You can suddenly play an imaginary piano, start a strange dance . . . it's terminal.'

Rosie, Alex and Bruce recoiled with a collective gasp.

'*What?* You're serious? . . . Poor Horace. Why, why didn't you tell me, Henry?' Rosie said almost inaudibly, then got up, walked over to Horace to put her hand on his shoulder, and turned to walk outside.

'Rosie, please. Of course I should have told you.' Henry followed her, but she pushed him away.

'I have to be alone for a moment,' she said, and closed the door behind her.

Henry inhaled and picked up his drink.

'Jesus, I'm sorry, Henry,' Alex said. 'Sounds like it *was* Hugo.'

'Alex, you're not to blame,' Henry said, looking out the window.

'Are you going to have a test, Henry?' Bruce asked.

'Yes, if Rosie wants me to.'

He opened the door and walked outside like a robot. His mind and stomach churned as he looked at Rosie sitting on a log, staring into the distance. 'Rosie, forgive me. You have every right never to see me again. But please don't do anything rash.'

'What a Christmas present. How *could* you? How could you avoid getting it? He's your twin brother.'

'He's not my identical twin. Please come back inside, I want to say something in front of everyone.'

Rosie sniffed and wiped the tears from her eyes. 'In a while, Henry. I'll come inside for the sake of the others. I don't know yet what I think.'

The mood was funereal. Not a word was spoken as everybody waited for Rosie. Ten minutes ground by, with Henry staring at Rosie through the window.

Eventually she appeared at the door, her face a mask of pain. She sat down on the sofa next to Mary, who took her hand.

Henry stood in front of the fireplace, wringing his hands. 'I want to say something . . . I believe I don't have the disease. I don't know why I believe this, but it came to me as I looked at Rosie's sad face a second ago. If she forgives me, then I will have a test, if that's what she wants.

'But there's something else. I started writing about relationships because I didn't know how long I had to live. I convinced myself that I was writing in jest, helping readers think about the sharemarket. I was really getting stuff out of my system. Anger and disappointment at the way the world seemed to be losing its way. All the while I kept Rosie in the dark. And you Alex, and Bruce. I've been a hopeless coward and have no excuse. I didn't want to lose you, any of you. Or to have you pity me.'

'That's why I've kept it quiet, Henry,' Horace said. 'I don't want pity.'

Henry looked at Horace and smiled feebly. 'It's now possible for us all to be tested for genetic diseases. A DNA test can tell us if we have a life-threatening disorder. And there's something else. This may seem a bit far-fetched, but it's been in my thinking. The events of September 11, and the horrors since then, are an omen. The Western world's had a DNA test and is found wanting. The prognosis is terminal unless there's a wholesale change in attitude. The worst diseases are greed and envy. The have-nots are bombarded with slick images. The system is geared up to make everybody slave their guts out for things that they hardly need, while the rest of the world starves. A breeding ground for the next suicide mission.'

There was silence. 'Quite a speech, Henry,' Alex said.

'Henry, that's noble stuff, but the world was always so,' Bruce said.

'But, *does* it have to be so?' Rosie said.

Everybody looked at Rosie, waiting for her to continue.

'I love you, Henry, for the person you are. You struggle with your conscience, and you're human. You're clever, but you make mistakes. It was a mistake not to have told me about the disease, but I can understand why you didn't. None of us knows how we would react until we're in the same spot.'

Henry's face lit up. 'Rosie. You forgive me?'

'I'll exact my punishment, don't you worry,' she smiled. 'Henry, if you love someone, you'll stick by them. How could you be any *more* difficult to look after?'

'This is wonderful. The best Christmas of my life,' Horace

said, looking like a man who'd had the weight of the world removed from his shoulders. 'Let's try to forget our troubles. Mary, it's time for your present!'

'Hey! Wait a minute, you Sinclairs. You've just told us that you're going to cark it, and now we celebrate?' Alex said with a sweep of his arm.

'I can't believe you just said that,' Henry joked.

'Yeah? Why?' Alex asked.

'Because *you're* the most fatalistic person I've ever met.' Henry fetched the bottle of wine and topped up Alex's glass.

Bruce had been sitting in shock watching the drama unfold. 'I understand why you wanted to ignore it, Horace. Faced with it, I think I would have done the same. Any one of us could be sitting on a time bomb.'

Horace took charge. He asked Henry to fetch Mary's present from the Kombi. Alex was to open more wine. Could Bruce light some candles? It was clear that Horace was doing his level best to lift everybody's spirits.

With Andy Williams dreaming of a white Christmas in the background – Mary's favourite carol, Henry handed the large, wrapped parcel to Mary, who gave it to Bruce. It contained a weaving, to be put on *that* wall, Mary insisted. It would cover up a mess of mud gap-filler.

Alex helped Bruce hold the weaving up against the wall, and they all moved over to study the masterpiece.

'It's amazing, Mum,' Henry said.

Bruce asked Henry to hold the weaving so he could look at it from a distance. 'Is it about Africa, Mary?' he asked.

'It's not Africa, silly,' Rosie said confidently.

'Where did you get the idea for that tiger, Mary?' Alex asked.

Mary was looking dejected.

'Tell them, Mary,' Horace said.

'No, let us guess,' Rosie said. 'I know, it's Cattle Dog, and that's the cabin, and that's the dunny! You did this from the way I described the cabin, didn't you?'

Mary nodded.

Light dawned – if only they'd had more wine they would have understood it immediately. That blob was Cattle Dog, and the lump he was standing over was the cabin. Cattle Dog had but a distant resemblance to a domestic feline. There was another structure to one side of the cabin which was difficult to fathom, but definitely standing at an angle. There were some interesting psychological overtones, but nobody volunteered them.

Now Bruce could understand the weaving's artistry, he was genuine in his praise. 'It's the best Christmas present I've ever had, Mary.'

'Told you everybody would love it,' Horace said.

Bruce gave Horace and Mary their present: a large fifties photo of a Morris Minor with a happy couple standing beside it. The Morris was the same colour as Horace's, and the couple looked like Horace and Mary in younger days.

Where Horace had found Alex's present – a large papier-mache hand holding a meat pie – was for him to know, but Alex was impressed. Rosie sniffed her perfume and scolded Mary. Henry had absolutely insisted that they not buy him a present, and he unwrapped his shirt with a shake of his head.

Henry had used some of his new wealth to buy gifts for Horace and Mary that he thought they needed desperately. They would be delivered the following week, but he gave them a card from himself, Alex and Rosie, with brochures tucked inside. Mary had often lamented not being able to afford Alpaca wool for her weavings, and Henry bought her reams of it. Then came the new washing machine, because Mary's was in worse condition than Alex's Kombi, and consented to wash only when it rained. And a new refrigerator.

Horace asked Henry how he could possibly afford all this. Henry said he'd explain later.

And then came Rosie's present, which Henry had left till last. Henry had suggested to Alex, Bruce and Rosie that they each should give presents only to Horace and Mary, but now he pulled a double-cross. He handed a small wrapped box to Rosie.

Thanks to its size and shape, everyone guessed what this gift might be. Rosie opened it nervously, her fingers shaking. She was looking at Henry with her mouth open.

She took the ring out of the box, climbed out of her chair, crushed Henry with an enormous hug and kiss, and fled from the room.

Alex filled his own glass, then noticed that Horace's was empty. Unsteadily he got up.

'You're looking a bit shaky, Alex,' Horace beamed. 'You know Christmas in Australia is about as good as it gets, except for the heat. The place shuts down. I said to Mary the other day that the work ethic has got a bit un-Australian of late, just like Henry said. Used to be you would get home at five to play with the kids. Now everybody works like a ferret to buy another microwave.'

'You're all getting a fair share of goodies,' Alex said, grinning, and momentarily let air out of the party balloon.

Henry chimed in: 'You're right Alex. None of us can afford to be righteous.'

Horace chortled: 'What did someone say? There are two types of people in the world: the righteous and the unrighteous. And the righteous do the dividing.'

'Spot on, Horace,' Alex laughed. 'Must've been talking about Henry.'

Just then Rosie came back inside fondling the ring on her finger, and began a discussion with Mary. Alex, observing, whispered to Henry: 'What sort of ring is it meant to be?'

'It's gold and has a sapphire in it,' Henry whispered back.

Alex dug Henry in the side. 'Dummy, what's it *for*?'

'Christmas, you drongo.'

'Christ you're a nerd, Henry. You're supposed to be a bloody expert on women!'

'Oh shit. You mean I should propose or something?'

'That's why she was emotional, you deadhead.'
'What, *now*? The ring's a ... stopgap ...'
'You mean like a bath plug, stop the water running out?'
'What are you two whispering about?' Bruce asked.

- 25 -

The days following Christmas were sober. Driving back to Sydney, the revelations in the cabin were so devastating that the thought of revisiting the disease in conversation was abhorrent. There was now an unspoken presence in their lives.

Henry applied himself to the book, Alex focused his efforts on the pie cart business.

The wrecker wondered about the need to register his work of art, saying there had to be a category for pie carts. No need, said Alex. The wrecker was dubious. It was essentially a trailer, to be towed around. It should be registered! But Alex, who couldn't be bothered with another beureaucratic obstacle, won the day. Reluctantly, the wrecker hitched the new Kombi to the new pie cart, and off set Alex on a glorious sunny day.

The spot that Alex chose for his pie cart was on the reserve close to the principal steps leading down to the beach. Henry, Rosie, Horace and Mary sat on a park bench and looked south along Arden Street eagerly awaiting the arrival of the pie cart like immigrants on the deck of a ship. Only Henry had seen it in its semi-finished state, and the reality was clouded in obscure imaginings. Henry had given up with his description when Mary hit an impasse at the open-air seats.

Not even Henry was primed for what they saw. The pie cart, painted in fashionable purple, bobbed and weaved behind the new Kombi like a live thing. A large flagpole was attached to the front and an unrecognisable flag fluttered in the breeze. The passage of such an unusual item did not go unnoticed, particularly as the Kombi constipated the flow of traffic. From their position by the side of the road Henry could see backed-up cars following at a funereal pace but there was no sign of any road rage whatever. 'Probably think they've stumbled on the tail end of a circus procession,' Horace joked. The pie cart leading half of Sydney into Coogee Beach made for an impressive sight.

Upon closer inspection, Henry could see that the flag was inscribed with an icon that looked like a hammer bashing a car. Ah yes, the logo of Wally the Wrecker.

The pie cart came to rest and was detached from the Kombi. Mary said in an aside to Henry that now she understood what he meant about the car seats. Rosie shook her head in disbelief, or profound admiration, while Horace was grinning with delight – his papier-mache hand holding a pie was stuck on the front of the roof. Slowly a crowd gathered, led by hordes of children. 'Pie in the Sky' was writ large on each side of the cart.

Alex parked his Kombi and strode back, puffed up with entrepreneurial pride. He unfurled a large awning over the serving window, attached it to poles, then entered the Kombi and stood, stooping, his head poking out through the servery. He reached back for a megaphone and boomed: 'Ladies and gentlemen, and especially girls and boys! Coogee's Pie in the Sky is open for business.'

Henry et al gathered at the window to congratulate Alex, who asked them to climb on the roof to eat the inaugural pies. Henry wondered how Alex had warmed the oven, there being no electricity connection. He peered inside and saw a gas cylinder, pleased that this time Alex had anticipated the need for heat.

A bunch of enthusiastic children rushed up and thrust coins at Alex. Horace suggested that adults should stand aside and let the children go first. Alex sold his inaugural pies to six children, who scrambled for the roof.

One small detail of construction that had escaped the wrecker's attention became clear as the children climbed up the ladder fastened to the Kombi's side. With six largish children on the ladder or the roof at the same time, the pie cart assumed a definite lean. Indeed, it rocked and rolled. After all, the Kombi had lost whatever residual suspension it had possessed about the time that President Kennedy died, making it swoon when a sparrow landed. This made life inside interesting for Alex, who suddenly lurched about. Children have little respect for design ingenuity, nor could they anticipate the difficulties of a proprietor attempting to smuggle pies from an oven when on a turbulent ocean, and proceeded to rock the whole thing with some vigour.

Alex, forced to finesse his customer relations program from the outset, grabbed his megaphone, poked his head out of the servery and nearly deafened a small child about to pay some money. 'This is an announcement,' he boomed for all of Coogee Beach to hear. *'You must sit still on the roof!'*

Fortunately Wally the Wrecker was on hand. 'No worries Alex, I'll build stabilisers. Er, it's a good idea to keep kids off the roof until I add a railing.'

All told opening day was a huge success. A very satisfied bunch of people, namely Henry et al, sat on the roof eating their pies, taking in the grand view, and waving to people at ground level. Mary hadn't been keen to climb up until Horace challenged her: 'Come on, old girl, your hip will be okay.'

Alex ran out of pies within two hours of opening.

- 26 -

Horace and Mary seemed resigned to the bank's march of appropriation, but Henry still hoped to save their house. First he had to finish his manuscript.

The sweep of the book was wrapped around Henry's original idea that people chose each other as shares. He sat at his computer and approached the end of the book with a chapter entitled 'Afterthoughts'.

'For most people a relationship is akin to a business merger, while, looked at from the outside, some relationships appear more like hostile takeovers. When a business merger is proposed, the first issue to be resolved is which chief executive will prevail in the merged entity. A relationship that works attempts to establish equality. Without a limbic brain connection, it is difficult to merge a road haulage company with a book publisher, for example. The cost of conflict is clear. Eventually the business and the relationship fails with substantial real dollar and emotional cost to all parties.

'In a merged entity like a relationship, there must be a reason why men and women voluntarily live together, apart from the parenting overlap. A baggage train of attitudes and expectations differentiate the sexes. It's a cliché, but women are right: men have to initiate discussion about sensitive issues, learn how to listen and clean the toilet. Women have to learn the art of signalling their intentions.'

Henry had devised a scheme that he was about to trial on Rosie. 'How to resolve conflict? Men can relate to yellow and red cards as used in football. A woman could use a yellow card to signal discontent. A man seeing his woman waving a yellow card could reflect on the range of possible causes. For some men this might encompass the entire spectrum of their behaviour, maybe taking a week. For other men, whose synapses functioned on a particularly Neanderthal level, it may take longer, like a month. A woman *has* to appreciate the inability of the male brain to engage in self-criticism, and be patient, and she is obliged to give notice of the place and time of interview.

'A yellow card signals a relatively minor, yet for many women a profoundly irritating misdemeanour, like the man leaving up the toilet seat, leaving out the butter, dropping clothes all over the place. A red card is serious, and is followed only by the sin bin in terms of gravity. The sin bin is appropriate for gross indiscretions, like infidelity, and could presage a team walk out.' Henry felt that he had committed just such an offence. Would Rosie really forgive him for not telling her about the disease?

'When approaching the interview she has arranged, the woman should adhere to the rules of engagement. This unfortunately puts the onus on her to deal with the matter in a problem-solving way, which is the only way to deal with some men. So simple,' Henry wrote, and wished that women could understand the male on this level. 'The woman should deal with each issue one at a time so that she is not a constant waver of yellow flags. And she should never, ever, link misdemeanours. The habit of linking misdemeanours is more popularly known as carping. It's perfectly understandable that carping occurs when the man is impossible to change. However, to advance the cause of conflict resolution, the woman might wish to try another tack. Perhaps a last-ditch effort to penetrate a thick cranium.' Like my own, Henry thought.

'To obtain a coherent response from some men, it is necessary for a woman to advance ownership of the problem.' Henry figured that this was key. He got up and walked around the apartment, refining his thoughts. 'Seemingly trivial issues, like the toilet seat, are symbolic of deeper resentments. Humour helps. Perhaps the woman should say that something in her psyche makes her scared to death by the sight of an open toilet seat. It's a deeply traumatic affliction, and she has no explanation for it, but she could only get her head around a toilet when the seat is down. A man can instantly relate to this, being possessed of a few phobias himself, being a problem-solver, and not wishing to explore the matter more deeply.

'If this fails she should padlock the toilet and hide the key. Stalemate is not the end of the world.'

Henry wondered how men would respond to his next bit. 'But I'm pessimistic about some men ever getting outside their locker-room heads, and here I have a few simple observations. There's a myth of masculinity for which Darwin is partly responsible. Great movement can occur in the battle of the sexes if men acknowledge how insufferably boring they can be, even to other men. To perpetuate the myth of bonding through inane talk about football tackles is doing a disservice to the intellect. To endorse mindless grunting about abnormal bra sizes is a step removed from the swamp. Thinking men hate bar-room chatter as much as women, but are afraid to say so, for fear of being considered wimps. But there's a caveat. Real wit and political incorrectness are the stuff of good fun. Men excel at this. Men have to continue to be men, whatever that means, even if evolution requires more self-analysis from them.' And this required an entirely new vocabulary of male talk, which he thought might be the sequel. He cracked his knuckles and shunted it off to Louise.

A letter of demand arrived from the bank giving notice of its intent to auction the cottage. A real estate agent, a Mr Winch, would call around and 'have a chat' with Horace and Mary.

Henry stood in the background as the agent considered the impediments to an open inspection. He was a youngish, impatient man who, it seemed, loved mortgagee sales because there was no need to be ingratiating. Power welled inside him as he strode around the house, screwing up his face. Henry observed his reaction to the car bodies, the weaving enterprise, and the general clutter. Horace followed him around wearing his old hat and his favourite slippers, while Mary materialised every so often with murder in her eyes. The reality of the situation was biting hard, and Henry felt sad to the point of tears.

Mr Winch rejected Horace's offer of a cup of tea. He stated the facts. They should get rid of the car bodies, they were an eyesore. The weaving enterprise should be closed down, for the same reason. A touch of paint would not go astray. After all, the bank was owed a lot of money, and any excess would flow to Horace and Mary.

He left, and Mary distributed tea. There was sipping and clinking, but not a word was spoken for some time. 'Dad, Mum, I have a plan. I'd like you to listen, because I've been thinking about nothing else.'

'Yes, son?'

'It was Alex who gave me the nudge, and we have him to thank for making me see myself for what I am.' Henry looked into his cup.

'For what you are?' Mary asked.

'Yes, Mum. A dope.' He looked up and met Horace's eyes. 'I'll get you out from under this mess. I'll be investing in shares, and I need about a month.'

'Investing what?'

Henry explained the seminars and his win, and his plan.

Horace sat cogitating. 'Henry, this is my fault. I can't expect you to bend your principles.'

'Dad, they're *your* principles. There's a bigger issue here. Somehow I have to support the float in my articles. The company is called Palamountain, and the guy behind it gives me the jitters. Normally I would have nothing to do with him, or his company. I'll be exploring alternatives, but I may have no choice.'

'He's quite right, Horrie. We're dinosaurs. The world has moved on,' Mary said softly.

'But *I* should be the one . . .' Horace mumbled forlornly.

'Cut it out, Dad,' Henry said. 'What'll you do, become a home handyman? And what about Mum?'

Horace nodded, pressed his lips together and looked over his bifocals at Mary.

'And the car bodies. If we wait for the agent to move them he'll just charge us.'

'I know, Henry. It was a silly idea, wasn't it?'

'Well, it might still work. You've had one offer,' Henry said.

'What'll it cost to move them?' Mary asked.

'Don't worry about that. Alex has a joint venture with Wally the Wrecker.'

Horace stared at a schedule the agent had given him. 'The first open inspection is mid-February. The auction will be early March.'

'That's time enough,' Henry smiled. 'Agreed?'

Henry floated around his apartment. His life suddenly had such purpose that he wondered whether he'd ever been happy before. Cruising for action, he phoned Alex and asked him about the car bodies. Did Alex think Wally could help?

'Pay him? Are you kidding, Henry? I've changed his life. He's never been happier. Reckons that he was born to the pie business. And Henry, good on you. About time you got off your arse, you know that.'

'Alex. You gave me the nudge, my good friend.'

'Me? Don't be stupid.'

Then, like a thunderclap, because that's how his staccato voice snapped over the answering machine, Eric phoned, and said that now Henry had a certain obligation, it would be timely to get together and discuss the float of Palamountain. Would Henry visit him on his new yacht? Moored at Rushcutters Bay. The Cruising Yacht Club. Andy, and maybe Rachael, would be there. 'I understand you've made quite an impression on my woman? Seven-thirty tonight. Right then, be there.'

★

The Rushcutters Bay marina was like a huge toy box. As Henry walked along the dock past enormous sailing boats with their rigging clanging in the light breeze, searching for berth twenty-six, he scanned between the tall buildings on the next peninsular hoping for glimpses of the Harbour Bridge and the Opera House above the oily water of the bay. He was suffering an acute case of the jitters. One boat after another pressed down upon him with rakish bows and enormous observation decks. He paused alongside berth twenty-six and gaped. Soaring above him wasn't a boat, but an ocean liner, with portholes and decks. The name *Palamountain* was inscribed on the side.

He walked up the gangplank and was greeted by Eric, who looked down from the upper deck. 'Here's our publicity machine, right on time.'

Henry, steeling himself for his mission, had taken time to don his version of casual power dressing. He'd put on his best floral shirt, old-fashioned short pants and longish socks, these making up the closest he could get to nautical attire. Andy and Eric, informal in crisp white shorts and sandals, were drinking white wine. They stood on the observation deck beside a table of giant prawns, lobster, and exotic salads. A young woman in a red silk sarong floated in and offered Henry a drink.

'Henry, missed talking to you at Rachael's party. Saw you briefly as Woody Allen, and a very good one, as I recall,' Andy said.

'Umm.'

'I remember seeing him. I think I was saying hello to Angie at the time, isn't that right Henry?' Eric said.

'Umm.'

'Help yourself to some lobster. How do you like my little boat?' Eric asked, leaning against the railing.

Henry, hating the attention from these two prize bulls, stuffed some lobster in his mouth to give it something to do. 'Very, umm, nice.'

The young woman reappeared and leant over the table. Eric

stroked her bottom as if she were his prize calf. 'Yvonne, you're looking fabulous.'

She turned, smiled a coy thank you, and sashayed back inside.

'Where do you get them, Eric? More stunning every time,' Andy leered, watching her depart.

'Rachael's coming straight from work. Best behaviour now.'

'Speak of the dragon,' Andy said.

They could see her walking along the dock. Henry was astonished as she appeared on deck. Rachael's hair was up in a French knot, her navy suit business-like but elegant, showing the ruffled cuffs of her blouse, and she wore minimal lipstick and blusher. She looked stunning, in total contrast to the teary mascara-smeared wreck Henry had last seen.

'Henry, it's wonderful to see you.' She gave him a peck on the cheek, squeezed his arm, then turned to Eric and gave him a quick kiss too. 'Hello Andy.'

They sat down at the table and a business agenda took over the proceedings. The Palamountain float would be priced at fifty cents. Rachael's float had been the experiment, and it had proven a stunning success. Now for the main game.

As Eric detailed aspects of the prospectus, Henry realised that he was privy to seriously inside information, and as a prospective shareholder, became alarmed. Behind Palamountain was a former gold-mining company. Like so many reincarnations, Palamountain was merely the listed shell for a biotechnology venture with a lot of hope and distant promise. The business model was based on early stage research into anti-viral agents from within the Australian Research Institute. A range of products would emerge from a torturous process of clinical testing. The most hopeful of these products was targeted at the HIV virus.

Henry flipped through the prospectus and recognised not one of the scientists on the advisory board. For any biotechnology proposal to have credibility, it was essential to have strong support from the best scientific minds in the area. There were affidavits from unrecognized foreign professors from universities not known for their biotech faculties. It appeared as though the support for the float would come from the devoted members of ITSSS Unbelievable. Eric said that, unfortunately, the underwriter had been unable to gather any institutional support.

Henry was crestfallen. He knew that Eric was a show-pony, but he'd hoped that Palamountain would have some substance. His plan to save Horace and Mary's cottage looked shaky. Rachael's company was substantial. It had a history of performance. Palamountain was built on hype and promise.

Henry was an ultra cautious expert in biotechnology. He'd suggested that many business models were premature, and investors were financing very early-stage research. Without any history of success a new company float was reliant entirely on the technology bubble. And it could burst at any time. Hasn't the dot-com hype taught us anything? he wondered.

'Henry, this is where you come in,' Eric said, catching Henry deep in thought. 'I want you to write a seriously supportive article on the prospects of the research.'

Henry's next trip to sit with Beth at the computer terminal took place a day later. Beth, blissfully confident, raved about the house she was proposing to buy. She'd had a wonderful Christmas, and her mum was in heaven, staggered that Beth could actually make so much money. It had changed all their lives. On and on.

Henry listened, pleased for her.

'Henry, I wonder what I should do. I could buy the house, now I have money for a deposit, but I'd still have to borrow.'

'What sort of house is it?'

'Just an old terrace in Erskineville. I couldn't afford anything flash. Do you know how much you have to pay? It's incredible what you get for three-hundred thousand. Tiny.'

'Yeah. Three-hundred thousand?'

'Yes,' she said dismally.

'And you have to pay tax, pay your mother her profit share ...'

'Well, my mum is prepared to lend some money. I'd then have to borrow one-hundred-and-sixty thousand. On my salary that's difficult, but I could just manage it.'

'Well?'

She turned in her seat and stared at him. 'Henry, what if I invest in Palamountain? It's a sure bet. Eric said so. Imagine it takes off like Rachael's company?'

Oh God, Henry thought. He stared at the screen and felt her eyes drilling him.

'What's the matter, Henry?'

'I'm very worried about Palamountain.'

She went quiet. 'Oh, by the way, what about coming to dinner?'

'Yes. I haven't told you about Rosie, my, umm, girlfriend.'

'You've got a girlfriend? Oh, sorry, I just, doesn't matter ...'

He turned toward her. 'Yes. She's heard all about you.'

'I'd love to meet her. Bring her along.'

'By the way, Beth, have you got, umm, is there somebody in your life?'

'No, not really. I've kind of given up on men. I just concentrate on my daughter. She gives me all the love I need right now. But, if I were a woman of substance, a woman of property ...'

'I tell you what. I have a close friend. He's unusual, and I wouldn't want you to think I was matchmaking ...'

She laughed. 'People are always trying to match me up, Henry. But if he's a friend of yours, I'd love to meet him.'

Henry brightened. 'I tell you what. Why don't we go to a restaurant. Save you having to cook. It'll be on me, to celebrate. I haven't taken Rosie out for ages. And I owe Alex ...'

'Is that his name?'

The following morning Henry sat frozen at his computer screen. He was unable to summon the wherewithal to write an article supporting Palamountain Ltd. He had not slept well at all, agonising about Eric's request – no, demand – that he highlight the float of Palamountain. Eric wanted him to draw attention to the forecasts in the prospectus, and say that the float would be oversubscribed – investors should climb on board.

He walked around his apartment, deep in thought. He was caught in a trap that he had vowed to avoid. As a commentator, he faced a conflict of interest that most of his fellow scribes ignored. Like them, he would have to declare that he owned shares in Palamountain, and this would detract from the impact of what he had to say, making him just another commentator. He had never used his own name, always hiding behind the 'Analyst' nom de plum. Was he now ready to step off his high-principled horse for the sake of his mission?

He sat back down at his desk, stretched his back and set to work. He researched his sources to find another example of a biotech company that would soon float. He wrote the article, forecasting the likely short-term success of Palamountain and one other hopeful start-up, but applying a mild caution about the untested business model. He finished the article by mentioning that he had shares in Palamountain.

- 27 -

The idea of going out to a restaurant grabbed everybody as a darned good one. Alex raved about the first week of his business. The beach weather had been terrific, and he'd cleared close to a thousand dollars. Alex sure wanted to celebrate. And meet Beth? He'd dress up.

Rosie hesitated. She'd kept the idea of meeting the attractive Beth as a distant possibility in her mind. She was on a crash diet, and had hoped that she would meet Beth sometime 'later on', if at all. 'Henry. Umm, that's fine. But Bruce is down for a visit on the weekend, remember?'

'I forgot. Bring him along. It'll be great to see him.' He sensed Rosie's reluctantance. 'Everything all right? You're not worried about Beth, are you?'

'Of course not.'

That Friday evening Henry was getting ready for Rosie and Alex to pick him up. Louise phoned. Her message wished him a belated happy new year, and let him know that the manuscript was with a publisher. 'She says it'll be out within six months. Congratulations, Henry. Bye for now.'

He heard the bell and scampered down the stairs assimilating this news. The Kombi idled in front of the apartment, and he shuffled into the rear seat beside Rosie.

She glowed in a new dress. Her hair was different somehow. And she was wearing shiny red lipstick, and eye make-up.

'God Rosie, you're looking fabulous!' Henry effused. 'What did you do to your hair?'

'Coloured it and ran some mousse through it.' She smiled and held his hand.

Alex was gripping the wheel. 'You wouldn't know about the colour, Henry.'

'No. Looks lighter.' Although he couldn't quite tell in the dark.

'I'm now officially a sort of blonde,' she said.

Then Henry noticed Alex. 'What the ...?'

Alex was wearing a wig.

They parked the Kombi down from the Greek restaurant, and as they stepped onto the pavement Alex stood, arms folded, awaiting Henry's reaction. He was dressed in a dark grey suit. The paisley green tie was huge, and looked like a giant bib. And the wig? Henry immediately thought of an Apache in a western movie. The hair was straight, and very long, and black. And it hid Alex's ears. It made him look, well, handsome.

'Doesn't he look fantastic?' Rosie said.

As they trooped inside Alex caused some of the diners to perform a double take. The combination of the suit, far too large on his thin frame, and the hair ... he looked like Geronimo who was sponsored to dress as a white man, but secretly itched to get back to hunting buffalo.

They walked over to where Bruce sat waiting for them. He was dressed in his business suit, and looked the part of the distinguished bureaucrat. Henry had never seen Bruce dressed up, and gave him a close inspection. He had Rosie's expressive large eyes; his thinning dark hair was grey at the temples. 'Bruce, you've stepped out of a magazine. You're all incredible.'

Beth appeared, looking around the restaurant and making her way toward the table. Henry noticed Alex freeze.

Henry introduced Beth, alive to any undercurrents. Beth took care to shake Rosie by the hand, and Henry could see that it was going to be all right. She sat down with Bruce on one side and Henry on the other. She'd made the sort of positive impression Henry had expected. What Henry did not expect, but might have if he'd truly thought about it, was the impression she would make on Bruce.

Beth had the full mouth, sparkling blue eyes and vivacious nature that would animate a garden gnome. For a man deprived of a woman in his life, she was tantalising. Alex just sat there, not saying a word. Bruce perused the menu, unusually quiet. Rosie and Beth made small talk, easily and warmly.

It came Beth's turn to order, and Alex chimed in. He was Greek, after all. He steered Beth around the menu, starching his voice with a curious inflection that had Henry concentrating. It made him sound like a sophisticated rock star, just for a moment.

'I'd recommend the moussaka,' he opined, and everybody

looked at him quizzically. 'On the other hand, there's a dish that has its origins in Mykonos, or is it Spiros? Have you travelled, Beth?'

'No, not much. Bali. New Zealand.' She smiled, catching glimpses of Alex over her menu.

'Umm, you live around here?' Bruce asked.

She turned to Bruce. Henry could see it. Rosie spoke about it afterwards. Alex almost saw it. Their eyes locked, but not immediately. Beth looked at him, turned away, then turned back for confirmation. 'Just like when we met, Henry,' Rosie said later.

Henry was sad for Alex, who was captivated, but largely ignored. In fact, Henry realised, Alex had fallen head over heels. His soupy eyes turned down at the corners, and his face was pained. He nodded in agreement with every one of Beth's utterances, shook his head in vehement support of her statement about property prices, handed her dishes before she was ready for them, and pushed his chair back to fly around and pick up her serviette.

Eventually it became obvious, even to Alex. At every opportunity Beth turned to Bruce, and Bruce engaged Beth. Bruce's boyish enthusiasm was infectious, and he'd found a similar quality in Beth. They prattled on and covered enormous ground, agreeing on virtually everything. Beth loved the country. She had always wanted to learn to ride a horse. Would she like to visit the cabin? Would she what? How wonderful would it be for her daughter Sarah?

After the main course Alex pushed his chair back and said he needed to check on his Kombi. Henry said he would join him, and they walked along the pavement.

'Alex, are you all right?'

'God, Henry. What a woman. I'm in love. How's it possible?'

'You're just a bit undernourished,' Henry said, putting his arm around Alex's shoulders and giving him a squeeze.

'What, too thin?'

'No. In matters of the heart.' He turned him around to face him. 'Alex, don't you see how fantastic this is?'

'Hey?'

'You're feeling something for the first time in ages. You're ready for someone at last!'

'Jesus, Henry. I'm ready for *her*, not someone I haven't met yet.' He looked down and scuffed his foot on the pavement.

Henry and Rosie put their heads together after Alex dropped them off at Henry's apartment. Bruce had volunteered to escort Beth home, and she had agreed, leaving Alex in a mild depression at the wheel of his Kombi.

'Rosie, how would a woman look at Alex?' Henry asked, lounging on the sofa.

'Well, he's got some great qualities, and a woman who wasn't put off by his looks would see that.'

'Alex is Alex,' Henry said. 'You never met Olivia.'

'Tell me about her.'

'She was the closest woman to an Alex I have ever seen. About ten years ago she and Alex met somewhere; I think he was delivering bread to her father's deli. He'd see her every day. She was a sweet, straight-forward person who appreciated Alex's energy and humour. But Alex wasn't interested, although they went out for some time.'

'Hmm. We'll have to think of something. I've looked at the women I work with. It will take someone very unusual.'

'You're not unusual, and you're with me,' Henry said.

'I'm not unusual? You say the sweetest things, Henry. I'm more unusual than you!'

'No you're not.'

'Yes I am.'

- 28 -

Andy, winner of the preselection contest for the seat of Bowers, was preparing for the unloseable by-election. He emailed Henry asking him to assist in the preparation of his maiden parliamentary speech. 'This is where I take off, Henry. Hitch your star to mine, and let's soar. Make it controversial, like that Pauline Hanson's maiden speech.'

In his new guise of action man, because that's how Henry was beginning to see himself, he found the challenge attractive. Andy's confidence in him was a compliment. Did he not touch on many political issues in his newspaper articles? Why not put his knowledge to use?

He sat at his computer and stared at the screen, cogitating. There were some fundamental problems brewing in Australia that, if not addressed, would cause vast misery in the future. The national savings rate was abysmal. Australia owed foreigners an amount equivalent to half the annual national income. Each year thirty billion dollars were added to this enormous sum. The dollar had been ravaged for this reason. Having an unstable currency was like having a house built without foundations. For all the talk of economic miracles and technology booms, Australia was but a mosquito on the backside of the world's elephant. What agendas would Alex, Rosie and Bruce bring to a maiden speech?

The only agenda in Bruce's life now was Beth. Henry obtained one version of the new relationship from Beth the next time they met at an investment seminar. Rosie obtained another version from Bruce over the telephone. Rosie's was more interesting, but there was substantial overlap in the two versions.

As Rosie related it to Henry, Beth and eight-year-old Sarah went down to the cabin the Sunday after dinner at the restaurant. The cabin had an interesting effect on Beth, as Rosie imagined it would. Rosie had to listen between the lines of Bruce's interpretation of events. She was expert at divining the truth from years of listening to Bruce and taking the square root of most things he said. 'Henry, Beth walked around with her mouth open for the first few minutes. Fortunately Beth, being the adventurous woman that she seems to be, experienced the cabin through her daughter's eyes. She began to see that Bruce was different; umm, eccentric; no wacky, and relaxed. She's even had a go at the leaning tower of dunny, Henry. "We could straighten that up, Bruce." And she tidied up here and there, fixed a meal. No sweat. She's a fine woman. I just hope Bruce doesn't let her do all the work.'

Henry inhaled deeply. He now applied the same analysis to his own rather stubbornly resistant ways, and had a good think. Maybe he should become a wee bit more compromising in matters domestic himself? Keep the place tidy, if it was obviously an issue for Rosie? Let her buy him scratchy clothes if it made her happy?

January saw another month of technology hype accelerate the growth in company valuations on Wall Street. Investment chat rooms on the internet were filled with hopeful rampers, mustering support for companies in the hope that their views would influence others to buy and force the price up. Palamountain would most likely tap into this mania, and succeed.

At the next seminar Eric harangued the true believers. Had he not delivered on Rachael's company? Yes! Was he not the deliverer of the best Christmas since Santa Claus first hitched up his reindeers? Yes! Palamountain would do the same – and much, much more!

Beth's face wore the glazed look of a true believer. There was an unstoppable momentum, and Henry realised that if he now cast doubt he would be seen as a wet blanket. His own strategy to invest in order to save his parents' home had become paralysed in analysis. He had researched alternative investments, wishing to disassociate himself from the hype and focus on fundamentals. He was hoisted on the petard of his own morality. Because he did not invest, he had no broker connections. He was never offered shares in new company floats, and was now confronted with a grim reality. Palamountain offered the only available prospect of delivering a windfall gain within the timeframe of the auction for the cottage. He had two weeks to decide.

Being action man was not easy. He had no fear of losing the fifty thousand dollars he was proposing to invest, but there was precious little chance of him making the four hundred thousand necessary to pay off the bank. No way would Palamountain deliver a ten-fold increase in value. He approached his dilemma like a chess player, evaluating each plausible move, and the clock kept ticking.

- 29 -

On a glorious sunny Saturday at the end of January, Henry and Rosie strolled down to the beach to visit Alex in his pie cart. Wally the wrecker's stabilisers functioned adequately. The metal struts were welded to the side and could be unhinged to buttress the ground, making the pie cart resemble a spider. Children on the roof were throwing paper wrappers at passers-by. They heard one of Alex's policy declarations boom out through his megaphone: 'No littering on the roof!'

They stood in line to buy a pie and were finally acknowledged by Alex with a smile. 'Be right with you,' he said as he suddenly rushed away, shouting over his shoulder in a gallop, 'I need more pies.'

They watched as he ran to his Kombi and came back carrying a box. To Henry's surprise, Alex seemed to have become an employer. Henry and Rosie moved away to sit on a park bench to munch their pies. When the lunchtime rush was over Alex appeared and introduced his employee as Mia, a woman in her mid- or late-twenties with copper-coloured dreadlocks and a flashing stud in her nose. She was wearing a caftan-like dress.

'How did you get involved in the pie cart, Mia?' Rosie asked.

Mia spoke dreamily, and kept looking at Alex. 'I stood in line waiting for a pie and got belted on the head by some rubbish the kids were throwing. Alex bellowed something, just like a moment ago. There has to be a better way to run this amazing business, I thought, and suggested to Alex that he could do with another pair of hands.'

'Congratulations. Alex, you're going to be a multinational,' Henry said.

'I think I might diversify. I went to look at some other pie carts and they sell pie floaters, you know, with peas.'

'Pretty messy, isn't it?' Rosie said.

'Yeah. I also need to stock more drinks. That esky on the front seat isn't enough. I run out within half an hour of opening.'

'And ice-cream. I suggested that Alex get one of those little ice-cream carts, with dry ice,' Mia said.

'Is it busy all the time, Alex? I guess it's going to be while the school holidays are on,' Henry said.

'It's a bit of a worry. Nothing much happens when it's wet, of course. I definitely have a seasonal business.'

Henry noticed that Alex was not his usual self. He seemed distant, even downcast, and he wondered if it was a carry-over from his disappointment about Beth. 'Have you had another good week?'

'Henry, it's good, but I'll never have another week like the last. Still, Wally the Wrecker is over the moon,' Alex gathered his legs and sat in the lotus position, looking up at them. 'Wally comes down here at the end of most days wanting to know the sales. Brought his wife and kids the other day. Asked me if I wanted to employ his wife. I'd just taken on Mia, so I couldn't. Besides, his wife's a bit fat. Mia's a contortionist,' Alex said, looking at her.

'Do you work full time?' Rosie asked Mia.

'No, just weekends, and if Alex needs me.'

A woman arrived, wanting to buy a pie, and Mia rushed off.

'Alex, she's a find,' Rosie said.

'Yeah,' Alex said, deep in thought.

On their way back to Henry's apartment Rosie asked Henry what he thought of Mia.

'Seems perfect. Quiet.'

'Don't you believe it.'

'What do you mean?'

'She's clever. And don't you see it?' Rosie asked. 'Men!'

'See what?' Henry walked slowly next to her. It was always a bit of a waddle, walking with Rosie.

'She's an Alex!'

- 30 -

Everything has its price, and so it was that being Henry was not a costless exercise. His thoughtfulness and gentle manner prompted those around him to judge carefully how long it would take for Henry to emerge from wherever he went when in crisis. Those with a bit more energy, which was most people, couldn't sit around idle while Rome burned.

Rosie and Bruce had a summit meeting in Bruce's Abbotsford flat about Henry and his parents' cottage. Bruce had invited Rosie for dinner, and they stood in the kitchen as

Bruce peeled potatoes. Rosie described the changes in Henry – how thanks to his genius for investment, as she put it, he had already made a pile of money from a standing start. But even Rosie, a beginner when it came to the commercial world, realised it was going to be a tall order for him to stump up four-hundred thousand-odd dollars.

Bruce looked at his sister's downturned face. 'Rosie, you've not said a word about Henry's disease. How does it affect you?'

She reached for a bottle of red wine and stood ready to pour, biting her lower lip. 'I've decided to put my trust in God and keep my powder dry.'

'Just forget about it? Aren't you going to insist he has a test? You're desperate for a baby, aren't you?'

'I think it will soon sort itself out. Henry always seems to know what to do, in his own time. On one level I'm afraid. What if he has the disease? I don't want to know.'

'Yeah. Well, I've thought about the cottage quite a lot.' Bruce cut the potatoes into small pieces. 'You know I made a fortune thanks to Henry.'

'Yeah?'

'I was quite touched by his speech at the cabin. I reckon I'd trust him with eighty thousand dollars for the cottage.'

'Wow, Bruce, you're a darling,' she said and gave him a hug. 'I've saved ten thousand, for umm, contingencies, and Henry doesn't know. That's ninety. What about Alex?'

Rosie called Alex to involve him in the discussion, more out of courtesy than hope or expectation. She got a remarkable response.

'Henry could easily double what we raise, I'm confident of that,' Alex said.

'I only wanted to let you know, Alex. I know you don't have any money.'

'What do you mean, no money? Just wait. I have an idea. I have to be involved. We can't let Horace and Mary get turfed out. How long do we have?'

'The first open inspection is next week. The auction is in a month,' Rosie said.

'No, I mean to get money for Henry to invest.'

'He said that this new float would be very soon. I'll find out. And another thing, Alex. What about Hugo? Are you going back to see him? I'd like to come along.'

'Phew. I don't know. I've put it out of my mind for now. I can't think about what Henry said at the cabin.'

'Me too,' Rosie said quietly.

Henry slicked back his hair and dressed up to go and see a bank manager. It was a long shot, but he was getting desperate. He'd never met a bank manager, nor had he really had much to do with banks, although he had recently deposited his winnings. He'd rejected the idea of a credit card years ago. What was the point?

He'd made an appointment at the Coogee branch of the Commonwealth Bank, and now he sat expectantly outside the manager's office. He had armed himself with projections of his earnings, and also an estimate of the likely returns from investing in Palamountain. Conservatively he calculated that the shares would double on opening. Palamountain, like the technology boom generally, was mostly hot air – but it seemed that investors couldn't buy enough hot air.

The manager looked up busily as Henry entered. He introduced himself as Kieron Synnott, and Henry recognised an Irish name. Knowing what he knew about the Irish, this was a mixed blessing.

Synnott looked Henry up and down and glanced at some papers. 'Henry Sinclair. You've recently opened an account. Healthy deposit. What can I do for you?' he said, knocking his thumbs together. He was in his mid-forties, and displayed the nervous manner that had beset all bank managers in this era of downsizing.

Henry explained his predicament and watched Synnott's

expression change from one of benign duty to plausible interest. 'You want a loan to bail out your parents? A mortgage over their property in Malabar?'

'Y-yes.' Henry was under pressure.

'How will you service a loan of four-hundred-and-thirty thousand dollars?'

Henry explained that he was earning about two thousand a month, in a reasonable month, and had limited expenses. He was only paying rent of one hundred a week, but there was the prospect that his landlord might jack it up. A realistic rent would be more like three hundred a week.

'But Mr Sinclair, servicing of the loan would cost you,' he performed a calculation, 'thirty thousand a year, *two and a half thousand a month.*'

'Yes. But I will at least double my cash reserve within the next month. And then I will do it again. In three months I will pay back the loan.'

'What? Based on share investments?' A condescending smile spread over the manager's face.

'Yes.'

The manager was used to wild optimism on the part of his clients, but he'd not met anyone as brazen as Henry. He was starting to enjoy himself. He knew a thing or two about investing in shares. He owned Telstra shares. 'What's your system? Maybe we could all get rich?'

Henry gave him a synopsis of the Palamountain transaction.

'And you say it's all blue sky?'

'Unfortunately, yes. But it will succeed.'

The manager turned in his swivel chair and smiled out of the window then delivered Henry the banking manifesto. 'Banks have to protect shareholders. We need security, which you may have in a property in Malabar, but just as important is loan servicing. You have to pay interest, Mr Sinclair. Unfortunately, Mr Sinclair, I have no confidence in the share-market. Now, a small personal loan, or credit card . . .'

★

Rosie hinted to Henry that she might have some funds to contribute to the investment. She and Bruce had come up with something. When would he need the money?

Henry smiled appreciatively, but suggested that she keep it. 'It's all too risky, but thank you for thinking of my parents. I love you for the thought,' he said.

'When do you need it? Don't tell me what I can do with my money,' she said, like Rosie.

'Well, if you must. But it won't be enough, whatever it is, so why do it?'

Alex phoned Rosie. 'I have thirty thousand dollars.'

Rosie was stunned. 'Where did you get that sort of money, Alex?'

'Don't worry about it. I'll have it in three days.'

- 31 -

The night before the application for shares in Palamountain was to be finalised, Rosie phoned Henry and said she was coming over, with Alex, just for a short while.

They all sat in the living room. Henry was edgy, his mind focused on the next day. It would see him investing his fifty thousand, and that would be that. His family's fortunes would be riding on a muscle-headed womaniser called Eric, and a fly-by-night outfit called Palamountain Ltd. He offered tea, wine, Drano?

'Come on, Henry, why the long face? We'll do it,' Alex chimed in. He seemed jovial, and Henry figured he must be over his depression about Beth. Henry wondered about Mia, and whether Alex saw any future there.

Rosie and Alex had decided to milk the moment for what it was worth. 'How much have you got, Henry?'

'Fifty thousand.'

'How much will you make on that?' Alex asked.

'It will probably double.'

'And you need, how much?' Rosie asked.

'Four hundred plus, you know how much,' Henry said, sipping a glass of wine.

'So, Mr Guru, investment analyst extraordinaire, technology saviour of the world, you need another, maybe, one hundred and fifty thousand?' Alex grinned.

'Yeah, maybe. What're you on about, Alex?'

'We can't tease him any longer, can we Rosie?'

'Guess not.'

Alex opened an envelope, very slowly, looking at Henry all the while. He passed over a note. 'We, the undersigned, have an amount of one hundred and twenty thousand dollars to invest in Palamountain, in the following proportions: Bruce Chadwick, eighty thousand. Alex Conomos, thirty thousand. Rosie Chadwick, ten thousand.'

Henry read the note several times, screwing up his brow, taking his glasses off, putting them on. 'What's all this about?'

'That's the world wildlife fund for the preservation of a cottage in Malabar,' Alex said, his cow eyes sparkling.

'Where the heck did you get this sort of money? And Bruce, putting in eighty-thousand? You're stark raving nuts, all of you. The money will go. It will just go to the bloody bank. You'll lose it. How would I ever pay Bruce back? And you, Alex. Where the hell did you get the money? Rob someone?' Henry was fuming, and started pacing.

'Settle down, Henry. I sold the pie cart to Wally the Wrecker,' he said, satisfaction written all over his face.

Rosie stared at Alex. 'My God, Alex...'

It was a done deal. Henry's protestations went nowhere. He was stunned by everybody's generosity, and unable to convince them that their money may be lost. It would be better just to give Horace and Mary the money, he argued, rather than invest it. But it became clear that his friends had boundless confidence in his ability to double the investment. The sharemarket contagion had affected even them.

He was able to swing an allocation of Palamountain shares to each of the others. After all, the members of ITSSS Unbelievable had absolute priority. Henry was conscious also of the tax implications. If they made a profit, the money would be lost to the bank, but they'd be liable for the tax. He faced potential bankruptcy. The only hope was that Palamountain would produce the sort of windfall that Rachael's company had provided.

The next day Henry and Beth sat at the computer screen and watched Eric's helper gather share applications from around the room. Beth signed the form, grinned at Henry, crossed herself and enclosed her cheque for eighty thousand shares. 'Gulp, here goes, Henry.'

Henry was taking the biggest gamble of his life. He looked at the application forms signed by Bruce, Rosie and Alex and felt dreadful. All told, he, Bruce, Rosie and Alex were sitting on three-hundred-and-forty thousand shares at fifty cents a share, not enough to bail out the cottage even if Palamountain doubled on opening. If there was not enough, then the mission had failed, but at least everybody would make money and they'd be able to provide enough for Horace and Mary to live on for quite a while. Henry swallowed as he put the application together. The allotment would be finalised in two weeks. The shares would hit the market on Thursday, February twenty-fourth.

Eric was out in front, sipping coffee and staring into space. Eric only appeared at the regular tuition seminars for important events. He caught Henry's eye, then Henry noticed him concentrate on Beth.

He came toward them and stood leaning on the computer

terminal. 'How are you Sinkers? Popped in your application? By the way, excellent promo article. Well done. My money was well spent. And who's this? Your partner?'

'Umm, this is Beth.'

Eric fixed Beth with the Eric look, the one manufactured to weaken any woman's resistance. He held out his hand, and Beth smiled back.

Henry sensed that Beth was nervous.

'We're all counting on you, Eric, ummm, Mr Schwartz,' she said.

'Your confidence is not misplaced,' he rumbled. Then he paused, not taking his eyes from Beth. 'How would you like to come to my private celebration? Just close friends. On my yacht, Henry. We expect the shares to be oversubscribed, and it will be huge. Black tie.' He transferred his attention to Henry: 'Can you manage that?'

'Umm.'

'Good. Saturday week. Nine o'clock. I'll really look forward to seeing *you*, Beth.'

He turned and walked among the rows of computer terminals, shaking hands here and there, pausing to suck up the adulation.

'Wow, Henry. What a surprise. We'll have to go,' Beth said, watching Eric.

Henry looked at her. 'I don't know, Beth.'

Beth turned to him. 'Hey? Come on, Henry, it'll be fun. I'll bring Bruce. You bring Rosie.'

'He only invited us. He was interested in *you*, Beth.'

'Was he?'

- 32 -

Alex had dreamt up another pie-cart idea, this time in Maroubra. But, as he mentioned to Henry, he doubted whether Maroubra was the beach of choice because it wasn't as popular as Coogee. Clovelly already had a cafeteria near the water. Bronte's shops were too close to the beach. Tamarama had a shop. Bondi? He said that he was seeing Mia on occasion; she was quite the businesswoman.

Andy phoned. Henry was aware that the by-election had been a humdrum, predictable affair, just as Andy had foreshadowed. Bowers was a blue-ribbon Liberal seat after all. The voters trooped out to vote, almost comatose, and the media took hardly any notice. Had Henry progressed with Andy's maiden speech? Could he look at the speeches of really successful politicians, like Bob Hawke and summarise the essential points? What was it about the speech, if anything, that set it apart and pointed to the future success of the politician? 'And Henry, I have to offer you a fee. What about six thousand as a retainer?'

Eric's invitation had a curious effect. Beth insisted that the invitation extended to her partner, and Bruce accepted, keen to experience 'the group' at close hand. Naturally Rosie was the same, and overruled Henry's objections. When the matter was brought to Alex's attention it almost caused an upheaval. How could they go and not take Alex? Wasn't he a foundation shareholder in Palamountain? Of course this Eric guy would want him there!

Henry was cornered. How could he deprive his friends when they had committed themselves so selflessly to Palamountain? They did have a right – well, sort of – to see the man behind their investment. He agonised, and phoned Rachael.

He explained his dilemma, saying he wasn't at all sure if Eric's invitation would extend to Rosie and Bruce—he couldn't bring himself to mention Alex. Rachael was adamant. 'If Eric invited you, then by all means, come, all of you. There'll be enough people there to be lost in the crowd. And Henry, it'll be wonderful to meet your girl, and to see you dressed in a dinner suit. In fact, I'm getting quite excited at the thought.'

Henry was experiencing more change than an Italian parliament. The prospect of wearing a dinner suit appealed to him as much as an invitation to levitate on prime-time television. Rosie was astoundingly excited by the idea. Her crash diet was living up to its name. She looked forward to seeing more of Beth, with whom she had conducted lengthy phone calls to dissect Bruce's character. It wasn't necessary for Beth to ask pointed questions, because Rosie anticipated her need. If Bruce only knew—he was shedding mystery like a nude model behind the drapes at art school.

All in all Eric's invitation appealed to the impossible-to-divine element that made women hunger for gossip about the sex lives of film stars. Henry only had to visit the dentist and flip through women's magazines to gather a truckload of material for his partner-choice hypothesis. He was helpless, and accepted his lot with grim determination.

It was not enough that the women were ganging up and getting excited about a night of incomparable tedium. Alex, surprising Henry, also had a secret longing to experience the lifestyle of the rich and famous. From the moment Henry mentioned the invitation, Alex had been resolute. He would take Henry shopping for a dinner suit. This was secret men's business.

A dinner-suit rental place, as you might expect, is vastly different from a costume rental place. An air of stuffy formality was not conducive to the arrival of two men who were as likely to be seen in dinner suits as penguins were to be found in the Simpson Desert. A very short, elderly man, who asked if they were in the right place, looked over his bifocals and examined his clients with intense curiosity. Alex took charge and swept his arm around the rows of suits and declared that he and Henry were indeed in the proper place.

The man walked over and looked down at Alex's scuffed sandals, and the long shorts out of which protruded two incredibly skinny legs, and the shoulderless frame that barely held up a grubby T-shirt with an equally disgusting meat pie on it. The tiny man had a way of arching his head back to see through the seeing part of his bifocals, which made it look to Henry that he was examining the bark of a rare tree. He stopped short of a close examination of Alex's head, presumably concluding that here was someone who would look awful even in a dinner suit. The man's sense of self and pride in his job, it was clear, had been buoyed by a lifetime of transforming the most unbearably unattractive clients. As he transferred his attention to Henry, who was dressed in a similar slovenly way, he realised he was confronted by the challenge of his life.

'Humph. You are aware that it would have been better to wear smart shoes to try on a dinner suit, and maybe a shirt and, dare I say it, a tie?' he said in a voice crisp with attention to detail.

Alex looked down at his attire. 'Oh, yeah. Doesn't matter. It's the fit that's important.' He grinned, and walked over to a suit.

'I'll find your size,' the man flustered, not wanting his suits fondled by Alex.

He took out a tape measure and asked Alex to stand next to a step-ladder and hold still. He measured Alex all over, getting up on the step and climbing down to write some numbers, clucking pessimistically as he went. Alex, wearing his look of bored resignation, kept rolling his eyes at Henry. Finally the little man turned from the desk where he was stooped over his calculations, and shook his head. 'Your measurements are all wrong,' he said with a gleam in his eye.

'Hey?' Alex said.

'We don't have a suit that will fit. You're too long in the arm, and too narrow in the shoulders, and your waist is, well,' he glanced down at his numbers, 'your waist is too small for your size.'

'Doesn't matter. Let me try on the closest thing.' Alex walked over to the rack once again.

The man saw that he had to comply and pulled out a suit. 'If this doesn't fit, that's it, I'm afraid.'

Alex went to try it on while the man applied himself to Henry who, he realised, was a similar, if not insurmountable, problem.

Another man was just making his entrance into the shop when Alex turned to look at himself in the mirror. He caused everybody to inhale with impossibility. The suit fit the shoulders because it was vastly short in the leg, and arms. Even Henry had to admit that the combination of sandals, T-shirt and Alex's long hair had made an impact that would be felt all the way down in the engine room of Eric's yacht. Alex looked like a homeless drifter wearing his infant brother's suit.

They all planned to meet on the night of the party at Henry's for a pre-party drink. In keeping with the pace of change, Henry shaved off his goatee. He examined himself in the bathroom mirror and wondered if anybody would notice. It made his face seem shorter, or rounder, or something.

Of course people noticed. The beard had been a Henry trademark. It had given him a Cossack-like appearance that only Rosie, or the czarina of Russia could have loved.

On entering Henry's apartment, Rosie shrieked, held her hand to her mouth and stared at her man. Bruce and Beth likewise forgot the drama of their own entrances, dressed up as they were, and shared in Rosie's bewilderment.

'Henry! You've shaved your beard,' Rosie gasped.

Henry was taken aback. He'd not anticipated such a reaction

and wondered if he'd done the right thing. Maybe she only loved him for his goatee?

'You look so much better, Henry,' Beth volunteered. 'Handsome.'

'Yes, Henry. It makes your face even cuter,' Rosie said.

Everybody had a chance to examine everybody else. Bruce looked as magnificent as Henry looked doubtful, and the girls made up for Henry's shortcomings. Henry had wondered how Rosie would find a formal dress to fit. He had been oblivious to her gradual weight loss. As he examined Rosie they were all secretly nervous about Alex, who was still to arrive. The women turned their attention on Henry.

As Henry and Alex had left the rental shop they had discussed shirts and shoes — for the first time in their long friendship. Henry didn't have shoes that went with a dinner suit, and he certainly didn't have a bow tie, or crisp white shirt. They'd decided not to hire these. The costs were starting to mount and, anyway, as Alex suggested, they could improvise. Why spend all that money on clothes they would only wear once? A bow tie was just a piece of black rag. But the shoes? They had trudged to the bus stop pondering this obstacle.

Beth looked like an Emmy-award winner. Everyone said so. Her dress was cut low at the front giving her the sort of cleavage that pirate women sport in old movies. Her shimmering hair was piled on top of her head, cascading down in wisps in a French way. Rosie, now that she was a blonde, looked amazing in her sequined dress. As Henry looked at her more closely he got the impression of a very large hand puppet. She'd done something to her hair. It was puffed up and made her face seem smaller.

Everyone stood stock-still as they heard the bell. Bruce grimaced for all of them, and Henry opened the door. The vision splendid sauntered through the door in a grand entrance. Alex had tied his hair in a pony tail, causing his ears to advertise themselves in a truly uncluttered way. His trousers were at half-mast, and he wore a very ruffled cream shirt, with a black silk scarf for a tie. And the shoes?

He pirouetted. 'Trallala,' he sang, allowing everyone a full-circle view.

'Alex!' gasped Rosie.

'What sort of shoes are they?' Bruce asked.

'I applied black boot polish to my sandshoes,' he said proudly.

'And the shirt?'

'I borrowed one of my mum's blouses.'

'And the tie?'

'Mum's silk scarf.'

They piled into Bruce's government car, a modern Holden, and set off in nervy high spirits. Bruce made everyone feel more at ease because he looked the part, and because he was used to high-level occasions. Henry described the yacht and Alex frothed in anticipation. Henry noticed that Alex stared at Beth at every opportunity, and was even boisterous. Maybe he was competing with Bruce for Beth's attention?

They arrived at ten o'clock. A warm breeze wafted around the marina, and they could hear a raucous babble of conversation in the distance. A young man in a white jacket greeted them at the top of the stairs and checked names against a list. Henry gave his name, and the man let them through, doubtfully. They had decided Henry should go first, followed by Bruce, then Beth. Alex should try to hide himself in Rosie's dress. Even so, the security man's sense of duty was under threat as Alex passed him meekly waving his fingers.

The open-air upper deck was festooned with coloured lights. A string quartet played in one corner, and fifty or so people were gabbing in full talkfest mode. Young women in fish-net stockings and frilly short dresses ran around pouring drinks.

Henry had an ominous feeling as he witnessed the bemused looks that Alex's appearance was beginning to generate. Starting at the immediate periphery of the gathering, elbows were nudging and conversations ground to a halt. He looked around for members of the 'group', wishing for the moment he could hide his friend. Alex, he knew, was feeling his way. What would the outcome be? He shuddered.

This moment, this night, was somehow a culmination of all the events that had had their birth at Eric's dinner party. He was melding his world with that of 'the group'. Would he stutter?

Alex reached for a glass of champagne that swept past on a tray. He managed it with a display of dexterity that was probably a fluke, Henry knew. But it gave him an air of competence, as he sipped, feet astride, nonchalantly gazing at people. Henry hoped that a shift of understanding was possible in the *haute couture* crowd, but the curious stares were as yet indecipherable.

Rosie and Beth were alive to the nuances, and Bruce fetched drinks to give everybody's hands something to do.

Louise filtered through the crowd, and gushed an airy hello. 'Henry, so nice you could make it,' she said, drink in hand. Louise was dressed in a tight lemon-coloured cocktail dress. Her face cracked with a smile as she sought an introduction. Henry introduced Rosie, making a point of putting his hand on Rosie's back in a sign of possession. Louise blinked and shook her hand. 'So, you're Henry's other half?'

'More like Henry's seven-eighths,' Rosie chuckled. Louise's eyebrow arched to the banter.

Henry introduced Bruce and Beth, then turned to Alex. 'And this is my close friend, Alex.'

It was apparent to Henry that Alex had decided that he was going to have fun. He was not in the least intimidated by the beautiful people or the billion-dollar boat, and met Louise with a bored, detached expression, holding out his hand with the resignation of a rock star. He saw a woman enmeshed in bullshit.

Henry saw that Louise had no idea what to make of his

jug-eared friend. Alex could contort his face to suit the circumstance, and thought that a Walter Matthau look of pained disinterest was appropriate for Louise. Of course, he had no idea who Louise was, introductions not being one of Henry's strong suits.

Louise, an expert in competitive facial expressions, responded in kind. Rosie said afterwards that it looked like two lepers rejoicing in the loss of a limb.

It was clear that Henry wasn't about to grace Louise with a curriculum vitae, and she constructed her own position in the scheme of things, which was an appropriate tactic considering Alex's insulting demeanour. 'We're all waiting for Henry to become a best-seller. I expect to have his book ready for launch very soon.' She looked each of them in the eye as if she had just announced a cure for cancer.

'That'll be nice,' Rosie said, thinking that Louise was not a person she would invite for dinner.

'Well, I hope you all enjoy the evening, even you, umm, what was your name again?'

'Me?' Alex half opened his eyes.

'I am looking at you.' Louise rankled.

'Sorry, what did you say?'

Louise was getting angry. 'Hard of hearing as well as incomparably uninteresting,' she grunted.

'Incomparably uninteresting? Oh, all right. I give in. You're more uninteresting than me,' Alex grinned.

'Is that a fact?' Louise hated coming off second best in front of an audience. 'Did your kid brother mind lending you his suit?'

'You're interested in younger men?' Alex was having fun.

'*You* look like you should be carbon dated. You're an insufferable boor,' she hissed through clenched teeth then sauntered off.

'Phew,' Henry muttered, and gulped his champagne.

Before anybody could offer a comment, Eric appeared, like

an ocean liner in a small harbour. He was on something, Rosie said later. 'Sinkers. Brought some of your fans?'

'Umm, th-thanks for the invitation, Eric,' Henry replied and made ready to introduce his friends.

Eric took over. 'I'm the captain of this good ship, Eric's my name.' He crushed Bruce's hand, and stood staring at Beth. 'I'm *very* glad to see you here, Beth,' he said, and Henry could sense Bruce bristle. Then Eric turned to Alex, ignoring Rosie completely. 'What have we here, a circus act?'

'Yep.' Alex exhibited his tombstone teeth. 'I'm known to disappear in a puff of smoke.'

Eric turned to the adjoining crowd. 'Hey, Dennis, Andrea, come here and meet Bozo the clown.'

Dennis and Andrea shuttled across eagerly.

'This here is my entertainment for the evening,' Eric said, putting his hand on Alex's shoulder and proffering him like an entree.

'Do you juggle, or eat swords?' Dennis asked with a smirk.

'No,' Alex said dreamily, and fell into his nonchalant pose, calmly surveying his audience.

'What do you do for a living?' Dennis asked.

'I'm in the pie-cart business.'

'Pie carts? Good idea.' Dennis knew not how to offer a rejoinder to this confident declaration and beckoned some others as reinforcements. New people started to crowd out Henry and his friends as Alex became the centre of attention.

Then Rachael appeared. Henry looked at her red dress, which was in two halves held together by cris-crossed string at the sides that made it obvious she wore no underwear. Henry thought that it must have been glued on. Not one to take her time in a queue, she pushed forward with an energetic hello for Henry, cutting through the throng gathering around Alex. 'Henry! You've shaved that disgusting goatee. This must be your lady,' she said, looking at Beth.

'Umm, no. Rosie's over there,' Henry said.

Rachael turned to Rosie and faltered. Rosie smiled warmly, and Rachael responded in kind. 'Very pleased to meet you. Henry has become my favourite person – after Eric.' She locked her arm in Henry's and looked pointedly at Beth.

After this momentary interruption the original Alex audience turned back on him. Henry and the others became a splinter group, with Rachael making small talk, gushing about the float, and Eric's amazing success, and how wonderful everything was.

In the meantime the crowd had adopted Alex, and he became an Indian mystic appeasing his anxious followers. Nobody would accept that pie carts were his vocation. Several women grilled him for the truth. Had they not seen him at the Sydney Entertainment Centre? 'Yes,' one woman shrieked, 'you're a member of the Grateful Dead.'

The crowd swooned. They were all secret Elton John and Barbra Streisand fans who wanted to be 'gratefully dead', but didn't actually have any idea who they were. Alex found himself accorded status that rather appealed to him.

'What's it like being a rock star?' one attractive believer asked. 'Do you have groupies?'

'Orgies?' asked another breathlessly.

Alex smiled knowingly, sipped on his drink, and winked at the woman.

'God,' she said with a nudge in her partner's midriff, hinting that it was high time they orgied a bit themselves.

And so it went. The evening gravitated around Alex, who began to offer serious commentary on the ills of the world. Alex, after all, was a philosopher, of sorts – he could be convincing to a crowd weaned on the Australian media.

The drinking accelerated, and the hi-jinx began in earnest, as Henry feared it would. He could see Eric, who had long left the crowd gathered around Alex, moving among the women like a shark. Rachael followed him like a fisherman, at a distance. Thankfully Eric did not pursue Beth – Henry put it down to Bruce's gate-keeping.

Henry and the others found a corner, marvelling at Alex, enjoying him enjoying himself, and taking in the evening. Andy, who had come late, held a passing conversation with Henry. He explained that he was now in serious political mode and engaged Henry accordingly, all the while casting his eye around. Soon Andy began to party like a returned submariner.

Then, when Henry thought it was about time to leave, the evening turned nasty. Many drunken revellers had already left. The string quartet had imposed sobriety on the night, but now the quartet finished its stint and loud rock music bellowed once again over the sound system.

Henry saw an attractive young woman coming up the gangplank. She was dressed in jeans and a halter-top, and seemed to be lost. She stood uncertainly for some moments, looking for someone. Henry had seen her before, he was sure of it. On Eric's yacht, serving food.

Then Henry observed her making a bee-line for Eric. The great man was leaning against the body of a woman pressed against the railing. She seemed to be enjoying his attention, drink held high in one hand, laughing in Eric's face. The young woman in jeans swept past and Henry caught sight of her wooden eyes and determined mouth. He was about to nudge Rosie, but she was absorbed in conversation with Bruce and Beth. The young woman tugged Eric on the sleeve. Eric, startled, grabbed her hand and led her away.

Henry didn't know what to make of the scene as he watched Eric drag the woman to the door leading downstairs. He turned back to the others and put it out of his mind – probably just another example of Eric wishing to father a good percentage of the next generation.

Moments later Henry excused himself and went down the stairs to the toilet. Just as he passed a cabin door it flung open and Eric stumbled out. He was pushing his shirt back into his trousers and attempting to pull on his jacket as he swayed from side to side. He saw Henry and blurted a command: 'Giss a hand, Henry.'

Henry obliged. Through the cabin door he saw the same, now near-naked, young woman lying on the edge of a bed. In that instant Rachael came bouncing from side to side along the corridor, drink in hand, hair dishevelled. She targeted Eric like a missile. 'Where have you been, darling? Been looking everywhere.'

Henry swallowed as Rachael was about to come within view of the prostrate woman. Eric's tie was adrift and his coat only partially done up. Henry hurriedly closed the door.

Rachael, suspicious, looked at Henry's wide eyes. 'What are you hiding, you naughty, naughty boy?'

Rachael had her hand on the cabin door before Henry could throw himself against it, or intercept her. No sooner had she pushed the door open than she wound her arm back and let fly with a slap to Eric's face that sent him reeling. Furious, she took off her shoe and belted Eric around the head. Yielding to the blows, he slumped to the floor.

Henry stood aghast as Rachael flew into the cabin and began shrieking at the woman. There was no response.

Rachael lifted the woman's head by the hair. Becoming concerned, she examined the woman more carefully. She turned to Henry. 'I think she's dead!'

Henry rushed inside and felt the woman's pulse, then checked her breathing. 'G-God, Rachael!'

Rachael shook her head in disbelief. Eric was slouched on the floor looking at the blood on his hand, oblivious to the drama in the cabin. He gathered himself and stood up, one arm propped against the wall, and poked his head around the corner. 'Shorry, Rashel. I do, I – love you, you know I do,' he slurred.

Henry and Rachael looked at one another, then back at the woman. Rachael covered her with a blanket. 'Henry, this woman was serving food at our business meeting, do you remember her?'

'Umm, yes.'

'Drug overdose,' Rachael said, more to herself.

'R-really?'

Eric, recovering his senses, staggered into the room. He swayed, but managed to lift the blanket. 'Shit!' He sat down heavily on the bed and put his head in his hands.

'Henry. You'd better leave,' Rachael said, squeezing him on the arm. 'I'll take care of this. Don't get involved. I'll phone you.'

'I – I can't just leave,' Henry said.

'What can you do? I'll fix it. Go now, please. Don't mention this to anyone. Please don't contact the police.' She looked steadfastly into Henry's eyes. 'The float.'

'The float? God, R-Rachael, you have to contact the police,' Henry blurted.

'Leave it to me, *please*,' she insisted.

Henry thought furiously. His instinct was to get the hell out of there. He felt sick. 'Rachael, you *must* call the police.'

'Just *go*!'

Henry stepped sideways past Eric, who stared at him through bloodshot eyes.

- 33 -

Alex had tired of being gratefully dead. So had his audience. He had gone back to telling pie-cart tales, and was holding the last couple spellbound at the prospect of investing in a global pie-cart enterprise.

Henry rushed onto the deck and approached Rosie, Bruce and Beth. 'We have to go. Now! Don't ask. Where's Alex?'

'What's wrong Henry?' Rosie asked.

Henry dashed over to Alex and grabbed him by the arm. 'We have to go. *Now*.'

Alex, smiling a goodbye to the couple, allowed himself to be led away by Henry. 'What's the matter with you? You drunk?'

'Come *on*. I'll explain later. Accident.'

They stood beside the car and waited for Henry to gather himself. Wringing his hands, eyes wide with shock, he told them what he'd seen.

'Bloody hell!' Alex said.

'Jesus!'

There was silence. The late-night traffic flowed past as they stood on the pavement. Beth held Bruce's hand, Rosie had her arm around Henry. Alex stood, horrified.

'We have to go to the police,' Henry said, white as a sheet.

'Of course we do,' Rosie said.

'What about what Rachael said?' Beth asked.

'What about it? Henry was a witness. He has to go to the police,' Rosie said forcefully.

'Of course he does,' Alex said.

'Let's go. There's a station in Kings Cross.' Bruce was firm.

They trooped into the late Saturday night jungle of the Kings Cross police station. An assortment of petty criminals, mugging victims and prostitutes sat around watching the entrance of a very unusual group of formally dressed party-goers.

The duty sergeant was listening to shrieking excuses for something or other by a scantily clad woman in high platform shoes. Henry et al formed a ruck around her and let it be known that, whatever trivial offence she had committed, it should wait. Their need was surely more pressing. Henry began to say this, but his explanation evoked merely a bored, irritated response from the sergeant. 'Just wait in line, will you,' he said.

Alex stepped forward. 'My good man, we are witness to a death. Maybe murder,' he said.

The sergeant blinked, adjusted his glasses and stared at Alex. He had seen his share of weird characters. He was an expert in weird. But the medium is the message, and the sergeant failed to take in the gravity of Alex's remonstration. 'Say again?'

'Look, just piss off, will ya. I was here first. Somebody pinched my handbag!' the woman with the platform shoes said angrily, shaking with the rings and safety pins that were holding her face together.

'Handbag? Jesus, lady, we're talking about murder!' Alex shouted.

'Murder?' Rosie and Bruce hushed in unison.

The sergeant's job was to mediate between the hordes of offended and oppressed that flowed through his station like a river. It was tiring to read between the lines of hysterical people. With a look of profound disinterest he again asked Henry and the others just to wait a second. He had to finish his report.

Thus mollified, they listened as the woman related the moment of bag snatching and a description of her assailant. 'He was slimy. Skinny, with jeans.'

'How much was in the bag?'

The woman was challenged. 'Don't know, exactly. Mascara, tampons. Hmm.'

'No. How much money?'

'Oh. Hmm,' she thought a moment. 'A real lot. All my wages for weeks.'

'Jesus. Is this Australian justice? She's lost her tampons, and we have a celebrity murder!' Alex took ownership of the high ground.

The sergeant looked up. 'Celebrity?'

'Yes,' Alex said smugly.

The woman, also, was suddenly alert. 'Yeah? Who?' she asked.

Another policeman appeared from a side room and whispered in the sergeant's ear. 'Colin, this guy here' – the sergeant pointed at Alex with a pen – 'says there's been a celebrity murder.'

'Yeah? Who's dead?' the young constable wanted to know.

'Umm . . .' Alex turned to Henry.

'I-it's probably not a murder,' Henry said.

169

'Now it's not a murder, Jesus Mary,' the sergeant sighed.

'If it's not a murder, shove aside,' said the woman.

'It's a drug overdose,' Henry said seriously.

'Is that all?' the sergeant asked wearily.

'But a woman's *dead*!' Alex cajoled.

'Who – or what – are you pretending to be?' the constable demanded, staring at Alex.

Bruce pushed through the melee. 'Sergeant, Mr Sinclair here has witnessed a serious situation. We wish to report it, and be on our way.'

'Okay, okay. I tell you what. Lady, take your tampon problem to the constable, here.' The sergeant nodded to the constable.

'My *tampon* problem? Sexist pig!' shrieked the platform woman.

The sergeant looked at his watch and sighed. He gathered himself and glanced at Bruce who, he was relieved to see, seemed to represent a saner segment of the population. Calmly, Bruce fed the policeman the sordid details.

The laborious process was interrupted by Alex, who kept making sure that there was no room for misunderstanding by injecting character references for Henry.

A female constable approached from another room. She pressed the sergeant out of earshot and it became apparent that she was talking about the incident on the boat. The sergeant came back. 'Which one of you is Henry Sinclair?'

'I am,' Henry said.

'I'll ask you all to remain for a while. I'll need details. Your names and addresses.'

'What's the matter, officer?' Alex interjected.

'Don't worry about it, somebody will arrive in a few minutes and explain,' he said.

They sat, tired and puzzled, in the company of bag-snatch victims and assorted felons. Alex, indignant, muttered about habeas corpus and the Geneva code. Beth showed the strain and clutched Bruce's hand, while Henry and Rosie were perched on their seats like canaries in a coal mine. Round and round went the discussion. Henry kept repeating that Rachael had insisted that he not contact the police. Why? And then he remembered that she had mentioned the float of Palamountain.

'Jesus, Henry, now I begin to see the light,' Bruce said.

'Of course! The scandal. She's trying to protect Eric,' Rosie said.

'Oh God. Yes.' Henry put his head in his hands. 'Play with fire, and you get burnt.'

'What?' Alex was confused.

A largish man in his mid-forties appeared and went straight to the duty sergeant, who pointed.

The big man came over and introduced himself as Detective-sergeant Michael Simpson. 'You're Mr Sinclair? You'll have to come with me. The rest of you are free to go, but be available for interview tomorrow. Your names and addresses will be taken by the duty sergeant.'

'If you want Henry, you'll want me.' Alex stood up.

The detective looked Alex up and down and frowned. Rosie pulled at Alex's hand to get him to sit.

'You heard me,' the burly detective growled. 'What's your name?'

'I'm allowed a phone call to my lawyer,' Alex said, chastened by Rosie's hand-pulling.

'Watch a bit of TV, do you?' the detective snarled.

'Thanks, Mr, umm, sergeant-detective. We'll go now,' Beth said, and pulled Bruce by the hand.

Michael Simpson hated the midnight watch. He instructed Constable Colin to do a computer search on Henry Sinclair, and said that he had to complete an interview at Rushcutters Bay. He would be back in an hour or so.

★

Simpson took off his battered coat, undid his tie, and sat facing Henry across a metal table in a tiny room. Constable Colin sat nearby. The computer search on Henry had revealed nothing. Simpson flipped through a notebook, then switched on a tape-recorder on the table. He stared at Henry, seeing a wide-eyed, pale, yet composed man. He tiredly recited the legal introduction to an interview. 'You're charged with possession of narcotics which have been found in your apartment. You have the right to remain silent. Anything you say can be used in a court of law as evidence. It's alleged that tonight you were on the motor cruiser owned by a Mr Eric Schwartz.'

'Possession? Of narcotics? In my apartment? Ummm, yes.'

'You were invited to a party.'

'Y-yes.'

'You were present when a woman by the name of' – he glanced at his notes – 'Yvonne Bierbaum died from a suspected drug overdose.'

'A-actually I was on my way to the toilet and I s-saw Eric Schwartz s-stumble out of a cabin. I looked inside and th-there was a woman . . . I don't know her.'

'How long were you downstairs?'

'I left my friends for f-five, maybe ten minutes, I think.'

'That lot who just left?'

'Yes.'

'Colin, run a search on all of them.'

A detailed interrogation ensued, during which Detective Simpson established the background to Henry's invitation. It was three in the morning by the time he finished. Henry was functioning on adrenalin.

The others were in shock. They had left the police station wondering what to do, and now stood on the pavement debriefing each other about the crazy events of the evening. Henry had asked Rosie whether she had the key to his apartment with her and asked that she wait there for him.

Rachael had wanted the incident kept quiet. So who had contacted the police? Bruce had a friend who was a lawyer, although she practised mainly in family law. Alex wasn't just going to leave Henry at the mercy of the forces of oppression, and suggested he go back to the police station. Rosie agreed. Bruce counselled against the idea. What could they do?

They concluded that, as the duty sergeant had told them, it was probably just a 'routine' part of the investigation – that the police were just holding Henry for questioning as the principal witness. They finally decided to call it a night. Rosie and Alex would sleep in Henry's apartment, and wait.

- 34 -

Rachael had watched Henry step sideways and retreat down the corridor.

Eric sat on the bed holding his head in his hands. She grabbed a glass and fetched some water. 'Drink this.'

Eric looked at the corpse as he drank. He mumbled that he needed to clear his head, went to the bathroom, and came back wiping his mouth on his sleeve. His face was ashen, his eyes rheumy from booze, yet he summoned his instincts. 'Rachael, we have a crisis. Here's what we have to do.'

He sat back down and fixed her with a desperate stare. 'This could ruin us. If the media get hold of this, we're history, the float's wrecked. Do you realise that?'

Rachael examined her man and saw him stripped of power. She was struggling with conflicting emotions. The shock of the beautiful young woman's death had dissipated the fury she'd felt at Eric's betrayal. Now she saw the woman as just another of the attractive ornaments he had to keep his business associates happy. She was seeing Eric, and her own life, in a new light.

Eric, as ever, was shrewd and convincing, despite his condition. He ticked off the facts. They had to weigh up all the hard work. There were Rachael's children to think about. Bad publicity would tarnish Rachael and her business. Eric was the driving force behind the Palamountain float and any scandal would sink it like a brick. They'd both made enemies, had they not? They had to move quickly. Henry was expendable.

'Henry?' Rachael reeled at the suggestion.

'Has to be him. He was pushing the drugs. Nobody knows anything about him. He's weird enough, with weird friends. Did you see that crazy?'

'Eric, what are you saying?'

'I'll fix it. Just relax. You don't want to be sucked back into the gutter?'

'I . . .' she looked down at the woman.

'No time to waste. I need your guarantee. Are we are united?'

'I . . .'

He reached out and grabbed her by the shoulders. 'Rachael. You've always impressed me as a clear thinker. I have to get Dennis onto this.'

'Dennis?'

'He's a fixer. He owes me. He'll do what I ask.'

'I can't stand him,' she said.

'Here's the plan. Do you know where Henry lives?'

'What? Why?'

'Just answer the question!'

Rachael crumbled under the Eric bulldozer. 'I have his phone number. Wait, he did tell me. He lives in Coogee. An apartment, flat. By himself.'

Eric reflected on this. 'Oh yeah. I remember taking down his address when he applied for shares. Can't be too many Sinclairs in Coogee . . . I heard *you* telling him not to go to the police. What was *your* game, dear accomplice?'

Rachael's head screamed. 'Christ, Eric, you can't be serious?

Why not just tell the truth? She overdosed. She had her own drugs ... wait a minute. Eric, did *you* supply the drugs?'

Eric gave no reaction.

'Oh, God! You *bastard*!'

'No time for any of this. Do you think Henry went to the police?'

'He's totally straight. I expect, yes, probably.'

He grabbed Rachael by the shoulders. 'We have time. Go get Dennis. Tell him to get rid of any guests, then to come straight down here. Hurry. I'm onto the police. The closest station is Kings Cross, isn't it? Henry probably went there. We suspect Henry gave her the drugs. We both found him here with her, didn't we? We just have to stall any attention, divert it to Henry, until Thursday. There's a fortune riding on this!'

Alex had to just about drag Rosie up the stairs to Henry's apartment. She was exhausted, and paused on the landing. 'I've had it, Alex.'

'Come on, we're here now,' he said, and walked to the door. 'Shit!'

He was about to put the key into the lock when the door swung open.

He examined the lock. 'Somebody's forced it. It's all splintered.'

They rushed inside, turned on the lights, and looked around. Everything was out of place, as usual.

'What the hell is going on?'

Rosie slumped onto the sofa. 'I don't believe this. A break-in? Henry's jinxed.'

'Should we phone the police?' Alex asked. 'Tell you what. I need a strong cup of coffee. Need to think. You too?'

Alex came back with the coffee. 'I think we should tell the police.'

Rosie pondered. 'Why now? In the morning. I'm too knackered. Henry'll be back soon.'

'Maybe the neighbours heard something. The door must have made a noise,' Alex said, and sat down next to Rosie. 'Bit of a coincidence.'

'You don't think it has anything to do with Henry being interrogated, do you?'

They sat talking quietly for half an hour. At the sound of footsteps they assumed Henry was back but two brawny plain-clothed police in their mid thirties appeared at the door, accompanied by a man holding a camera. One of the men flashed police identification, asked Alex and Rosie to identify themselves, and produced a search warrant.

The policemen stood over Alex and began a flurry of questions. How long had they been there? Where were the others, Bruce and Beth?

'The door had been forced open,' Alex said, mouth dry.

Detective constable Cunningham went to the door and called his partner. They came back. 'You're saying the door was like that when you got here?'

'Yes, officer,' Rosie said in exhaustion.

The policemen looked at one another. 'We have to search the apartment. Sorry.'

There began a horrendous destruction. The detectives emptied cupboards, rifled through bins and stripped the bed. Alex and Rosie sat aghast.

Suddenly one of the policemen called out from the bathroom. 'Here it is, Martin.'

He emerged with a small plastic bag in his hand, tore the bag open, wet his finger, and tasted the white powder.

'I'm afraid you'll have to come down to the station,' the detective said.

'You're joking. What's in the bag? What's going on? This is disgusting. You can't just come in here and destroy the place. We have rights . . .' Alex waved his arms around.

'Just relax bud,' the detective glared at Alex and made a call on his mobile phone out of earshot.

- 35 -

Jail. No amount of mental gymnastics could prepare them for the impact of steel bars.

Alex was handed a toothbrush and blanket, and thrust into a cell with three other desperados. He stood in the darkened space looking at the lumps snoring in the bunk beds. It was nearly dawn, Sunday morning, and he was a wreck. There was nothing for it but to sleep, if at all possible, and he stretched out on the impossibly hard mattress. Charged with possession?

Rosie lay in a cell unable to sleep, with another woman oblivious to her arrival.

Henry, in a cell with one other man, stared into the void. His life paced up and down in his mind. He was not worried about jail, not in a way that somebody else might worry. He was innocent, and was surrounded by a loving network of support. His worry had more to do with the unfortunate timing of it all, and his involvement with 'the group', which was becoming a festering swamp. What would happen if the scandal hit the press and the float failed? His friends had committed money that they could hardly afford to lose. He bore the cross of a risky investment and the imminent auction of the cottage; everything else paled. Narcotics in his apartment? He tried to remember whether he even had any aspirin.

And then, of course, he had no knowledge that Rosie and Alex were also behind bars, or that Rosie was on the other side of the brick wall of the Kings Cross station exercising her own vivid imagination.

If he were asked, Alex would say with some defiance that his nerve and character had been supremely tested in a number of forums. Because he never had to spend mental energy on considering his image as a chaser of women, or as a second-row forward with the Randwick rugby team, he tended to think of himself as an island within a world that stood to suffer from a rising sea. This made him feel a tenuous affinity with others whose circumstances were also subject to the whims of fate. He opened his eyes when he was shaken by one of his cellmates.

'Hey, mate. Wake up. You'll miss breakfast.'

Alex stared at a deplorably ill-kept set of teeth in a youngish face that had been hit by a truck. 'What?'

'Yeah, mate, wouldn't want to miss out on scrambled eggs, would ya?'

Alex swung his legs out from the lower bunk and was narrowly missed by other legs that were being lowered from the upper bunk. His three co-criminals sat themselves on the bunk opposite and commenced a getting-to-know-you session.

His toothy alarm clock introduced himself as Richard, popularly known as Maggot, while his friend on the left was Blowfly. The other guy was merely Robbie. Alex felt he should also have an alter ego, and his mind searched for something suitably parasitic. 'I'm Leech,' he said disconsolately, rubbing his eyes as the drama of the previous evening registered.

'No kidding!' said Blowfly, pleased to expand his circle.

'What're ya in for?' Maggot wanted to know.

Alex yawned and looked around the cell. 'Don't actually know.'

'Oh, carn. Ya must know,' Blowfly said.

'What did you lot do?' Alex asked.

'Robbed a petrol station. Nearly got away with it. Had about two grand, mate. Cigarettes, and Maggot here stuffed enough chocolate bars in to feed a bloody army,' grinned Blowfly.

'Chocolate bars?'

'Yeah. Bit of fun, mate,' Robbie rejoiced.

'How'd ya get caught?' Alex asked, slipping into stride.

'Camers. Maggot set off an alarm,' Blowfly said.

'Wasn't me,' Maggot said.

'Camers?' Alex asked, nodding his head knowingly, but seeking more explanation.

'Yeah.'

It went differently with Rosie. The woman in the opposite bunk stirred at seven o'clock. Rosie was numb from worry and lack of sleep, and wasn't ready to meet her fellow inmate. She was in her mid-twenties, and was a motorcycle gang moll judging by her leather jacket, which Rosie saw had the words 'Body Snatchers' written on it. Rosie was more or less ignored as the woman went about her morning ablutions in the three-metre concrete cell.

Henry's fellow inmate was a drifter who welcomed the new day with a coughing fit that sounded like two Dobermans fighting to the death. Henry lay on his back, his head on his hands, glancing across occasionally to check whether the man was about to expire.

Eventually the grey, balding man in his late sixties or early nineties looked across at Henry. 'Owryagoin?'

'Not bad.'

'Whatareyainfor?'

'Drugs.'

'Got any?'

'No.' Henry wondered if the man was still drunk. He could barely sit up.

Bruce and Beth arrived at the station at ten o'clock. They had telephoned Henry's apartment and got no answer. Then they had telephoned the police station.

The duty personnel had changed shifts. Bruce and Beth had slipped into casual wear and brought a change of clothing for the others, although Bruce's outfits were likely to be a poor fit for Henry and Alex, and perhaps Rosie would have to continue wearing her sequined dress. Bruce had mumbled that

Alex and Henry needed to make some sort of impression of normality. The phone call had established that Henry was in jail. He was so shocked that he didn't enquire about Alex and Rosie, thinking that they would be waiting at the station. The station was empty, as could be expected on a Sunday morning. Beth and Bruce looked around for Alex and Rosie, charged up to the desk and asked the duty constable where Henry Sinclair was, Beth refusing to believe that Henry was in jail.

'Who are you?' asked the constable.

'Friends.'

'He's inside.' The constable looked bored.

'Really?' gasped Beth.

'Yes,' he replied with a look that said, people are so bloody naive.

'What's the charge?' Bruce asked.

'Are you a lawyer?'

'No.'

'I'm afraid he should be represented,' the constable said.

'Jesus Christ,' muttered Beth.

'He'll do,' said the constable, with the flicker of a grin.

'Have two others been here this morning, friends of Henry?' Bruce asked, thinking that he would have seen Alex and Rosie by now.

'Checked in last night.'

'You mean Alex Conomos, and Rosie ...' Beth looked around the station again.

'That'll be them, inside, cell numbers six and eight,' the constable said, glancing down at a manifest.

'Are you saying they're in *jail*?' Bruce was getting fidgety. This constable was so darned nonchalant.

'Afraid so.'

'What for?' Beth gasped.

After some questioning, and based on the fact that Rosie was his sister, Bruce excavated the details. Henry, Rosie and Alex had been charged with possession, and a magistrate would be likely to set bail in a hearing on Monday morning. Bruce and Beth were advised to seek representation for their friends, quickly, otherwise court lawyers would step in.

Bruce and Beth retreated to confer. The constable did not elaborate on the charge and it made absolutely no sense. Sitting on the bench seats, they reviewed their options and decided Bruce would make some phone calls to find a lawyer. He wondered whether to contact Horace and Mary. Beth thought not at this stage. 'We don't want to worry them. Anyway, what would we say?'

Bruce phoned his acquaintances. They despaired about finding anyone on a Sunday. So he called a twenty-four hour legal hotline, wondering about legal procedure.

- 36 -

Detective-sergeant Simpson was no minnow in the cesspool of crime. He could sympathise with people who committed crimes of passion, or with those whose downwardly mobile circumstances elicited unfriendly shoves against the well-heeled establishment, but could never abide crimes committed by the rich. He had a face like a detective, long suffering, with a round-shouldered body that showed the effects of fast food taken on the run. He had arrived at the yacht following a telephone call from an Eric Schwartz reporting a death. There Schwartz had accused Henry Sinclair of involvement in the death of the woman. It was alleged that Henry Sinclair, seeking to protect himself, was on his way to Kings Cross police station. So, for the second time that night, back from the station, Detective-sergeant Simpson trudged up the gangplank of Eric's yacht and greeted his sidekick. 'The media arrived?'

'Yeah. It's that dickhead, whatshisname,' said Cunningham from the Homicide Squad.

'Not Ace Ventura?' Simpson muttered. 'Where is he?'

'Waiting down there, end of the dock. Told him you'd give him a briefing when you got back.'

'Where's that Eric fellow, and his girlfriend? And have forensics arrived?'

'Yeah, combin' the joint now. Eric Schwartz is in the stateroom.'

'Stateroom is it? Have forensics taken a swab?'

'Both Eric and his girlfriend finally agreed, although Schwartz objected.'

'Our rich friend protested against having his precious saliva pinched? Interesting. What do you think?'

Detective-constable Cunningham stood with his hands in his pockets looking out over the oily water of Rushcutters Bay. The light was changing with the breaking dawn, bathing the yachts in yellow parchment. 'I reckon our rich mate was nervous.'

'Anything else about Henry Sinclair's apartment?'

'Yeah. You heard that the front door had been forced open?'

The lot of a police roundsman was not glamorous. It meant tapping in to the police radio network at all hours, listening for the lead that might become a headline scoop. Hearing policemen and women berate each other in the early hours would have a linguist speculating on new directions for the English language. But Dieter Lollinger was not cut from ordinary cloth. He was ambitious. He spent his off-hours glued to detective dramas on television. At the tender age of twenty-three he had set himself the goal of becoming the top investigative journalist at the *Herald*. His colleagues were in no doubt that he would succeed, and had nicknamed him 'Ferret' in their bafflement at his ability to sniff a story.

Many in the media thought of police roundsmen as ambulance chasers, following the police around like crows. Dieter did not disagree. His Swiss-Australian accent imparted a sing-song lilt to his conversation that amused his listeners and deflected attention from his razor-sharp intuition. Just as dogs tend to resemble their owners, police roundsmen adopt the mannerisms of the detectives they have to second guess. Dieter was shortish, podgy, and his coal black eyes were overcast by a verandah of curly black locks. Michael Simpson reckoned Dieter looked like a gollywog.

Dieter would have ignored the police radio operator's reference to yet another drug overdose were it not for the mention of a luxury yacht. His competitors, also glued to the same radio frequency, obviously had ignored it, and Dieter interviewed Simpson alone at the bottom of the gangplank as the sun crept over the horizon.

Fatigue and irritation were rit large on Simpson's face. 'Hello again, Sergeant,' Dieter said, notebook poised.

'Routine, Dieter. Forensics doing their thing. The deceased a young woman, early twenties, cause of death to be revealed in an autopsy.' Simpson leant against the railing and wished he was in bed.

'Who supplied the drugs?' Dieter asked, the question coming out like a Strauss waltz.

'Had your ear glued to the radio?'

'Of course. Any names?'

'Of course not.'

'Who owns the boat? You know I'll just check. You could be helpful, Sergeant.'

This was a ritual, a game of cat and mouse. The media could seriously advantage a career, or sink like a stone someone who was arrogant, unapproachable, evasive. And Ace Ventura was not to be treated lightly, in spite of his ridiculous immaturity. 'A Mr Eric Schwartz.'

'Anything about him?'

So it went. The police had cordoned off the boat as a major crime scene, which lent depth to Dieter's suspicions. Simpson had the inflection in his voice that Dieter recognised as icing on an interesting three-layer cake.

'Who lives in Coogee?'

The police knew and Dieter knew that a drug overdose was a clouded matter. If anybody wanted to commit murder, this was the way to do it. It was almost impossible to prove that a person had overdosed as a result of somebody else administering a cocktail of drugs, particularly if the victim had a history of addiction. There was nothing more tantalising to an ambitious roundsman than the possibility of murder in the upper echelon of society. Nor for the police, for that matter.

A newspaper is peopled with a curious array of misfits. Not unlike politics, people are attracted to journalism for subterranean motives — the exercise of power is a drug.

In their storehouses of information journalists can be secretive librarians. For a young, ambitious roundsman to tap into the knowledge resident within the sometimes paranoid minds of his colleagues requires acute negotiating skills. Nothing can be gained by revealing a promising lead to a superior if the juicy morsel is devoured and our roundsman elbowed out of a front-page story. Dieter understood the game. A senior mentor was a prerequisite. Someone who knew the ropes, knew the Sydney social scene and had his finger on the pulse, yet was prepared to share information with a promising upstart who was appropriately sycophantic.

At nine in the morning Dieter crashed, exhausted, in his sparse bed-sit in Balmain, keen to make some phone calls later that afternoon.

Henry did a lot of his living inside his head. This was generally a pleasant experience — after all, he knew most of the people who lived there. He was well acquainted with stubborn Henry, he fought constantly with procrastinating Henry, but he despised glum Henry. Glum Henry fought for attention whenever the pendulum of optimism swung toward its pessimistic twin, and the fight could be won when the weight of evidence was overwhelming.

By three o'clock Sunday afternoon, glum Henry was hogging the limelight. He'd been acquainted with all the facts: Rosie and Alex languished in jail; they were all charged with possession of narcotics; there were more serious allegations to do with the woman's death; the auction for the cottage was a week away; Palamountain would float on Thursday. And his bloody cell-mate wouldn't stop coughing — it sounded like the man's internal organs were engaged in a bar-room brawl.

Henry had gleaned all the facts when he telephoned Bruce, having decided that this was his only recourse, and having been informed by the duty constable that Bruce was searching for a lawyer. He also discovered that bail was likely to be set in court on Monday morning. Bail?

Rosie reacted to her situation by lying in her bunk bed and staring into space. In her mind she was atoning for her life's misdeeds. She recalled leaving a clothing store knowing that the cashier had undercharged her. She berated herself for siding with a colleague against a workmate when it went against her instincts. She had toyed with the idea of forgetting to take the pill so that she could fall pregnant to Henry. Now she slipped into depression, convinced that she would spend the rest of her life in jail. 'What goes around comes around,' she mumbled over and over again.

Alex faced his predicament in an Alex way. He decided to run a lifestyle seminar for his cellmates. His credibility as a man of commercial substance given a boost by his description of the forthcoming globalisation of pie carts, he hectored Maggot and Blowfly into forming a partnership between themselves, and going straight. Robbie, a cynical boy, spent the afternoon scoffing, but Alex had won over the others, no question about it. How much for an old Kombi? Councils were bending over backwards to push local enterprise. Who doesn't eat pies? The Chinese would love them, they don't have a chance to eat meat. How do you imagine McDonald's started?

Dieter sat up when he heard from his mentor that Eric Schwartz was well-known around the business traps of Sydney. Further phone calls revealed that many people considered Eric to be the worst incarnation of the flamboyant entrepreneur. He had a past that was compared to Alan Bond – lowly beginnings and a streak of spectacular business successes that stemmed from questionable buying and selling of companies. He'd made numerous shareholders very poor, but himself very rich. The most interesting aspect had to do with his widely known circle of close friends. Had Dieter heard of Andrew Finley, the new golden boy of the Liberal Party? Then there was his girlfriend, the founder of a substantial recruitment company, a Rachael Quinlan. He mentioned others who were associated; prominent stockbrokers and bankers. His circle of friends was known as the 'feeling frenzy'. Dieter did a double take. He was told that no, the 'l' shouldn't be a 'd' – they fed on opportunity like sharks, but they did it with feeling. His last piece of advice was: 'Don't get in their way.'

Dieter resolved to follow up with more research. In the meantime there was a court appearance in the morning. His investigations had revealed that someone had been implicated in the death of the woman, and that this person would be up before the magistrate. This information dampened his ardour – perhaps Eric Schwartz had nothing to do with the tragedy on his boat.

- 37 -

For an ordinary citizen like Alex, lawyers, and the justice system generally, operated on an incomprehensible level. Alex concluded that contact with the legal system should be avoided as keenly as a performance of *A Streetcar Named Desire* put on by a local theatre group that he had had the misfortune to experience. The ritual and props were like a staged performance. The acting, because that's what it was, was generally on a par with Harry Squat the deli owner, who was dragged in to do Kowalski at the penultimate moment because the designated Kowalski had the flu. There was glazed incomprehension in the courtroom on the part of everyone, which was a precursor to rigid catatonia. It appeared to Alex as if no one had remembered their lines, and the plot was so mangled that the poor old guy sitting out in front just kept mumbling about a case that must have been being heard in another court.

He sat with Henry and Rosie in the front row of a room that served as a staging area for the main event. People shuffled about, herding other victims in and out, and all the while some foreign language was being mumbled by insufferable boors who clearly wished they were somewhere else.

The reunion had all the emotion of three reunited hijack victims. Alex looked like he'd withered away in a Thai jail, so lost was he inside Bruce's shirt and slacks. Henry was similar, but looked almost like a western citizen, while Rosie, still dressed in her sequined dress, looked like she'd made a wrong turn for the Opera House. After hurried rejoicing at being reunited and a flurried three-way conversation to try to bring everyone to the same point of ignorance, they sat down meekly, when instructed, but elicited the curious stares and sniggers from all those present. They sat at the front of a crowded room, waiting to be called before the Magistrate next door, and were informed that someone had been appointed to represent them.

Then, to Henry's left, because he was sitting closest to the door, a woman appeared and asked the duty clerk to point out Henry Sinclair.

She moved over and began with an apology: that she'd only just been informed of the case, and had barely had a chance to absorb the details. The woman established that she belonged to the firm contacted by Bruce. She looked dishevelled, as if she had given birth to triplets about two hours before, and Henry had a sinking feeling that their fate was in uncertain hands.

Just then a hugely impressive man in a flash suit appeared next to Henry and interrupted to say that he was Anderson Charters from Higginbottom and Charters, that he was proposing to deal with the case, that he had been instructed, and that the woman should retire. There occurred some credential exchanges and the woman disappeared, gratefully.

The lawyer was in his mid-thirties. He wore slicked-back brown hair and spoke with assurance, making it plain that Henry, Rosie and Alex were not to worry, that he was instructed not to reveal who had hired him, and that this morning's hearing was just a formality to set bail. They would shortly be released.

Alex wanted to know who would pay bail, and how much would it be, and why were they there in the first place, and would he act for them while he prepared to sue the government? Henry told his friend to shut up with such vigour that the others just stared.

Eventually they were summoned into the next room to appear before the magistrate.

The magistrate dispensed justice like a worker in an abattoir. He listened to the incomprehensible drone of some woman standing out in front while burying his head in his hand as if he didn't want to hear any more. He referred to some date in the future and looked down at a case list for his next victim. It was just as Anderson Charters said. Henry was impressed with the man's grasp of the facts, and his knowledge of their characters, and his understanding that they had never committed an offence and that bail should be minimal. And so it was. There ensued some lengthy discussion about the amount of bail and who would post it, and dates for hearings. Anderson Charters undertook to act as surety, which caused the magistrate to peer closely at him through his glasses. Henry was released on ten thousand dollars bail, Alex and Rosie on two thousand each. Alex discovered that they would only be liable to pay the money if they failed to show up. Bruce and Beth observed the proceedings from the rear of the courtroom. Dieter Lollinger scribbled furiously to one side.

Outside the courtroom everybody talked at once, with Bruce and Beth adding to the confusion. Anderson Charters was adamant that he would not reveal who had hired him to represent them, leaving everybody befuddled. Dieter Lollinger, who hovered in the background pretending to be waiting for his turn in court, overheard the conversations.

Anderson Charter's job was done, and he wouldn't be drawn on what would happen next. He said that they would find out soon, and that he would await instructions, and he left. Which was the moment that Dieter introduced himself.

At first he was ignored, being smallish and having the sort of sing-song voice that sounded like he wanted to sell roses. But he won Beth's attention, and she shouted at the others to be heard. 'Shut up a minute. This man is a police journalist.'

Dieter explained what he was about, causing everyone to give him undivided attention. Dieter had found out that Henry was a respected freelance journalist who worked for the *Herald*, among other publications. Unfortunately Dieter did not read the financial pages of his own paper and had never heard of Henry. A quick mobile phone call cleared that up, and he approached his questioning convinced that the trail to

Eric Schwartz was getting warmer. It took a couple of calls for him to establish that Henry was an enigma, but finally he was put on to someone who knew that Henry Sinclair had an unsullied reputation as an honest broker. His source was surprised at the mention of drugs, but ended by saying he couldn't say for sure whether Henry was the type, he'd never met him.

'We work for the same paper, Henry,' Dieter said. 'Both journos, sort of.'

'Umm,' Henry was about to correct him.

'You know all about deadlines and editors,' Dieter prompted.

'Well, technology articles, and finance . . .'

'Yeah, must be full of characters,' Dieter suggested.

There was something about Alex that made people listen to him. Henry spoke too slowly, and whenever a pause occurred in Henry's recollection of events, Alex hurried in. Dieter saw something in Alex that resonated with his own view of the world, and he also saw a loose cannon, much loved by journalists. Dieter scratched on his notepad when Alex told him about the broken door, and the drugs obviously planted in the flat, and that Henry was only gone for ten minutes to go down to the toilet, and that Henry was a saint, and they knew no one at the party, and they'd never met the dead woman, and what the hell would Henry's motive be?

It sounded convincing when Rosie came in and said that Henry just wouldn't cheat on her. Dieter was bemused when he stared at Rosie's outfit and her hairdo, which had come adrift through her ordeal, but his face registered nothing. He was, after all, used to strange people. Dieter looked at Henry and couldn't imagine him as a philanderer, or drug user, although he couldn't be totally sure about Alex. But what made it all sound credible to Dieter was the openness with which everyone spoke. No one questioned his right to be asking the questions, nothing was guarded.

While Alex was venting his knowledge, it occurred to Henry that they were imparting the kiss of death to Palamountain.

If this journalist probed Henry's suspicions, then he would uncover Eric's involvement, and perhaps past drug dealings. Days before the float, it would tarnish the image of Palamountain. The share price would probably collapse on opening.

Upon their return to Henry's apartment Henry, Alex and Rosie confronted the mayhem instituted by the police search. It was not a welcoming sight, despite a history of mayhem. They sat quietly, sipping tea, wanting to debrief, to share this amazing experience and ponder a way forward. Bruce and Beth had to leave shortly to get back to work. Rosie had asked for the week off, not knowing what to say to her employer, and thinking that she faced a future of unemployment. Nobody would hire a criminal. Everybody was downcast for everybody else, not least because Henry explained that all their money was now at risk, and that the journalist was the last straw, and that would be that. Henry insisted that Horace and Mary should be kept out of it, at least for now. There seemed nothing for it but to wait for Anderson Charters, the mysterious lawyer. Round and round they went, speculating on who could have hired him on their behalf.

Eventually Beth and Bruce left, and Henry set about making a late lunch of sandwiches.

- 38 -

When first Detective Simpson arrived at the yacht on Saturday night, actually in the wee hours of Sunday morning, he sat opposite Eric and Rachael and summoned his policeman's instincts. Body language, spoors, the weather. Some people have the skills to read the signs. An Aboriginal tracker can tell how long ago a goanna sashayed through the dirt—the untrained eye would see a smudge. A detective prospered because he could read the tremors of untruth like a seismologist, or the flickering cadence of emotions like a Geiger counter. As he sat listening to Eric and Rachael, Detective Simpson affected a casual disinterest and scribbled in his notebook.

He had learned to clarify the muddy waters of lies and obfuscation. In his scheme of the criminal mind, people were either goldfish bowls or house bricks. A goldfish bowl had nothing to hide except the goldfish, which was the truth, and the truth swam around in tight circles. All was honest bluster and sincere denial and finger-pointing over shoulders, and much was said but little was gleaned. A housebrick, common variety, sat square with rectitude, buttressed by a wall of social justice and position in the scheme of things. It was an effort to penetrate a housebrick and prise it away from the righteous cement that held it in place. Detective Simpson had, in Eric and Rachael, two shining stereotypes. His first interrogation went like this:

'And you say you saw Henry actually come out of the cabin as you both came down the stairs?'

'We were coming down the stairs, for, umm, you know Sergeant, when you're in love and you're the hosts, and there's no time for each other . . .' Rachael gushed.

'You came down for a bit of a snog.' Simpson cut through the custard.

'Yes,' Rachael said, putting her hand on Eric's.

'I turned a blind eye. I should have done something, but you can't help people with an addiction,' Eric said, with an unblinking stare. He sat composed, square, like a brick.

'You think this Henry may have been a trafficker? Who was the girl, how come she was dressed casually, not one of the invited guests?'

'She's someone I've employed as a hostess, to serve drinks, that sort of thing,' Eric said, and Simpson observed Rachael's slight reaction as she pressed her lips.

'Why would she have arrived without an invitation, and no duty to perform?'

'She snuck on board. I had no idea,' Eric said.

'What, just to have a good time with Henry?'

'I don't really know, Sergeant, and now, if you don't mind, it's late and we're bushed,' Eric said, making to stand up.

Rachael offered that Henry had said he was going straight to the police station, which made Eric falter and sit back down.

'Why would he do that?' Simpson asked.

'He's a bizarre character. You should see his druggy friends,' Eric added.

'I'd ask that you submit to a routine saliva test for our forensic people. Merely common procedure. Please remain here. I'll be back shortly. Kings Cross station, I presume?'

- 39 -

Henry sat next to Rosie on the sofa. Alex was sitting on the armchair, gazing into space. 'The auction is next week, Palamountain is supposed to float on Thursday,' Henry said morosely.

'I've got to get this dress off before it grafts itself onto my body,' Rosie said, getting up and walking into Henry's bedroom. 'Shit! Damn, darn!' She came back into the living room. 'I've taken my clothes to the dry cleaners!'

There was the sound of footsteps outside the flat, then a knock on the door. Henry went to open it. '*Rachael?*'

Alex stood up, hearing Henry gasp her name. Rachael entered, looking at Henry, staring around at the wreckage. She took off her sunglasses. Everybody reacted. 'Bloody hell,' Alex said.

'Sit down, Rachael, you remember Rosie and my friend Alex.' Henry took her by the elbow and led her to an armchair.

There was bruising around one eye, which she had attempted to cover with make-up. Her upper lip had swelled, and there was a hint of blood in the corner of her mouth. She was dressed casually in slacks, her hair tied back in a pony tail.

'I'm so sorry Henry, all of you.' She started to sob, slowly, then she shook with emotion and Henry gestured to Rosie for tissues. Rosie, wide-eyed, shook her head. Alex raced to the closet, fetched a towel, and handed it to Rachael.

Henry knelt on the carpet in front of her, confused, upset, wanting to console her. 'What happened, Rachael?'

Rachael wiped her eyes on the towel, then blew her nose, and looked at Henry through teary eyes. 'Henry, I don't know how to tell you this, but Eric is on a rampage. I, I was pressured by him to tell a lie about you to the police. I was an idiot. I've been an absolute fool. He's a pig. I knew it in my heart, but ... you know, since I met him I've moved into that huge penthouse, changed my wardrobe, been going to the gym, bleached my hair. God, I'm a successful businesswoman, people think I'm strong. I've been weak as water. It hasn't been me. And when I saw what he would do, and that he probably gave that woman the drugs, and then tried to pin it on you ... and I'm caught up in the thick of it. Eric says that perverting the course of justice, which is what we have done, gets twenty years.' She began to sob again.

'Did *you* hire that lawyer?' Henry asked.

'Yes. I didn't sleep at all, and I had to do something, and Eric clobbered me. He can't control his anger. But look, Eric found out that there's a journalist snooping around. He'll pull out all stops to prevent his name getting in the paper before the float. He was in a rage when he found out about me helping you ...'

'Did you tell him?' Henry asked.

'Yes. I couldn't live with the idea that you'd been caught up in this mess, and in jail ...'

'So why do you think he's after Henry? What would he do?' Alex asked.

Rachael looked at Alex and blinked. 'Umm, he snarled at me, and said that Henry was his ticket out of this mess, and that I haven't seen what he's capable of, and what was I doing jeopardising his life's work . . .'

'You're saying that Henry's in danger?' Rosie said quietly.

'I think Eric is capable of anything. He's just not rational. I kept at him just to stop this stupidity. If the girl was an addict, why not just go to the police with the truth?'

'Doesn't that mean all of us are in danger?' Alex asked.

'Maybe, yes,' Rachael mouthed softly.

Alex was winding up. 'This is unbelievable! I do think, staring out the window, that we're in a flat in Coogee, not Sicily. People just can't kill people to keep their names out of the newspapers!'

'Shut up, Alex. Okay, here's what we do.' Henry got up from the floor. He stood clasping his hands and commanded attention. 'We're going to get out of here, now. To the cabin, in your Kombi, Alex. He'd know your car, Rachael. I have the journo's number, and the police. You have a mobile phone Rachael?'

'Yes.'

'Well, let's get out of here.'

Outside Henry's flat a man sat in a car and spoke into a mobile phone as he watched everybody pile into Alex's Kombi. As the Kombi left, the BMW 735 slowly followed.

They arrived at the cabin in the late afternoon, strung out from an endless discussion.

They had sat quietly in the Kombi listening to Rachael describe the first heady days of her involvement with 'the group'. She'd felt a contagious excitement to be suddenly among such powerful people. Imagine being caught up in a bid to have somebody become Prime Minister, and Eric was so persuasive, and Louise was so articulate, and . . .

Henry said that they should phone the journalist, and the police, and everybody went quiet.

'Henry, it would mean the end of Palamountain,' Rachael said. 'If we hole up in this cabin for a few days, the scandal will blow over, and Eric will have his successful float, and get screamingly rich, and his motive to silence us all will fade away.'

'There's something in that, Henry,' Alex said.

'Perhaps Rachael's right, Henry,' Rosie said. 'The cottage.'

'The cottage?' Rachael asked.

Rosie explained how they'd all become involved in Palamountain.

'I knew you'd made some money on the float of my company, Henry,' Rachael said.

'I now understand why your company was sold so cheaply. You would have made much more money had you priced the shares sensibly. It was Eric who pressured you, wasn't it?' Henry asked.

'Yes. He wanted my company to deliver a windfall for his investors, and then we'd all make a bucket of money on Palamountain.'

'But there's a problem, isn't there?' Henry said. 'Your company is substantial, Rachael. There's only bluster and bullshit behind Palamountain. It's just an ego thing for Eric, to show he can do it, isn't that right?'

'I guess so,' Rachael said.

'And you've already done well, haven't you?'

'Oh God, yes. I have more money than I ever thought possible,' Rachael said.

'So, let's expose Palamountain for what it is. How could we live with the idea that ordinary investors, mums and dads, will end up paying for something that's all hot air and run by a criminal?' Henry said.

'Wait a bloody minute, Henry. You've already forked over our money,' Alex said.

'We took a gamble, just like all the marshmallows. At least we had some idea what we were doing,' Henry said.

'I don't understand the difference,' Alex said.

'The difference is that now we really know who and what is behind Palamountain. Before, we could take an honest risk, based on the euphoria of the market, cross our fingers. We took a gamble to save Horace's cottage. Now we know for sure that there's a gutter rat behind it. I'd read bits and pieces about Eric over the years. There was a lot of smoke, no fire. Now it's burning.'

'But that will mean that we'll lose our money, Henry, and the cottage will go,' Rosie said.

'It's like knowing that the ferry has a leak, and we're on the dock watching innocent people going on board, and there's a big storm brewing,' Henry said. 'How could you live with the idea that you've prospered at the expense of innocent people?'

'Henry's right,' Rosie said, and squeezed his arm.

'Aren't Horace and Mary innocent?' Alex asked. 'Am I not innocent?'

'Yes. Let me put it to you this way. I made a huge mistake. I was uncomfortable with Eric, and Palamountain, but went along with it because I thought it was a chance. I'm no different to anybody else yet I'm supposed to be the bloody expert! It's highly likely that the news on Eric will come out with or without us. Who knows what the police have uncovered. So we should do the right thing.'

Rachael watched the exchange. 'You're prepared to sacrifice your money – and your friends' – because of the principle?'

They turned off the freeway onto the Marulan exit. As Alex drove the Kombi around the exit ramp he glanced into the rear-vision mirror. He noticed a car. Didn't he see it before? He'd been preoccupied with the discussion. 'Guess what, don't turn around, but we're being followed.'

'What?' Rosie gasped.

'Don't turn around!'

Alex drove past the truck stop along the ribbon of road leading out of the small Marulan township. The BMW went in the other direction, and they breathed easier. At the intersection he turned right onto Brayton road to travel through the undulating farmland, and checked the mirror. There was nobody in sight.

'Okay, time to phone the journalist. And what about the police?' Henry asked.

'I'm not sure, Henry,' Rachael said.

'What's the matter?'

'Well, I'm implicated in this whole affair, and haven't had time to speak to my lawyer.'

'But if somehow Eric has followed us ...'

'What could he do? Bruce has a shotgun in the cabin,' Alex said.

'Oh, Alex!' Rosie chortled.

Henry phoned Dieter Lollinger's number. An answering machine asked that he leave a message. Henry spoke as quickly as Henry was able. The mobile phone was starting to give out. He gave the number of the cabin and Rachael's mobile number. Rapidly he stated that Eric had gone berserk, that he'd hit Rachael, who had hired the lawyer, and that they'd all sped away for safety. Rachael, likewise left an urgent message for Anderson Charters.

Rachael entered the cabin like a space voyager. 'I *have* led a sheltered life,' she mumbled, and everybody laughed.

Henry watched her negotiate the entrance and thought about this woman. Her daring, noble act to intervene on his behalf had changed the balance. He was actually getting to like her.

It was getting dark. Alex lit the pressure lantern, and Rosie did her best to show Rachael around, avoiding the dunny, and suggesting to Rachael that she'd be better off going bush. Time to drop your drawers over thorn bushes, she said. Rachael replied she'd never ever simply, well, she couldn't imagine, wasn't there another way? What about in the middle of the night, and sleeping, and food?

Food was a problem. Henry had said that they should buy some provisions, but Rosie, anxious to keep moving, and thinking that they'd be safe in the cabin, had said that there were always tins galore, and that there was plenty of booze, and they'd make do. By the time that Rosie and Rachael returned from their inspection of the ablution facility, Alex had begun to organise a meal.

Henry used the wall phone to call Dieter Lollinger. Again there was the answering machine, and he repeated his message. Then he left a message for Bruce. Rachael made another call to Anderson Charters, and narrated the turn of events. Should she call the police? Charters said that he would handle it.

To add some cheer Alex lit the fire, even though it was warm outside. Rosie found a bottle of vintage port, and they sat staring into the flames, sipping, while Alex opened tinned food. Rachael declared that she couldn't remember the last time she'd eaten out of a tin. If only her children could see her. Rosie asked about her children, and Rachael said that they were with her mother, and that her mother was ignorant of her predicament.

'Rachael, what will Andy and Louise do when they find out?' Henry asked.

'Oh God. Andy will flip. I think he's got most to lose. You know how much the media love it when politicians get caught up in this sort of scandal.'

'Will your business be affected?' Rosie asked.

'I don't think so. Depends on what happens.'

Alex got up to relieve himself, walked out of the cabin and stood on top of the rocky outcrop. He gazed into the darkness, bracing himself against a stiffening breeze, and chanced to look over his left shoulder. Through the treetops he spied two sets of headlights at the gate to the property. Quickly he did what he had to do and rushed inside. 'We have company!'

- 40 -

Michael Simpson was acting on his hunch. He found out that Eric was a successful businessman whose company would float on the stock exchange that week. Drugs and large amounts of wealth were too tantalising a combination to be ignored. Fancy yachts owned by ostensibly honourable people could easily shift quantities of drugs. Simpson insisted that an autopsy be performed as quickly as possible. On the Tuesday morning he consulted the forensics expert who had received a preliminary report from the coroner's office.

Simpson had supposed there might have been intercourse, and the report confirmed that traces of Eric's semen were found on the woman. But then came a breakthrough. The woman was pregnant.

'With Eric Schwartz's child?'

DNA tests were still being performed.

There was a history of addiction.

A plausible motive was established. Eric Schwartz wanted to rid himself of a woman who may have been pressuring him as the father of her unborn child. If she was an addict, then there were all manner of complications that Eric Schwartz would do his best to avoid. But using Henry Sinclair as a foil? That was poor judgement, and Simpson began to see that Eric Schwartz was out of control. House bricks would do anything to avoid exposure.

Late Monday afternoon, several messages had been left for Simpson. One was to call Dieter Lollinger, urgently. Another, embedded in the list, was a request to contact Anderson Charters, a name he did not recognise.

Simpson did not get his messages until shortly after he received the forensics report on Tuesday morning. At the same moment someone handed him an article from the *Sydney Morning Herald* that almost caused him to spill his coffee.

Simpson phoned Dieter. 'Well?'

'Sergeant, a message was left on my answering machine late yesterday by Henry Sinclair. Before I tell you what it was, have you any information you could share with me?'

'No.'

'Well, I don't know whether it was important after all.' Dieter played a dangerous card.

'Look, Dieter, Ace Ventura, bloody Lolly whatever your name is, don't go playing your journo's games with me,' Simpson said, his blood pressure on the rise.

'Okay, okay. I have a job to do as well, Sergeant. Actually, I was about to tell you anyway. Henry Sinclair said that he and his friends have fled to a cabin in Marulan, near Goulburn. Rachael Quinlan is with them. She had been beaten up by Eric Schwartz, and she was afraid that he was after them all.'

'Really? Why didn't you get this to me earlier? Did he give an address?'

'No, just some numbers. '

'Have you called them? '

'The ordinary number is dead, the mobile is out of range.'

'Shit! Okay, give them to me.'

Alex's announcement exploded like a bomb.

'God! What'll we do?' Rosie went white.

'How do we know it's Eric?' Henry asked.

'It'll be Eric,' Rachael said. 'He's such a sneak – he would have turned around and followed from out of our view.'

'Okay. We can't take the risk. We have minutes. We separate. Alex, go find the shotgun, I'll take it,' Henry said. 'Rosie come with me, you and Rachael get going. We'll go over the back fence. Quickly.'

As Henry doused the lamp Rosie poured water on the fire. A hiss of steam, then a pall of smoke wafted around the cabin.

'Oh shit,' Alex turned back. 'Can't see. Bring that torch.'

Henry found the torch and followed Alex into Bruce's bedroom. 'Come on, where's the gun?'

'Over here.' Alex was pulling at a drawer to an old chest. He tossed the contents out in a frenzy and handed the shotgun to Henry. 'You know how to use this?'

Henry stared at the repulsive object and exchanged a frozen look with Alex, as they confronted a reality that was frightening and ridiculous at the same time. 'I can't believe I'm holding this, Alex.'

'Would you actually use it?'

'Dunno. If Eric's flipped, what do we do?'

'Yeah. Henry, what's happening?'

Alex looked pinched as he searched the drawer for cartridges. Henry opened the gun. It was empty of shells.

'No bullets,' Alex said.

'Oh well,' Henry said.

At the door they turned to one another. 'Good luck, Alex,' Henry said, and gave Alex a quick hug. Rosie and Rachael looked uncertainly at the shotgun, then Rosie also gave Alex a hug. They disappeared into the night.

Henry, dragging Rosie by the hand, sped up the hill into the gum trees as fast as Rosie's legs could carry her inside her cumbersome dress. This was not very fast – she shuffled forward like a Japanese geisha. There was a half moon and a patchwork of clouds skittled across the sky, giving them some sense of direction.

'Lift your dress, Rosie.'

'What?'

'It's slowing us down.' Henry stopped, lifted the front of her dress in a bunch and handed it to her. He could see headlights approaching the cabin. Rosie started to gasp before they had gone more than fifty metres. 'Slow down, Henry, I can't go any faster,' she puffed.

Henry looked back at the cabin. The cars had arrived. The clouds parted momentarily, and he strained his eyes to see two torch-beams darting about, first shining over the Kombi, then entering the cabin. Within moments a stabbing light came up the hill toward them. He could see another light going in the opposite direction and remembered Eric's fitness and strength. Henry wondered if Eric would be doing the dirty work himself.

As Rosie gathered herself Henry was lost in her wheezing, which sounded very asthmatic, He could see that the flashlight was moving fast. He looked into the gloom of the trees and remembered a huge termite nest. 'Quickly, over here!'

Their pursuer was a mere hundred metres away when Henry stumbled and fell heavily over a fallen branch, his fall causing a branch to crack. 'Damn!'

Rosie, with the momentum of his tugging hand, fell on top of him. He moaned as her weight crushed his face in the dirt.

'Sorry, Henry, you all right?' she flustered as she rolled to one side.

'Shhh. Come on, quickly!' he whispered. The shadow of the three-metre-high termite nest sprang out at them. He dragged her behind the nest and they pressed themselves against the mound, breathing like bellows in a steel mill.

Henry craned his neck. The torch was coming directly for them. He clutched the gun at his waist and gulped, putting his hand over Rosie's mouth to muffle her heavy breathing.

Alex took Rachael's hand and they paused at the top of the rocky outcrop. Given the intermittent visibility it would be dangerous to descend, and Alex remembered well how precarious the slope was in that direction. But there were deep fissures and over-hanging ledges in the cliff immediately beneath them. They could hide there. He fell to the ground on his backside and gestured with his hand for Rachael to do the same. He slid down the six-metre rock face on his bum and jolted to a halt. 'Come on, it's okay,' he whispered to Rachael.

Rachael, who had watched him slide into the dark, assumed the same posture, but now was afraid of the slope. Gathering her courage, she pushed forward with her hands and slid down until she banged up against Alex's back. There they sat like two children on a slippery dip. Alex turned his head to whisper over his shoulder. 'Rachael, did you ever think someone like me would piggy-back you to fame and fortune?'

She was stuck, legs astride Alex, totally dependent on him to move away, her hands resting on his bony shoulders. 'What a time to be cracking jokes!' she hissed.

They were wedged in a fissure. The only way forward was to climb the next rock, or jump into total darkness on the other side. Alex thought that they might as well just sit there. It was comfortable enough, what with her pneumatic build.

'Well? Are we going or not?' she whispered.

'Where do you suggest?'

A flashlight beam stabbed at the trees around them. Alex lay back on Rachael, pressing her flat on the rock ledge. Someone was standing above them, on the very spot from which they had descended.

Eric Schwartz bounded up the slope, flashlight in hand. He wondered how Dennis would handle the rough terrain and the dark. Dennis was grossly unfit, but they had to split up. It was obvious that there were only two exit directions from the cabin; the far side was far too steep. The smoky interior had told him that the fire had just been put out. Had Rachael spoken to the media? He had rushed inside the cabin and cut the phone line. He'd also found Rachael's mobile phone in her bag on an armchair.

Eric's instincts were smooth bearings inside a well-oiled machine: infallible when it came to outguessing others. He based his actions on his hunch that Rachael was deeply implicated, and would avoid the police and media. Henry Sinclair and his friends were a different story, but Eric guessed that they'd be under Rachael's influence. She was surely more persuasive than muttonhead Henry. Sinkers was a dud, just like he remembered from high school. Eric had never understood the group's infatuation with him, wanting merely to use him.

He heard the sound of a breaking branch.

The flashlight stabbed here and there and came to rest on the termite mound. Eric approached it, then swept the trees with his torch.

As they saw him jog to the rise Henry shoved Rosie around the other side of the mound. 'We have to make a run for their cars. Could be our only chance.'

'You've got to be joking.'

'We'll just wait here a couple of secs, let him disappear over the rise. You can make it. Gather your dress. No, take it off.'

'What? Henry, are you sure this is the moment?'

'Come on, take it off, quick. It's too restrictive.' He pulled up the dress and eased it over her head.

Rosie stood in a slip. 'Henry, this is pretty embarrassing.'

'Okay, *now*!'

Henry grabbed her hand and they retreated back down the hill, at first gingerly, Henry checking over his shoulder for the flashlight. They gathered speed and, because they were travelling downhill, Rosie managed to stoke up a head of steam. Within fifty metres of the cabin he could see the beam of the flashlight once again appear at the top of the rise.

Eric found the dress. The sequins glimmered in the torchlight. Then he looked down the hill and could see a large, whitish figure, and another, scampering toward the cabin.

Henry raced for the first car, tore open the door and checked for keys. There were none. Quickly he raced to the other car, aware that the erratic light was seeking them out. Again, no keys. He dismissed any notion of driving the Kombi. It would be too slow. He grabbed Rosie by the hand and they raced in the direction that Alex had gone. Suddenly a torch shone in their faces and a voice yelled for them to stop.

Alex heard the voice. He squeezed Rachael's shin.

Blinded by the powerful beam, Henry and Rosie stood, panting. Henry thought about the shotgun, but let it drop to the ground. He couldn't see whether the man had a gun.

Moments later Eric appeared, and also directed his beam. 'Well, Sinkers and his fat girlfriend, without her clothes,' Eric snarled. 'Well done, Dennis. Where's Rachael?'

'Dunno. Nobody could move down that ridge in the dark. She must be hiding just over the back.'

'Okay. Henry, get in the cabin. *Move!*'

Dennis found the pressure lantern and ignited it.

'Can I find something to wear?' Rosie asked.

'By all means. Please do,' Eric said. 'Dennis, keep looking for Rachael.'

Dennis left the cabin, and Eric looked around, then helped himself to the bottle of port. He drank greedily. 'What sort of cheap shit is this?' He spat, and chucked the bottle, shattering it in the fireplace.

Rosie, scrummaging around, found a white sheet and draped it over herself. Eric ordered her to sit down next to Henry, and then sat, staring into the fireplace.

Henry wondered whether Eric had a gun. Perhaps he was bluffing? He looked at Eric's haggard face, seeing a desperate man, and wondered. His mind drifted to the dead girl. Eric must have done something to cause her to kill herself, or maybe he had killed her. If that was the case, then they were in serious trouble. And Dennis? Henry recognised him from the party. He looked like a banker, hardly a criminal, and seemed nowhere near as threatening as Eric. In fact, Henry decided, he and Alex could overpower him.

After a few minutes of silence, Eric got up and walked over to Rosie. 'Give me your sheet.'

'What? Why?' she said.

He grabbed her by the hand and yanked her up. 'Just do as you're told, fat girl.'

Rosie undraped the sheet and Eric took it. He went to the kitchen and rummaged in a drawer, retrieving a sharp knife. He began to tear the sheet into long strips.

Henry exchanged a look with Rosie. Should they charge at Eric and try to knock him out? He was not confident of his own strength, but figured Rosie would be a great ally in a fight. His face still smarted from where she had merely fallen on him. He saw Rosie glance across – perhaps she had read his mind – and Henry nodded at a shovel propped up against the wall.

'Don't even think about it!' Eric snarled. 'I'll belt you over the head with it before you could say sh-sh-shovel.'

He told Henry and Rosie to sit on chairs and began to tie them up, feet first. Then he stuffed strips from the sheets in their mouths, blindfolded them and tied their hands behind the chairs. Then he left the cabin.

Alex and Rachael had formed a strange physical bond as she sat like a bookend against his back. Alex had never in his life been so close to a well-endowed and attractive woman, and the allure of Rachael's perfume had him thinking that it may be high time for him to form a relationship with a woman, rather than a Kombi.

But he cancelled thoughts of a marriage proposal when he heard voices immediately above. After a moment's panic, Alex realised that they had not been discovered. They were hidden in a dark moon shadow. But whoever it was up there had only to direct a torch downward, and their number would be up.

'She can't have gone far without a torch' – he recognised Eric's voice – 'it's pitch black down there, she must be holed up in one of these crevasses.'

'Rachael,' Eric yelled. 'It's lover boy. Come out, come out wherever you are. I'm not going to hurt you.'

The torchlight flitted all over the place. Alex lay flat on Rachael willing them both to disappear inside the rocky face. Then the game was up. The torches beamed on them like a laser.

'What have we here? Rachael, naughty girl. You shouldn't be so intimate with a stranger. Good God, I believe it's Bozo the Clown!'

Henry tried to wriggle out of his bondage. Eric had tied the strips tightly, and the gag in his mouth meant that his efforts at communicating with Rosie came out as a series of hollow grunts. Rosie responded with an equally obscure barrage. Altogether, they sounded like a family of chimps heralding the arrival of a predator. Then the door flung open, and Alex, Rachael, Eric and Dennis came inside.

'Henry, Rosie, you all right? What're you doing in your underwear?' Alex rushed over.

'Back off, Bozo. You'll get your chance to eat sheet.' Eric laughed at his own joke. 'Get it, Dennis?'

He instructed Alex and Rachael to sit on the floor.

- 41 -

Dieter Lollinger engaged in an intense discussion with his mentor at the newspaper. He knew he was on to a headline-grabbing story, but his evidence was disjointed, anecdotal and definitely relied on leaps of faith. In short, the sort of story editors hated.

As he strung out the details like washing on a line, his mentor's attitude began to change. Given that Dieter had the foresight to bring a tape-recording of Henry's phone message, and the fact that Henry's credibility had been established, and the fact that they had uncovered the imminent float of Palamountain, the brew was tantalising. His mentor had sought the advice of the financial editor, who had confirmed the importance of the story—it would affect the fortunes of prospective investors. He encouraged revelation of the details.

They had to decide immediately, as first they'd need to run the story by the legal department in case there was scope for a defamation action and contempt of court.

But the facts were indisputable: death due to a suspected drug overdose had occurred on flamboyant businessman Eric Schwartz's boat; a police investigation was underway; several people were implicated; Eric Schwartz and Rachael Quinlan had disappeared, and were not returning phone calls, and no-one knew where they were.

At least an immediate release of this information would alert readers to a follow-up story when more evidence came to light. The financial editor decided to run with the story, including a reference to the circle of high-profile people who were connected to Eric Schwartz. The headline would be: 'Will the Ship Float?'

Michael Simpson was attached to the phone, his tensed lower jaw exposing his bottom teeth in a grimace, and making the tendons in his neck stand out. He couldn't get through to Bruce, whose number he had from the police report taken at Kings Cross police station, and was getting increasingly desperate. He had his people phone around for Eric Schwartz and Rachael Quinlan and they confirmed the lead that Dieter had given him. Nobody knew where they were. Mobile phones were not responding. Something was up, and it was up in a small town called Marulan. He decided that he'd better get going, and that he would remain connected by telephone to his office. The local constable at Marulan confirmed that Bruce Chadwick was well known in the area, and lived out at Canyonleigh Road, ten kilometres from the township. It was ten-thirty on Tuesday morning before Detective Simpson left for Marulan.

It was about ten-thirty on Monday evening when events unfolded within the cabin. Henry gleaned that Eric was not completely deranged. The man was out of control, but hopefully not stupid, and had nothing to gain from killing people. He merely wanted to keep things away from the press and the police until midday on Thursday, when Palamountain would register its first transactions as a listed public company. Henry thought that it may be Eric's strategy to sell a large percentage of his shares on opening, and thereby make his pile of money. Whatever happened thereafter was in the lap of the gods.

Eric assumed a directorial attitude. Sitting in an armchair, legs crossed, cradling a glass of red wine, he began a speech. All the victims were aligned on one side, while Eric and Dennis sat opposite.

Henry thought that the hiss from the pressure lantern was a suitable background noise. Henry and Rosie were still gagged and blindfolded, she sitting in an undignified position in her slip, while Rachael and Alex sat on the floor, arms clasped around their knees, looking up at Eric.

'What a stupid lot you all are. I know that you're all going to get rich in the float, and here you are, sitting at Daddy's knee, with the river of gold days away, and you would risk it all? Dennis and I are only here to protect you from yourselves. That's why I hit you in anger, Rachael. I couldn't believe that you could be so stupid,' he said.

Alex cleared his throat. 'Umm, could you untie Henry and Rosie. It's silly for them to be sitting like that, don't you think?'

Eric stared at Alex. 'Dennis, this Bozo here has to be the strangest marshmallow I've ever seen.'

'He's the king of meat pies, didn't you know?' Dennis said. Dennis, in his mid-forties, was bloated and flabby from a desk-bound life nurtured on meat pies.

'Meat pies? He doesn't look like a carnivore. Okay, Bozo, go untie your friends.' Eric grinned.

Alex untied Henry and Rosie, who rubbed their wrists and ankles. Rosie looked fiercely at Eric. 'Would your royal haughtiness allow me to get another sheet?'

'A cheeky fat person? Oh goodie. What's your name, Fatso?'

'I don't believe I have to give you my personal details — you've seen enough of them already,' she replied icily.

'And a riveting look it was.' Eric smiled as he watched her draping another sheet around herself. 'Isn't it interesting that you're all sitting there like mackerel, while I sit using only my voice as a weapon. Have I threatened you? Do I have a gun? You're marshmallows, snivelling, weak shoestrings. I crack my knuckles, and you shiver in fear. And I thought you were different, Rachael. You all have Rachael to blame for this inconvenience.'

'What do you want to do with us?' Henry asked.

'Henry ... you're the strangest character I've met. Strange at school, now even more hopeless. You have a bit of a brain, but it's gone walkabout.'

'Eric, the fact that you don't understand him tells me everything,' Rachael said coldly.

'As for you, my own true love, I clearly misjudged you. I thought you were a winner.'

'You reckon *you're* a winner?' Alex said.

'Bozo! Who put you together? You look like a wheelbarrow of human spare parts. If a committee designed the camel, you must have been designed by a soccer crowd,' Eric said and choked on his own joke.

'Well, we can sit and insult each other all night,' Henry said.

Eric sucked air and checked his watch. 'You're right, for once, Sinkers. We're going to escort you away from this luxury. But just excuse me a minute.'

'You can't leave,' Dennis said.

'Dennis, now don't you become a marshmallow. Where's the loo? Come on, even you lot have to relieve yourselves sometime. Oh, doesn't matter. The whole place is a toilet.'

'Outside right,' Alex said.

'Dennis, take that shovel and stand over them. They try anything, belt them on the head.' Eric chuckled, and opened the door.

Dennis brandished the shovel above Alex's head. He stood side-on to Rosie. She looked at Henry and then, in an instant, raised both her legs and horse-kicked Dennis in the thigh, sending him staggering against the wall. Henry and Alex jumped up, Rosie grabbed Dennis's arm holding the shovel, and Alex put a headlock on him. Rosie bit his arm and Dennis yelled, dropping the shovel. Henry picked it up just as Eric raced back inside doing up his fly.

Henry, shovel raised, turned to Eric, who stood at the door scowling.

'Now, now. You are a silly lot.' Eric reached inside his pocket and pulled out a gun. 'Put it down, Henry.'

Henry dropped the shovel.

'You're a desperate, stupid man, Eric,' Rachael said.

'Sit down, all of you,' Eric said tiredly. 'Enough horseplay. You all right Dennis?'

'Yeah,' Dennis mumbled, rubbing his arm.

'Okay. I'm going to get you to drive the cars. Henry, you drive the BMW with Dennis. Alex, I presume that heap outside is yours. You drive the Merc. Rachael, Fatso, with me in the Merc. Any stupid moves ... Now get going!'

'Wait just a bloody minute!' Rosie screamed, causing everybody to freeze in astonishment. 'I have to go to the loo myself, if you *don't* mind.'

This took the heat out of the moment.

'I'll embarrass myself. I wouldn't want to destroy your beautiful car, Mr High and Mighty.' Rosie stood with the sheet around her, moving from foot to foot.

'Er, all right. But hurry up,' Eric said gruffly.

Rosie took a torch, shuffled outside and approached the leaning tower of dunny. It was dark and she gingerly shoved open the door to peer inside, shuddering at the cobweb-festooned interior. She threw off her sheet and attempted to enter, barely able to squeeze past the door sideways. This approach wasn't going to work and she tried a rear-end-first thrust. The whole point was to wedge herself tightly inside, to waste time and frustrate Eric. Summoning her will, she heaved her rear end through the door, wrinkling her nose.

After five minutes of restless waiting, Eric gave Dennis his gun and went outside. 'Fatso, you still alive? What's keeping you?' he yelled angrily.

'Sorry, Mr, umm, Eric. I'm stuck. Can't get out. It's so embarrassing.' She feigned a sob.

'What? You're joking!' Eric tore open the door and was blinded by Rosie's flashlight. 'Give me the light,' he snarled.

'God, you have no shame. Can't a woman have a second of bloody privacy?' Rosie screamed at him.

'Listen here Fatso ...' Eric ran out of steam. 'Well, hurry bloody up!' he sighed, and shut the door, folding his arms in a huff.

Rosie started to sob again.

'Shit!' Eric yelled and raced back inside the cabin.

'What's happening?' Dennis asked.

'Fatso's stuck in the bloody toilet, would you believe?' Eric mumbled and grabbed the shovel.

'Is she all right?' Henry asked as Eric sped out of the door. 'You know she has a weak heart.'

Eric muttered, 'Weak heart, hey,' to himself as he again stood outside the dunny. He found a gap in the logs and began to prise them apart.

'What do you think you're doing?' Rosie sobbed.

'Shut up!'

Eric strained to use the shovel as a lever. Finally, seeing that this would not work, he put his shoulder to the whole thing and attempted to rock it. Remarkably, and because the structure was not secured to the ground, the entire dunny moved quite easily.

'Hey! What're you doing?'

'You either come out voluntarily, or I'll just push it over,' he said through gritted teeth.

'Okay, okay,' Rosie said, and pushed herself out like a wine cork.

Henry rushed over to embrace her as she entered the cabin. 'You all right?'

They were shunted outside, Eric brandishing his revolver like a cowboy. As they opened the car doors, Henry called out to Alex to remember to put on his seat belt, and Alex nodded, thumbs up, a fleeting look of incomprehension sweeping his face.

- 42 -

Horace had left messages on Henry's answering machine. The auction was due the next week, Tuesday, and there were matters to be discussed. There was no answer at Rosie's. Alex's mother had no idea what had become of Alex. 'He's never been away this long without telling me.' Bruce wasn't contactable either. His secretary said that he was at an executives' retreat. Phones were not permitted. Horace and Mary became frantic, and phoned the hospitals, then the police.

★

Henry thought furiously. He engaged the gears of the BMW and, with Dennis sitting beside him, followed the tail-lights of the Mercedes as they bounced their way over the dirt track to the gate. He watched Alex get out and undo the chain, then Alex drove forward to let Henry through. Henry stepped out and refastened the chain, then they continued.

This was definitely not what Henry had anticipated. The fact that they were being taken somewhere else was nerve-racking. He oscillated between feelings of disaster and calm, trying to assess Eric's character, coming back to the conclusion that Eric was likely only to hold them for some days. Until the float. But kidnapping was a serious crime. How could he possibly think he would get away with it? He must be planning to leave the country with his winnings. Then nothing made sense, and Henry's fertile imagination saw them all rot, tied up in a house in the bush.

He spoke not a word to Dennis, and wondered whether to appeal to him on some human level. The tail-lights of the Mercedes were shrouded in dust.

Inside the Mercedes, Alex was preoccupied with his own assessment of their plight. Of course he had never driven a car like this one, and he was immensely impressed. He glanced across occasionally at Rosie, who stared grimly out of the windscreen. Then he thought about Henry's last comment. 'Fasten your seatbelts' — why would Henry say that? He checked to see that both Rosie's and Rachael's seatbelts were fastened, then looked in the rear vision mirror and saw Henry driving dangerously close to his tail.

Eric had put the gun back in his pocket and sat leaning forward directly behind Alex, watching Alex closely and observing the road ahead.

They turned left onto the paved road leading to Marulan and the freeway to Sydney. The Mercedes picked up speed, and Henry followed closely, as Dennis instructed him. The speedometer climbed to one hundred. Henry glanced down and saw that Alex was accelerating, then followed in kind. One hundred and ten, twenty. Dennis started to get anxious.

Inside the Mercedes Alex decided to act. He pushed his foot to the floor, thinking he understood what Henry had been trying to say. Eric yelled at him to slow down, then put his arm around Alex's neck from behind and began to apply pressure. Rachael pounced on Eric, and he lashed out with his free hand, sending her sprawling back in her seat. Rosie strained to bite Eric's hand from her position in the front seat. He shoved at her head with his open hand, and pushed her heavily against the side of the car. Alex gagged and dropped his foot from the accelerator.

Henry was following along at one hundred when the Mercedes slowed. He pressed on the horn, braked and braced himself as he ran into the back of the Mercedes with an enormous crash and a tearing jolt. The BMW's air bag inflated, much to Henry's surprise. The Mercedes bucked into the air, slewed sideways, and the two cars careered into a ditch.

Henry had slowed to about eighty at the point of impact, with the Mercedes still travelling. He hadn't wanted to risk injury to the others. As it was, he had prayed that they would brace themselves when he pressed down on the horn. But the impact had been far more savage than Henry expected. Steam hissed from the front of the BMW, which was a mess of crushed metal. Henry looked quickly at Dennis, who sat, mouth open, eyeballing his air bag.

Henry squeezed past the inflated bag and ran to the Mercedes. Eric had bashed his head against Alex's headrest, and sat groggily holding his forehead. Henry opened Alex's door. Alex had hit his head on the steering wheel, but not badly. He groaned, as he ran his fingers over an emerging bruise. Rachael was slumped on her side, motionless.

Henry raced around to Rosie's door. He yanked it open, and Rosie rotated her head rubbing her neck with her hand.

Henry shouted, 'You all right, Alex?' as he examined Rosie.

Alex staggered out of the seat and looked about, delicately upright.

Dennis squeezed out of the car. Alex saw him approach, and looked about for something hard to hit him with. He grabbed a rock from the side of the road. Dennis opened the Merc's door and checked Eric, who was still moaning and holding his head. Alex lifted the rock and brought it down on Dennis's head with a crunch. As Dennis collapsed on the road beside the car, Eric fumbled for his seatbelt, pushed his legs out of the door, then started to get out. Alex's feet almost left the ground as he raised the rock above his head.

The sound was rather off-putting. Eric crumpled in a heap beside Dennis. Alex stepped back to survey his handiwork, then grabbed the revolver out of Eric's pocket and shoved it in his own.

Henry was preoccupied with Rosie, but had absorbed the spectacle of Alex unleashing his anger. 'Well done, Alex,' he yelled.

Rosie summoned a feeble smile. 'Henry? What happened?'

Alex stepped around the car and opened Rachael's door. She was starting to stir, and pushed on the seat to sit up.

'You okay, Rachael?'

'Oh, my head,' she moaned, feeling the back of her neck.

The ping of cooling metal and hiss of steam were the only sounds to be heard as they stood on the deserted road in a moment of collective thought. Minutes later, headlights approached from the direction of Marulan.

A Land Rover pulled up, and a shrivelled old man lowered the window. Alex stood next to it and began an explanation. He saw a wobbly look in the old man's eyes.

'Whadyasay?'

Alex tried again, but the old man merely stared at Alex, then looked at the crushed cars. 'Jeez. Accident?'

'This guy's useless. Drunk as a skunk,' Alex said.

The old man stepped out of his car, leaving the engine

running, and staggered in their direction. His initial momentum propelled him at some degrees from the main event, and he followed his left shoulder into the ditch, where he fell over.

'God, what's come over the world?' Alex muttered, and jumped into the Land Rover to drive it to the side of the road.

Henry confirmed that neither Rosie nor Rachael had suffered serious injury, then examined the rear end of the Mercedes. It was buckled beyond recognition. He looked at the old man's Land Rover, which had a front cabin and a utility tray at the rear. He checked the tray as best he could in the light still shed by the headlights of the Mercedes, and found some jump-start leads. 'Alex. We have to tie Eric up.'

With some effort Henry pulled Eric's arms behind him, and began to wind the cable tightly around Eric's hands. Henry's and Alex's heads were in close contact as they bent over Eric's body, and Henry looked up into Alex's face. They grinned at each other like schoolboys.

Henry had to use all his strength to twist the jump leads around Eric's hands. He then examined Eric's head, which was dribbling blood onto the road. 'God, you really thumped him, Alex.'

'Is he all right?'

'Yeah. Head his size, you could have used a sledge-hammer and made no impression. He'll be sore when he wakes up.'

'What about Dennis?' Alex asked.

'Better tie him up too,' Henry said.

The old man was hovering over them. 'Who's the prisna? Is that a crim?' he slurred. 'Yus ain't police are yus?' He looked at Alex quizzically and seemed satisfied on that score, particularly when he noticed Rosie getting out of the car in her sheet.

Rosie walked slowly around the car, and there began a standing around and recollection of events. It was all so unreal, Henry said.

'I figured you were trying to tell me something, Henry.

Quick thinking about the seat belts. I was expecting a crash. You can think like a snake when you have to,' Alex said.

In the meantime Henry found some old oily rope inside the man's Land Rover and tied Dennis's arms behind his back.

The old man had watched the bizarre activity as if in a dream, wobbling around, wringing his hands. 'Yus kipnapers? Umm, I'm, umm goin now,' he said, and started for the Land Rover.

Henry led him by the elbow to sit down in the back seat of the Mercedes.

'Are ya gonna kipnap me too?'

'No, just wait a sec. You shouldn't be driving anyhow,' Henry said.

Dennis stirred and started to moan. They bent over him and propped him up against the side of the car. He complained of a massive headache. Blood oozed down his face. Eric was told to sit down next to Dennis, and he likewise took some time to regain focus. His hair was matted with blood that had run down one side of his face, making him look far more damaged than he actually was. Henry had guessed correctly that Alex's thin arms could hardly deliver a deathly blow.

Between them Rosie, Alex and Henry decided that they would pile everybody into the Land Rover and head back to the cabin. It could be ages before another vehicle came along. There began a debate about calling the police. The mobile phones were useable near Marulan, but would not work when back in the cabin. Rosie knew that the police station in Marulan was unmanned at night. They couldn't drive to Goulburn. Tiredly Henry suggested they use the wall phone in the cabin.

They prodded Eric and Dennis to their feet and told them to wriggle onto the back tray. The old man was confused about this latest twist and began to protest. Henry and Alex escorted him to the utility tray.

'Can't drive it from there,' the man slurred.

'You're not driving it. We're just going to Bruce Chadwick's cabin for a while. You can leave from there,' Henry said.

'Bruce? I know him. Is he here?' He looked around.

With some turning him around and some shoving and prodding, the old man crawled up and looked disbelievingly at Eric and Dennis sitting with their backs against the driving cabin.

'Hey, yus bleedin.' Then the old man's bloodshot eyes surveyed Rosie as she beached herself like a whale on the tray, propelled by a rear-end shove from Henry.

Everyone was sitting on top of everyone else and Henry wondered whether the Land Rover could handle the load. It was too tight a fit for Rosie in the front with Rachael and Alex, and he had to be in the back to keep an eye on Eric, who looked like a prizefighter who had lost his world ranking. Blood was still oozing down his face, and his head hung, probably from concussion, Henry thought. Dennis stared at his fellow passengers as if seeing them for the first time.

Alex turned the key, yelled out of the window for everybody to hold on, and the Land Rover lurched forward.

The trip was uncomfortable in the extreme for the mass of humanity clinging to the rear tray, but soon they were bumping their way up the dirt track to the cabin. Alex laughingly began a rendition of 'Waltzing Matilda', changing the words to 'Waltzing ta kill ya'.

Henry, Alex and Rosie basked in their relief. Never had the cabin looked so good. Henry immediately went to the phone. 'The line's been cut.'

They would have to wait until morning. Henry would drive the old man's truck to the police station.

The cabin assumed a festive air as they shed the stress of their ordeal. The old farmer was pleased to join the party. It was Eric's turn to be tied to the chair, and he accepted his fate with a hangdog expression quite at odds with his former all-conquering mien.

The old man slumped back in an armchair and began an open-mouthed snore that shook the timbers of the cabin.

The fire popped and spluttered, Alex opened some tins of food, and Henry filled Eric's glass with wine. He declined with a grunt.

The events had taken their toll and it came time to think about sleep, and how to guard Eric and Dennis. Rachael wiped the congealed blood from their faces.

'I want to talk to you all,' Eric said.

'Talk away,' Henry said, sitting next to Rosie on the sofa, with Alex on her other side.

'How much would you be likely to make in a lifetime?' Eric asked sullenly.

'Who are you asking?' Henry said.

'You, Henry,' Eric answered.

'I would expect to write two or three articles a week,' Henry replied.

'You know what I mean,' Eric said.

'What's the point of such a stupid question?' Alex said.

'I can make you all rich beyond your dreams.'

Rachael came in: 'Eric, you never give up, do you? Can't you see that these people don't speak the same language.'

There was loud staccato snoring as the old man climbed the steps to apnoea, then everybody watched, alarmed, as his breathing stopped altogether. Then breath was vented in a cascading sigh, adding a surreal quality to Rachael's remark.

Henry and Alex would take shifts of two hours each to keep watch. Henry checked Eric's and Dennis's hands and tied more rope around their arms and legs. He found some aspirin for their sore heads and spooned food into their mouths. As Henry bent over Eric, spoon poised, he looked into Eric's desperate eyes. 'Who's the marshmallow, Eric?'

- 43 -

Tuesday morning was heralded by the cackle of a kookaburra. It was also ushered in by an article in the *Sydney Morning Herald*. Henry checked his watch. It was six-thirty, and he looked down from the loft above the kitchen to wink at Alex, who was sitting watching Eric, Dennis and the old man snoring together like an Easter Island choir.

'My shift,' Henry said.

By ten in the morning, breakfast had been consumed, and Rachael said that she had never enjoyed baked beans so much in her life. Henry was alert to a whispered conversation between Eric and Rachael, and wondered about that. Dennis complained of extreme pain in his back and wrists and Henry checked to see whether the ropes were cutting off the supply of blood to his hands. There appeared to be no problem. Eric sat staring into space like a prisoner of war. The old man had struggled to his feet and wondered where he was.

Henry asked him to drive him to Marulan – he wanted to make a phone call and make sure the old man was capable of finding his way back home. As Henry and the old man were about to leave the cabin, Henry paused at the door and motioned to Alex to come outside.

'Alex, this is probably my paranoia speaking, but keep an eye on Rachael.'

'Say again?'

'I saw her whispering to Eric. Hasn't she changed sides rather quickly?'

'Crap! She's not acting, Henry . . .'

'I hope you're right. Don't let her out of your sight until I get back. Just a precaution. I rather like her, and I hope I'm wrong. Money does strange things to these people.'

★

By eleven o'clock Henry was sitting opposite the constable in charge of the Marulan police station. He was informed that Detective-sergeant Simpson was on his way. Messages were relayed, and Henry spoke to Simpson by phone. As best he could, he narrated the events, needing to repeat himself, as his fuzzy brain mangled bits of the story.

Simpson, together with Detective-constable Cunningham, the local constable and Henry drove to the cabin in the early afternoon. Henry had handed over Eric's revolver to Simpson and begun to intercede on behalf of Rachael, explaining that she had been threatened by Eric to fall into line. Simpson accepted it all with a policeman's stoicism.

As the car approached the cabin Alex, Rachael and Rosie stood on the verandah grinning like lottery winners.

'Had yourselves quite an adventure?' Simpson said, as he stepped out.

'Just a typical day for us, sergeant,' Alex grinned, and Simpson recognised the strange excitable chap he had first seen at the Kings Cross police station.

'You again?'

They trooped inside and the policemen stood over Eric and Dennis. Simpson had his hands on his hips as he glared at Eric. 'So Mr Schwartz, we meet again.'

Smudged and congealed streaks of blood on Eric's face were combined with a bluish yellow bruise that had started to puff up one side of his forehead.

'You are charged with perverting the course of justice, kidnapping, and, what else precisely?' Simpson turned to his offsider. He turned back to Eric and rather formally advised him of his right to remain silent.

Dennis looked almost as bad as Eric, and started to shake. 'I had nothing to do with it, sir. Schwartz blackmailed me, forced me to go along,' he spluttered.

'Oh, blackmail is it? Add that to the list,' Simpson said, and couldn't prevent a smirk forming at the edges of his mouth.

Simpson turned to Rachael and asked her to follow him out of the cabin, telling the officers to untie Eric and Dennis from the chairs and handcuff them. Then he led Rachael to the edge of the rocky outcrop. 'I figure you must be worried, Ms Quinlan,' he said.

'Very.' Rachael stood, looking down the slope, seeing her hiding spot in daylight for the first time.

'Henry Sinclair told me what happened, and he has done his best to speak for you. You should have told the truth on the night of the girl's death, you know that. I happen to believe him, but ask you to act as a witness. I can't guarantee how it will go for you when all this hits the courts,' he said, looking in the distance.

'Of course I'll be a witness. I want that bastard behind bars more than you know.'

'I think I can guess,' Simpson said. 'He had sex with the girl on the night.'

Rachael flinched, and closed her eyes.

'She was pregnant,' the detective said.

'With Eric's child?'

'We don't know yet. And another thing. There was an article in the *Herald* this morning.'

There was one item on Simpson's agenda that he was saving for last. He wanted to savour it. Eric's offsider, Dennis, had no stomach for his ordeal, and was primed for some serious inter-rogation, particularly while his defences were at rock bottom and he was without legal representation.

Simpson and Rachael again entered the cabin, and he had a quick word with Detective Cunningham. Cunningham escorted Eric out to the police car, and asked the constable from Marulan to keep an eye on him. The two detectives then asked everybody to vacate the cabin and confronted Dennis.

Simpson let it be known that he was tired, dog tired, and wished to go home. He asked Dennis if he had anything to say, warning him that anything he said could be used as evidence. Dennis sat handcuffed in an armchair, his face bloated from fatigue and worry.

'You could make it easier for yourself. You already mentioned that there was blackmail involved, which could get you off the hook to some extent. I'm very keen to find out whether Henry Sinclair and his friends have anything to worry about. I think you could show some cooperation, which Detective Cunningham and I will point out in court. Now, isn't it true that the drugs were planted in Sinclair's apartment?'

'Umm, look Sergeant, I, this is an enormous humiliation. My wife and kids . . .' Dennis swallowed.

'Well? Detective Simpson is trying to help you. You've got to pull yourself together,' Cunningham said, with aggression.

'Yes. The drugs were planted. Eric made me do it.'

'Did Sinclair have anything whatever to do with the girl's death?' Simpson asked.

'Umm, I, I believe not.'

'You believe not? That's not good enough. I'm sure you know not.'

'Yes.'

- 44 -

How Alex had driven the Kombi without falling asleep was a miracle, because Henry, Rachael and Rosie slept all the way back to Sydney. Rachael asked that she be dropped off to catch a cab in Liverpool. 'By the time this old bomb makes it, I'll be a grandmother,' she laughed in parting. 'I'll be in touch soon. Thank you for everything – from the bottom of my heart.'

Henry, Alex and Rosie trooped into Henry's apartment and Henry turned on his answering machine. Horace's multiple messages of concern were interspersed with ones from Andy and Louise. Bruce and Beth both rang, concerned. Bruce apologised, saying he had been uncontactable. Then Dieter Lollinger's sing-song voice asked Henry to return his call, urgent.

Alex simply had to go home and sleep, and Rosie felt that she had better go see her employer and Bruce, and explain her absence. Henry had to assure his parents that all was well and he thought he had better do this face to face.

After Henry propped his bicycle against the wall he took off his helmet and smiled weakly at Horace. Horace gripped him by the shoulders and looked steadfastly into Henry's eyes. 'Where have you been son? We've been worried sick.'

Henry sat down in the living room after giving Mary a hug. She looked him over, brow furrowed, to tell him he'd lost weight, and looked awful, and whatever had he been doing?

Cup of tea in hand he sat on the lounge while Horace and Mary gave him their undivided attention.

'I've been in jail,' he said.

'Jail?' They looked at one another.

'I was accused of being a drug trafficker.'

'Explain that, son,' Horace said.

'Dealing in drugs, you know, selling them,' Henry said.

'Why would you want to do that, Henry?' Mary asked, edging forward in her chair, wringing her hands.

'I don't quite know how to tell you this, because I find it almost impossible to believe myself. I'm okay now, and you don't have to worry. Someone accused me wrongly, and Alex, Rosie and I got caught up in a police investigation when a girl overdosed.'

They were speaking a different language. Horace avoided reading bad-news stories. He often said that there were enough tragedies that he couldn't avoid hearing about to bother with researching even more of them. Any references to drugs were definitely off his reading list.

Henry watched total incomprehension besmirch the faces of his parents. It was intriguing to Henry that he could pen complex articles with great clarity, yet become lost in a maze of emotional clutter when it came to telling a story. He began again, and took his time.

Henry was aching for sleep. Nevertheless he persisted with his explanation and eventually hit pay-dirt as the deep furrows in Horace's brow softened to mere ditches, and they all sat pondering.

Then it came time for Horace to tell Henry about the developments on the auction front, and Henry asked whether they were resigned to the dismal prospect of moving out.

'Yes. Really no choice is there?' Horace said.

'There is faint hope,' Henry said. 'We'll get back *some* money from the Palamountain float. I can't say how much. You should know that Rosie, Alex and Bruce chipped in with what money they had to buy the cottage. I only need a ten per cent deposit, then I have a month to settle. We may yet be able to do it. If not, there'll be some money for you to live on.'

'They chipped in? Henry, what are you saying?' Mary asked.

Henry had no time to sleep. He thought it best to answer the phone messages, and dialled Dieter Lollinger's number. Eventually they connected, and a conversation ensued between two individuals whose body clocks came from the same time zone.

Dieter had hardly slept, so enthused was he by the revelations that he had uncovered. He was dying to speak to Henry, to piece together a story that was assuming fantastic proportions. Against Henry's protestations, he insisted that he drive right out to see him.

Then Henry returned Andy's call, wondering what sort of

reception he would receive. He felt an unusual degree of anticipation as he dialled the number.

'*Henry!* Jesus! I'm besieged with phone calls from Louise, let alone my political bosses. What the *hell* has been going on? I've had a journalist snooping around, I haven't had a clue what to say. That newspaper article was very damaging. Just because I'm connected with Eric. The float's tomorrow! For Christ's sake, we've all got our life's savings. What's your role in all this? Is Eric guilty? Will more shit hit the fan?' He was hysterical.

'Umm. I don't know what to say. Eric's in jail, I think.'

'Jail? God!' There was some heavy breathing, as if Andy was hyperventilating.

'I have to go. I'll have to speak to you later,' Henry said.

'No! *Don't go.* You have to explain. Christ, will there be more publicity?'

'Probably.'

'Jail? What for? Drugs? What's he been up to? I left the party on the yacht, and then heard nothing until this journo, and then the article ...'

'I'm very sorry, Andy. I haven't really slept for days. I've been in jail as well,' Henry said, and it occurred to him that he was not stuttering.

'*What?* And what's happened to Rachael? Can't find her.' The future Prime Minister was having his first real crisis. 'Look, I found out where you live, I'm on my way.'

It went almost identically with Louise, although her hysteria was more tied up with the bad publicity surrounding Palamountain and her lost fortune. She had no idea Henry had been in jail. Henry couldn't get a word in before she also signed off and said that she was on her way. Henry scratched his aching head and looked around at the domestic chaos, thinking that this was not the moment he would choose to have 'the group' around for afternoon tea. The apartment looked worse than it did the day they took off for the cabin, as if all his possessions had been animated through their liberation, never again voluntarily to be shunted back into cupboards and drawers. He lay down on the sofa and fell asleep.

The front door to Henry's apartment was ajar. Dieter Lollinger looked at the splintered wood, then knocked. And knocked. Eventually he entered and absorbed the unholy mess, then called out to Henry. He found him on the sofa and shook him awake.

'Wha, what?' Henry slowly sat up.

'Sorry, Henry. I'm probably as tired as you. Can we talk?'

Henry made a cup of tea, glanced at his watch and wondered how long he'd been asleep. Not long, and he attempted to clear the curtain of fog from his brain.

He looked across at Dieter's curly black locks and the dark eyebrows arching for answers. 'It's quite a story. Will you be publishing it in tomorrow's paper?'

'Front page,' he said.

Henry started to tell him everything. Eric's rampage, the kidnapping, the future PM's bad publicity – when suddenly in walked Louise, dressed in her business suit. No sooner had she taken in the turmoil with open mouth than Dieter introduced himself, and she sat down, deflated, unsure how to proceed with the enemy sitting pen poised over his notebook. Then she seemed to recover from her shock and suggested she wait outside. In the midst of getting up to leave, there was a loud knock and Andy strode into the room, distinguished in a grey suit.

'Andy?'

'Louise?'

Everybody stood in the available space, which was not very available – they were looking down at their feet, conscious of stepping on Henry's underwear. Then there ensued some very close-quartered eye-gazing. Henry was still dressed in Bruce's clothes, and his unshaven face and haggard expression blended well with his domestic circumstances.

229

Andy took charge, and asked who Dieter was.

'We've spoken on the telephone, Mr Finley,' Dieter said.

'Have we?'

'Andy, we should just go outside a minute.' Louise led Andy by the elbow, with some force, while Andy stared at Louise's hand as if it were some evil thing. 'We'll be down on the street,' Louise said as they left.

Henry couldn't help the slightest smile forming at the corner of his mouth as he watched the chastened exit. He remembered Andy's confident outburst in which he boasted about his politician's skill at sniffing all the angles. Andy was being bisected by his own geometry, and it was not a good look.

'God, Henry, that was "the group" forming a tight defence. Andrew Finley I recognise, who was the woman?'

'Louise Hatfield, she's my agent.'

'Say again?' Dieter was now at sea.

'Umm, yes. Well, I've written a book about the sharemarket and, oh it would take too long to explain.'

'Henry, you're a character, if you don't mind me saying. Are you telling me that that woman is important to you?'

'She has a tough job. Too many authors all wanting her attention. Is she important to me? I don't really know. She thinks my book will do well.'

'When does it come out?'

'Soon, I think.'

'So you're not afraid of having her exposed as part of "the group"?'

'Well, I don't know whether she's done anything wrong. I'd leave her out of it, but that's your decision.'

'Henry, I have it from the editor that the float of Palamountain will crash. He's helping me with the story and if I get it published tomorrow, then it's curtains. Palamountain is essentially Eric and his believers.'

'I know. I have shares in Palamountain.'

'*What?*'

Henry explained his investment and how it arose. Dieter wrote it all down.

'So let me get this right. You're trying to save your parents' cottage. All your friends have invested. You stand to go down the, how would you say, plug? So does your parents' cottage?'

'Yes.'

'In a nutshell, you have an awful lot riding on the success of this float?'

'Yes.'

'Why are you talking to me?'

'Because ordinary people are going to suffer when this mess comes out.'

'But ordinary investors are already sucked in.'

'We all deserve what's coming to us.'

Dieter, judging by his expression, obviously needed time to reflect on Henry's revelation, and got up to take his leave. 'Henry, I don't know how my editor will treat this story. Have you been contacted by the other papers? We may have a scoop.'

'Nobody else.'

'Thanks.'

'It's okay.'

After Dieter left, Henry had to confront the unpalatable next step of inviting Andy and Louise back into his apartment. He sighed heavily, trudged down the stairs and found them standing under a tree, looking besieged. They trooped back up and Henry apologised for the mess, making room for them to sit down.

'Henry, we really need an explanation,' Louise said.

Henry sat forward in his armchair and wiped his face with his hand. He repeated his story and watched the expressions change from horror to worse.

'I'm finished,' Andy whispered, white as a sheet. 'Labour will crucify me. Parliamentary privilege. Any mention of drugs ...'

'We've lost our life's savings, Andy,' Louise mumbled, her face etched like a granite slab. 'What will happen to the share price, Andy?'

'If this comes out in tomorrow's paper, you can expect sellers to dump the stock on opening. It will hit rock bottom. We'd better get our sell orders in. Henry, I want to ask for your honest opinion. Is there any chance you can get that little journalist, God, just a bloody kid, to hold off on his story for just one day? I'd make it worth your while,' Andy said, and looked at Henry expectantly.

Henry shook his head. Slowly he looked at their hopeful faces. He got up, his body tight with anger. He walked to the door and opened it. 'Get out. All you two can think about is your reputation and your money.'

- 45 -

Henry set the alarm for nine in the morning. He'd phoned Rosie after Andy and Louise left and discovered that she had already held lengthy telephone calls with Beth and Bruce. He asked her to organise a meeting in his apartment for ten-thirty, to watch the float on his computer. He quickly mentioned the visits he'd just had, and ended by saying that he was bushed, but that it would all be out in the paper the following morning.

Henry muffled the alarm clock's piercing beep with a wooden hand. He wanted only to turn over and sleep some more. The day's importance then imprinted itself, and he dragged himself out of bed. His first plan was to fetch a copy of the morning paper and see what Dieter Lollinger had made of the story.

As he staggered to the shops he felt like his was the walk of a dead man. Maybe a wombat would waddle unknowingly to its fate? And that fate might be a truck bearing down a highway, ready to splatter the poor animal all over the road. He felt as if his private life was about to be revealed on prime time television, and that somehow he stood to suffer, no matter how innocent his involvement may have been. He knew enough about newspapers to be worried that their slant was unpredictable. As a man who had spent his public life sheltered behind a nom de plum, his feelings were confused indeed. He had a considerable readership, of that there was no doubt, but he had never really thought about it because his writing was depersonalised, and people only knew him for his opinions. This was different.

All these feelings were knotted together as he approached the news stand, and he hovered, wondering if there would be a crowd of people all reading about him, ready to point and jeer. He felt naked.

Then, closer to the point of picking up the *Herald*, and still averting his eyes from the headlines, he had a thought. Maybe the moment of opening the paper should be shared with the others? No. They already would have seen the paper. If the story had a positive slant on Henry, surely they would have phoned. And if he was crucified along with Eric and Palamountain they would have done nothing? Just what did he expect?

He walked out of the shop and watched from afar as people picked up the paper. Certainly the news was not like a declaration of war on Indonesia, judging by the way people tucked the paper under their arms. It was tantalising, fascinating for him to speculate on his deliverance or execution.

He turned around and walked home, thinking that his feelings were too interesting not to share. If only Alex and Rosie were with him. He needed them to witness his apprehension. They'd tell him that he'd flipped his lid to be so worried.

At ten-thirty Alex and Rosie arrived together, brandishing the morning paper. 'How's it going Henry? Sleep well?' Alex grinned as he walked inside.

Henry was fixated on the newspaper that Alex had tucked under his arm. He gave Rosie a kiss.

'Beth and Bruce should be here in a minute. You look strange. Anything wrong?' Rosie asked.

'I'm glad you're here. I haven't had the courage to open the paper,' he said sheepishly.

'You're a nutter Henry.' Alex smiled and sat down next to him. He opened the paper to a headline story: 'A Lone Sailor on the Ship of Greed'.

Henry was shocked. He adjusted his glasses and read: 'This morning at eleven o'clock another biotech hopeful, Palamountain Ltd, will have its debut on the stockmarket. It has become mired in tragedy and deceit, and has thrown up a hero and a villain.' He looked up to see Rosie's adoring smile.

'Henry, you're a bloody hero,' Alex said.

On close reading it appeared that Dieter Lollinger had interpreted Henry's quest to save his parents' house as a mirror image of the greed and violence perpetrated by Eric. Dieter and his editor had given Eric and the float of Palamountain a mighty broadside, warning investors to tread carefully. Each member of 'the group', except Louise, was mentioned.

Henry became agitated as he read the address of his parents' cottage in Malabar, and that next week would see an auction which, if successful, would allow Henry's retired parents to live out their lives where they wanted to live.

With the arrival of Bruce and Beth, and the retelling of stories about their ordeal, they gathered around the computer screen to watch the debacle.

Rosie was sitting on one of Henry's old kitchen chairs which actually belonged in a 1950s' kitchen and looked too spindly to support her weight. She was twisting the ring on her finger, staring at the computer screen, a sheen of perspiration on her forehead evidence of the level of tension. Beth, with her prospective home and her mother's savings at stake, shifted from foot to foot in the background chewing her fingernails. Bruce, trying to soften the blow, offered fatalistic comments. Alex kept mumbling that it was their collective karma to be poor. What was the worst that could happen? They could become rich?

Henry had primed everybody to expect a disaster. He reminded them that they had purchased the shares at fifty cents. Alex had sixty thousand, Rosie twenty thousand, and Bruce one hundred and sixty thousand. The scandal would most likely mean that the shares would debut at perhaps forty cents. The question was whether there was any interstate interest which was not yet as exposed to the Sydney Palamountain scandal.

Henry had counselled everybody to place sell orders at thirty-five cents. He hoped they could salvage something on the way down, and that perhaps that the initial price would fall through forty cents. He was wrong, and they watched with a collective sucking in of air as the price opened at thirty cents and found resistance at eighteen cents. People were dumping the stock.

'Shit!' Alex said. 'My thirty thousand dollars is now ten thousand eight hundred. I'm still rich!'

'Should we sell, Henry?' Rosie asked.

'Bruce, Beth, I'm most worried for you,' Henry said.

'Wait a while Henry. You remember what happened last time. The price will come back up,' Beth said confidently.

'Maybe,' Henry said. 'The market might think that the shares have been oversold.'

'Greed will come back to haunt with a vengeance,' Alex said ghoulishly. 'Trouble, trouble, toil and bubble, buy, buy, buy you silly investors.' He waved his arms over the screen.

'Alex, you're a wizard,' Beth said, as the price started to recover.

Alex milked his power for all it was worth, pulling at the screen with both hands, cackling like a witch, and the price continued to recover.

'Now, Henry,' Beth said, as the price faltered at twenty-nine cents.

Henry looked at everybody. Bruce nodded, and Henry pressed the sell key.

It took half an hour before all shares were sold. They sat on losses averaging forty per cent, and Henry's fifty thousand dollars had been reduced to twenty-seven thousand. At the end of the day, Palamountain shares were trading at sixteen cents.

'What an interesting way to lose money,' Alex said quietly.

- 46 -

Following the collapse of Palamountain the mood was not exactly festive. There were a few 'Oh wells', and a number of 'Could have been worses', but there was not a lot to say. The exercise had been a gigantic failure, and Henry felt responsible. As the unhappy investors trudged out of Henry's apartment in a state of gloom, he mumbled apologies, and everybody agreed that they would be in touch over the weekend. Rosie desperately wanted to stay over, but sensed that Henry needed to be alone. The auction for the cottage was doomed, because it was obvious now that Henry would be unable to bid.

An hour after Henry closed the door on Rosie and Alex, the phone rang. He wondered whether to answer it, then thought he would monitor the call. He was in no mood to talk to anyone.

'Henry. Hugo. You're a star ...'

Henry raced to intercept the call. 'H-Hugo,' he said, pressing the stop button on his answer machine.

'How are you Henry?'

'Th-the more important question is, h-how are *you*?'

'Been better. Look, time I came over for a chat. Read that the cottage will go under the hammer next week. The newspaper's made you into a hero, Henry.'

'W-when?'

'What when?'

'W-when are you coming over?'

'No time like the present.'

'Umm, sure, come on over.' Henry put the receiver down, shaking.

Whatever stress had been induced by financial failure, it was a trifle. He rushed around the apartment picking up clothes. He then waited, sitting at the kitchen table, his research folder on Huntington's disease staring at him. There was a knock on the door.

He had not seen Hugo for six years. As he stood in the living room and watched his twin brother enter, he felt his heart pound.

'So, baby brother, how goes it?'

'Umm, g-good, well, o-okay.' Henry was flustered.

'Going to get me a cup of tea?'

Hugo had aged, terribly. He seemed to move normally and sat down on the lounge. Nonchalantly he stretched his arms out on the backrest, staring at Henry. 'Are you pleased to see me? You still look a mess, young brother, and your humble abode is even more humble.'

'Umm . . .'

Hugo's face contorted itself in a grotesque spasm, then his hands began to grope the air. He launched himself from the lounge, then back down, crossed and uncrossed his legs, all the while grimacing and contorting his face. Nothing was still; a bundle of human parts in constant motion.

His face was still recognisable for its good looks. Hugo's large brown eyes were wrestling Henry's in an unflinching show of sibling superiority. It was as if Hugo was trying to dominate Henry all over again, while drowning in his own desperate condition. The disease was approaching the beginning of the end, and Henry could see that before too long Hugo would need constant care.

'Tea?' Henry scurried into the kitchen and put the kettle on.

The timing was sweet. Hugo could not have orchestrated a more opportune time to catch Henry at a low point.

Henry placed the tea in front of Hugo. 'White with one?'

'You remember? What else do you remember, dear brother? Do you recall that I was once able to sit without my body doing this crazy dance? Do you realise that I am coherent? In spite of the way I act, my brain is still functioning? On and off?'

Hugo's body again denied him and began another round of awful jerking. 'Henry, I give myself about eight years. You've done the research. You know that most people commit suicide before it gets too bad. You can understand why, seeing me like this.'

'Y-yes.'

'Still stutter? Poor baby,' Hugo spat. 'And now, to top it all off, Henry has become a media darling, a hero. What could be more selfless than saving his parents' cottage? I wonder how long it will be before you come down with it. Maybe you missed out? Maybe Horace only gave *me* the present.'

'Umm.' Henry could see that Hugo was ratcheting out of control.

'Is that all you can say, you piss-weak piece of slime?'

'W-what do you want me to say?'

'Anything. Let's have an opinion from the world-famous columnist.' Hugo's face twisted in a muscle spasm that threw his mouth into a dreadful sideways shift. His hands suddenly reached out in front as if he was playing an imaginary piano. 'I was the one, Henry. I went back into Horace's past. Uncle Sean told me. On the trip to Ireland. I was twenty-nine. He was on his last legs. Was I aware that Horace's relatives had died mysterious deaths? I did the research. I deserved the PhD, Henry. *I* had the guts to have a DNA test. Horace didn't want me to. *I* wanted to show him that *I* had the courage. Our dear loving father went ballistic. Wasn't my fault that the Sinclair family tree is . . .' He spasmed, twisted from the sofa to writhe on the floor. Then he repositioned himself.

'Yes?'

'Yes? They protected you from it, Henry. You were the precious do-gooder, went to uni, did all the right things. I'm the black, shitty sheep. When did you find out I had it? When did Horace even bother to tell you?'

Henry's mouth had dried to dust. The famous Hugo aggression.

'Yes, he told me. He was in denial. He didn't want to know. What was the point?'

'The point?' Hugo swept the coffee table with one arm, making his cup fly across the room and shatter against the wall. He was drooling, and snarled at Henry like a dog. 'He threw me out, Henry. I came back and told him that he had this dreadful gene. He had a fifty per cent chance to pass it on to you, and to me. Fifty-fifty, Henry! You could live with that? I couldn't.'

'H-Hugo. It's a tragedy. Horace will come down with it, so might I. Why would I want to know? You chose to have the diagnosis. Horace tried to argue with you. You and Horace clashed long before any of this came out. He didn't desert you. You left the family. Why?'

'Maybe I was a bit mad, even then. Maybe something told me I'd be mad.'

'But why take on a business, and involve Horace like you did?'

'He *owed* me. I wanted to make a squillion. I've lived four lives in the last four years, Henry.'

'*Why* did he owe you?'

Hugo spasmed. 'Because he gave me the bloody disease! Is that good enough? He's killed me!'

'Th-that's just rubbish. It's not his fault!' Henry started to shout.

Hugo stood up. He kicked at the coffee table and missed,

falling back onto the sofa. He lay with his face in a pillow, writhing wretchedly. Then he straightened himself and became rigid. Henry went over to turn him on his back.

'Keep away from me!' Hugo snarled. He relaxed and pushed himself to a sitting position. 'I'm nowhere near this bad normally. Must be the stress. You want to know why I blame him? The bloody question you have to ask, you dumb shit, is *whether he knew before he decided to have us*!'

Henry's world disintegrated. It came apart in tiny fragments of understanding. He lowered himself into the back of the chair and placed his head between his hands, staring at the floor. No matter how often Horace said that he had only found out about the disease twelve years ago, Hugo would never believe him. There was too much poison between them. No wonder there had been a wild argument, and that Horace didn't want to talk about it. How could he ever prove that he didn't know he had the disease?

With Henry devastated, Hugo's facial ticks and muscular spasms subsided. Gradually he sat still, watching Henry. Then, slowly, but in seeming control, Hugo stood up and walked behind Henry's lounge chair. His hands trembling, he stooped over the back of Henry's head as if he were cutting a rare flower. He jerked some strands of hair from Henry's head.

'Hey?' Henry jumped up, alarmed. 'What? What's going on? What did you just . . . My hair?'

Hugo dropped the strand into his wallet, which he stuffed back into his pocket, smiling malevolently. 'You shouldn't live your life in the dark, Henry. You shouldn't have a girlfriend and not tell her . . .'

'What do you *know about her*?' Henry was ranting, his face ashen, realising full well that the strand of hair could be used in a DNA test.

'You know I've been observing you Henry.' Hugo smiled his twisted smile.

'Hugo, please. What have I ever done to you? Why do this?'

'I'm doing you a bigger favour than you will ever know, young brother.'

'You've *got* to believe me when I tell you that my girlfriend knows. I've *told* her!'

'Oh, really? I don't believe you. You're like Horace. Shift the burden onto your partner. Shouldn't your partner know what you know, to make an informed choice about you? Aren't you compounding Dad's error?'

'Wait. W-wait. You're wrong about Dad. Horace said that he only found out about the disease twelve years ago.'

'And you believe that? Well, we'll see. In the meantime at least *you* will find out, and your girlfriend will leave you. Just like Mignon left me, Henry. Nobody sticks around.'

- 47 -

Henry spent the next few days sagging under Hugo's revelations. Whatever he did to distract himself only put the cap more tightly on the bottle. What Hugo had said made enough sense to focus his mind on the moral dilemma that he'd tried to suffocate for years. What right had he to let anyone love him – the friendship could end in a train wreck of muscular spasms, grotesque grimaces, dementia and early death.

Hugo had left the apartment almost controlled. There was nothing; no warmth, no date for another visit. How would he cope with the disease alone? Wouldn't he soften, relent, allow the family to help?

Alex and Rosie each phoned to say that Henry could use their remaining money to put down a deposit. Neither asked Henry why he was so subdued – everybody felt crushed. When Bruce also offered his money, Henry felt sick. Bruce's generosity sat in his conscience like a sea urchin. Bruce knew how Henry had misled his sister.

Henry approached Tuesday with cannon balls squatting in his gut.

Horace and Mary were running around the house tidying up. Henry arrived with Alex and Rosie in the Kombi. There was little conversation. Henry had explained that, even with the money the others had offered, there was too much risk that he could not complete the purchase, and the deposit would be lost. It was game over. Rosie held his hand.

The auction was to take place in the front yard. The agent, Mr Winch, had personally rung all interested parties to change the venue from an office in Kingsford when he read the front page of the *Sydney Morning Herald*. Never had he been involved in a sale that had attracted front-page attention, and he thought he would indulge himself. He was considering a political career.

Horace and Mary were their normal selves. Mary had dressed for the occasion, and Horace had swapped his slippers for his going-out shoes. As he put it, this was his concession to the final move in his life, but one.

The day was bright and sunny, with a mild south-easterly blowing from the sea. The agent shifted his portable podium to capture as large an expanse of lawn as possible, making sure that the television cameras he expected to arrive would focus on his left profile. He was dressed in his best dark-blue suit with a bow-tie that seemed rather an overstatement whenever the eye shifted from him at the podium to the fibro cottage behind. Horace nudged Henry and said that he should be selling a harbourfront mansion.

Amid these preparations, the crowd began to gather. The Italian delegation from Antonio's side arrived like a bed of flowers, so colourfully were most of the women dressed. Henry watched some twenty people, along with a woman in black he took to be Antonio's mother, gather themselves on their side of the lawn and arrange folding chairs for the elderly. At the same time another group of bright dresses and short squat men in suits and balding heads arrived from Luigi's side and positioned themselves opposite. Henry, standing in the centre, felt a chill in the neighbourly ambience. There was some cursory head nodding, but it looked to Henry that both villages were gathered on opposite sides of a medieval battlefield.

Cars clogged the street. Dieter Lollinger arrived with a photographer. And, sure enough, there was a television camera. And another. Horace said he was getting giddy from turning around to see who would arrive next. The Pope? Henry, asked for a few words by the TV reporters, protested that he really was too nervous, and that he really didn't warrant, and maybe after the auction. The fact was that Henry only had one imperative. Hugo.

He stood next to Horace, who was starting to enjoy himself. Henry couldn't concentrate on the auction, even though it had been his preoccupation for months. He could only see Hugo writhing around in his living room. The tension rose in him. 'Dad. I have to have a quick chat,' he whispered in Horace's ear.

'What? Now?'

Henry steered Horace by the elbow, muttering to Mary, Rosie and Alex that they would be back shortly.

'Where are we going, son?'

'Just around the back, for a moment. I have to ask you something.'

Henry stopped behind the house and confronted Horace. 'Dad. This is the most important question I have ever asked you. Everything I believe in turns on your answer. I have to know the truth.'

'Goodness, Henry. What's the drama?' Horace took off his hat and stared at his son.

'Hugo paid me a visit. He's in a bad way, Dad. He was angry. He told me something which may explain him, and also goes a long way to explain why you would willingly sign over the cottage to him when you knew that his condition wouldn't allow him to run a business.'

'Yes, son?'

'Dad. You said at Bruce's cabin that you only discovered you had the disease twelve years ago. Hugo doesn't believe you. He thinks you knew that you had the gene for Huntington's disease before you and mum decided to have us.'

'Oh God!' Horace put his hand to his forehead and went to the back door. He lowered himself to sit on the step. 'Son. Hugo has been eaten up by that question. I can never prove this, but you can ask your mother to confirm it. I had no idea, son.' He grabbed Henry by the arm and looked into his eyes. Tears started to form. 'This tragedy goes from bad to worse. The disease runs your life. Once I found out that it was in the family I was determined that you not be told. If the disease was going to get you, it would, in its own time. The fact that Hugo has it means that I have it. I must have passed it on to him. He wanted to have a test that would tell me whether I was the carrier. Mary and I wanted to protect you. But it's okay for me. It will hit me soon, and I've had a good life. Hugo was always cocky, brash, egotistical. So we had the biggest argument of many, when he went off to have the test.'

Henry stared into the distance. He could hear the auctioneer begin his preamble. As far as Henry knew, Horace had never lied in his life. The Sinclair tragedy assumed an even more poignant edge as he thought about Hugo's unshakeable belief. Hugo was determined to blame someone for the cards that had been dealt him. 'Thanks Dad. I expected that answer, but I wanted to be sure.' He helped Horace up and they walked back.

'What about Hugo, son? Will he see us?'

'I think he's lost.' Henry stopped and put his hand on Horace's arm. 'Dad. You should know. Hugo pinched a strand of my hair for a DNA test. He's determined to find out if I've got it.'

'Oh, God.'

'Ladies and gentlemen, do we have an opening bid?'

They returned to stand next to Rosie, Alex and Mary. 'Where have you been, Henry?' Rosie asked.

'Just having a quick chat with Dad,' Henry replied and squeezed Rosie's hand.

Henry caught Dieter's eye and smiled. At least a hundred people were milling around. The bidding began in earnest. From four-hundred-and-ten thousand it quickly rose to half-a-million, then faltered. Antonio stood with his arms folded, wearing sunglasses, a mirror image of Luigi on the opposite side, also in sunglasses. They each affected a nonchalant attitude that contrasted sharply with the frenetic waving of fans by the women immediately behind.

The auctioneer started to milk the crowd for incremental bids. Prime location, best development potential, surrounding houses worth a million. Somebody else was bidding. The bids rose from five hundred thousand to five seventy-five. The crowd was making room for a well-dressed man who stood at the rear and held up his folded newspaper to bid. Anderson Charters, Rachael Quinlan's lawyer. The auctioneer recited bits of the story as it had appeared in the newspaper, and put the spotlight on Horace and Mary, and Henry.

As Henry watched Anderson Charters make his bids, he shook his head and closed his eyes in quiet thanks. Could Rachael, the woman he'd found so repulsive when he first met her, be their saviour? Each dollar over four hundred and thirty thousand would go to Horace and Mary. Already they had one hundred and forty thousand to see them through for some time, medical expenses notwithstanding. Henry felt the stress leave his body.

The auctioneer was having difficulty getting bids from the Italian delegation, which conferred in serious asides. Then suddenly he concentrated on a person who had arrived at the rear of the crowd. Somebody was making his way forward from a taxi, causing people to step aside.

Henry turned around to see what people were staring at. Hugo.

Hugo strode forward with an occasional spasm, but managed to negotiate his way with some control. He was dressed in a white suit and hat, with a red carnation prominent in his lapel, like somebody from a movie set.

The auctioneer cleared his throat and went back to the business. He was calling for final bids, saying that the gentleman at the rear had the running – were there any offers over five hundred and seventy thousand? Once, twice, sold!

Henry didn't hear a word. He inadvertently squeezed Rosie's hand with such force that she recoiled. 'Henry? Who's that?'

The crowd parted, sensing that something dramatic was happening. Hugo stood unsteadily, and then jerked his hand in an uncontrollable flourish.

Alex hushed: 'That's Hugo, isn't it? He's the guy I saw in the house in Newtown.' He moved to see better as Henry and Rosie slowly walked toward Hugo.

Mary started forward, accompanied by Horace. Bruce and Beth, who had been to one side of the Sinclair family, followed them. Dieter Lollinger pushed past some people, alert to another twist in the Sinclair story.

Hugo stood, assisted by a walking cane. He wobbled unsteadily then glared at Horace. Mary took Hugo's arm and Hugo pulled it away.

The attention of the crowd was divided. Anderson Charters' bid for the house had won, and he was speaking to the auctioneer.

Alex stood immediately behind Henry, alert to what he now knew was a crisis. The crowd withdrew to form a circle of distant, curious observers.

'Hugo, you're back?' Mary asked, overcome.

'I have something for Henry, Mum,' Hugo said, his gaze fixed on Henry.

Henry stepped forward.

Just then Anderson Charters caught Henry by the sleeve. 'Excuse me, Henry, but I have a letter for you. It's from Rachael Quinlan. She insists that you accept the cottage as her gift.' He pressed an envelope into Henry's hand and disappeared through the crowd.

Henry half concentrated, and gave the envelope to Rosie. The brothers' eyes were locked together. Hugo rocked and twitched. The moment played out in slow motion in Henry's mind. Oblivious to the concerned looks of Rosie and Alex, he waited for the verdict.

'Henry. I have your fate in my hand.' Hugo brandished an envelope.

Horace's face registered fear.

'Well? Let me have it. By the way, Hugo. Horace had no idea. He couldn't have known, thirty-four years ago.'

'Maybe. Do you want to be like me, Henry? This is Rosie, is it?'

Rosie nodded.

'Do you want to have children with this man?'

Rosie was trembling, mouth dry, gripped by fear.

'Henry. You're clear as a bird. I'm happy for you.' Hugo handed Henry the envelope, and turned around. He waved his stick at the taxi, and made to walk away.

Henry shook and began to collapse at the knees. Alex could see that both Henry and Rosie needed his support and he grabbed them by their arms. With vacant eyes that gradually began to refocus, Henry swallowed, looked at Alex, turned to face Rosie and bound her tightly to him. Tears fell in a torrent from his eyes as he tried to bounce her around the lawn.

Author's note

Why would a novelist seek out the opinion of friends? They're hardly going to tell you that your story is rubbish.

Some friends tell you a lot from what they do not say. It's in the shuffling of their feet.

In any journey, the potholes test the suspension. In the process, the work becomes a community project. And this book is all about community.

Some people I wish to thank have been of enormous help throughout the years I've been writing this and other books. I've always waited for Carol Bacchi's opinions with a gulp. If she thinks I have not dealt with a character convincingly, she tells me. Nena Bierbaum tells me most by what she does not say, even while she casts her keen editorial eye over the language. Elizabeth Guilhaus has been an inspiration as I've researched my stories. Jane Sloane has given me acute responses for which I am exceedingly grateful. Gordon Pender is my oldest friend, and tells it like only old friends can. Norton Jacobi has let me know exactly where the manure is hidden, and with kindness. When I hear Ken McNally's contagious laugh over the phone I know I'm on track. Andy Charter's comments suggest he should be the one writing novels.

For professional input along the way I wish to thank Tom Shapcott, who manages both to give razor-sharp critiques and to provide the essential confidence boost. Sophie Lance of Jenny Darling and Associates believes in 'intelligent humourous fiction'. I hope she's not disappointed. She helped enormously. Joanna Parsons Nicholl appraised the work cinematographically and has the best camera eye in the business.

Michael Standing provided valuable advice. Many thanks also to Su Cruickshank, Bruce Russell, Roz and David Watkins, Marjorie and Howard Muller, Michael Guilhaus, Samantha

McKinlay, Mike Bowden, Alex Karydis, Breda Carroll, John Taylor, Mark Cunningham, Michael Gray, Ciaran Synnott, Dr Michael Kay and Paula Winch.

My special thanks go to Michael Bollen and Sheree Tirrell of Wakefield Press, who helped reshape the work.

Shauna Carroll was involved throughout and commented on each paragraph. For her, a private dedication.

Fred Guilhaus, Adelaide, 2002
fredgx@ozemail.com.au

Wakefield Press has been publishing good Australian books for over fifty years. For a catalogue of current and forthcoming titles, or to add your name to our mailing list, send your name and address to

Wakefield Press, Box 2266, Kent Town,
South Australia 5071.

TELEPHONE (08) 8362 8800 FAX (08) 8362 7592
WEB www.wakefieldpress.com.au

Wakefield Press thanks Fox Creek Wines
and Arts South Australia for their support.